Worth The Fight

Cover art by Kari March designs~
https://www.facebook.com/Karimarchdesigns/?fref=ts
Formatting by: T.a. McKay
Editing by T.a. McKay , Ellie Aspill and Nicola Haken

DEDICATION

To everyone who has ever had to hide who they are. To the people who have to live a life that isn't theirs just to keep other people happy.

This is for you, may you find the courage to be who you really are.

AUTHORS NOTE:

As much as I've tried to keep the facts in this book as real as possible, it remains a work of fiction so I took artistic license with parts of it. It may not be fully true to life, but sacrifices need to be made for the sake of the story. So on that note, read on … and I hope you enjoy!

PROLOGUE

Zeke

I pound my fist into the bag, enjoying the feeling of my muscles flex as I release the power that's built up in them. My muscles contract as I pull my fist back, getting ready to strike again. This is what I love most about training, the control, the precision, and the power. There's no better feeling in the world than connecting perfectly with the punch bag, knowing that if it were flesh, it would have left some serious damage.

People think that fighting is all about anger and rage, but it's not. There's a rhythm to it, a reason for every movement, it's almost like a dance. You need to be light on your feet, agile, and have the skill to dodge every hit thrown your way. After that comes the strength and how much power you can pack into every single punch.

I feel pressure on my wrists and a burning sensation in my knuckles that lets me know that this workout will leave marks. I smirk to myself before throwing my body into a full round house kick. I apply as much force into my leg as I can and the bag jolts away from me, swaying as I feel sweat dripping down my back. I jab and duck, avoiding my imaginary opponent.

Jab, jab, duck.

Jab, jab, uppercut.

I'm lost in my rhythm, concentrating solely on making sure my form is better than perfect. I'm so consumed in what I'm doing that I don't hear the footsteps behind me. But I don't miss the hand that grabs onto my shoulder though. The sudden contact makes me turn and instinctively pull back my fist to punch whoever's touching me. I manage to stop myself just before I connect with a face that's full of shock. *Ethan.* He stands still as all the color drains from his cheeks and a look of panic flashes in his eyes. I would feel bad if the guy didn't annoy me to the point of distraction.

"What?" I know there are people who might think I'm being rude if they heard me, that I'm an asshole, but little do they know that I'm being as nice to him as I can possibly manage. If I had my way and could do whatever I wanted, I would punch him every time I see his annoying little face. Especially now that he's interrupting my training time, this is as nice as it's going to get.

"Coach wants to see you," he mumbles as I turn away from him and get in a couple more hits on the bag before I remove my wraps. Ethan tries to help me but with one glare he quickly moves away. I throw my wraps at him when I pass and head towards Coach's office. Coach's name is actually Eddie, but I don't think I've ever called him that, he even introduced himself as Coach the first time I turned up here. I can't remember ever hearing anyone calling him by his name either, not even the guys who are older than him.

I knock on his door and enter before he can respond. He's called me to his office so he knows I'm coming. He's sitting behind his desk with a huge diary laid out in front of him and I know he's checking out the scheduling for the upcoming fights.

"You wanted to see me, Coach?"

He looks up from the diary with a start like he's almost shocked to see me standing in front of him. That's when you see the fighter he used to be. He might not have the body or stamina to be in the ring anymore, but when he focuses on a task it's the only thing in existence. That's what every fighter needs, there's nothing as important as your concentration, your composure and your form. You need to have that one single goal, that drive when you get into the ring. The moment you step through the ropes the world could go up in flames and you wouldn't notice.

"Yeah, Zeke. How's the training going?"

I sit in the chair across the desk from him and lean back, putting my feet up on his desk. He stands and walks to the corner of his office, grabbing a towel from the rack on the wall. He throws it to me before knocking my feet off the desk. It's our usual routine and one we've done a thousand times but it doesn't make it any less comical to me. I take the towel from my lap where it landed after it hit me in the chest, and wipe the sweat from my face and shoulders as Coach walks back round to his side of the desk.

"S'all good. I'll be ready to face Man-eater next week. And while I'm on the subject, what a stupid fucking name? How can he expect anyone to take him serious with that?"

I watch Coach take his seat again, his eyes never leaving me as he lowers himself onto the chair. "You're still dropping your left shoulder, that's gonna lose you the fight."

I use all my strength to try and resist rolling my eyes. It's the same critique I've been getting since I started fighting years ago, and well, this year I haven't lost a single fight yet.

"You know who could probably help you with that? Ethan. You know, since he's your coach and all."

I grind my teeth, my jaw aching from the sudden pressure. "Trainee coach, and one I never asked for. You know I think the guy's an ass. He doesn't know how to do his job and I have absolutely no need for him."

Coach sighs and he leans forward towards me with his arms resting on the desk. "Zeke, he's going to be your coach one day. When you hit the big time I won't be able to give you the time you'll need. You need someone who will be there for *you*, no one else." I've heard this speech so many times now and, as usual, it falls on deaf ears. I don't want Ethan as my coach, I want Eddie and I'm pretty sure when I hit the big leagues he'll give in and train me. After all, I'll be the one bringing in the big money. All I need to do is win the fight next week and I'll be one step closer to hitting the UFC. That's the dream, and the one I'm planning on living very soon. I've spent my entire life training for this so winning is the *only* option. I was good at school, and smarter than anyone realized, but when my dad made me fight I knew I had found my passion. Suddenly, there was nothing more important than my next fight.

I look out the office window and see Asha walk past, throwing her long dark hair over her shoulder as she catches me looking. She smiles at me, biting her lip and giving me that shy look that won her my attention last time. I don't even know why she's here, all she seems to do is strut around in her very tight gym clothes. I haven't seen her use any of the equipment, the only thing that she seems to *do* is the fighters. I rise from my seat and walk to the door, more than ready to get a little relief for the day.

"Zeke, I'm not done with you yet. We need to talk about Ethan, about you letting him help you."

I wave my hand over my shoulder, not willing to have this discussion again. It bores me and there's something, or maybe that should be someone, much more exciting that I want to do. "It's not something I want to talk about. The guy isn't my coach, he never will be. You will be following me into the big leagues, old man." I walk out of his office just in time to see a smiling Asha walk into the locker room and I feel my body harden in anticipation.

I start to follow her when I hear Eddie hollering behind me. "Hey less of the fucking old, and I'm not going anywhere, boy. You hear me?"

I smirk. It's the same answer every single time.

CHAPTER ONE

Zeke

My knee bounces in time to the music playing through my headphones, the built up tension from my nerves is too much to keep in. I'm always like this right before a fight, the need to get out into the cage overwhelming, and it's even worse tonight. This is *the* night. This is what all these years of training have been for. Tonight is the final fight with Rage, and when I win, it will pave my way into the bigger arenas, into the main stream and hopefully into the ring with the UFC. That will mean bigger fights, more money, and a lot more respect. It will take just this one win to change my life.

I hold my hands out in front of me as Ethan tapes them up. I hate him doing it, this isn't his job and I don't want him touching me, but the cut man is late and the officials don't want to hold up the fight. Both fighters agreed to allow our coaches to tape us up and let the ref check them before we leave the locker room. I wanted Coach to do it, but he's already ringside which leaves me stuck in this situation with Mr. Incapable. I zone out, trying not to focus on the clusterfuck that this fight is becoming. There's been so many things go wrong already and I haven't even left the locker room. This isn't helping my focus at all. I close my eyes and listen to my music, trying to clear my head. I want to be able to block out the world, but the only thing I can concentrate on is Ethan and the fact that he isn't using the right wraps. I think all sportsmen have silly traditions once they get a winning streak, a routine that they don't deviate from. My red Meister wraps are something I've been using all year and they're not the ones currently being wound around my hands.

"They're the wrong wraps. Take them off and get the right ones." My voice is so loud that even I can hear myself over my music. Ethan jumps slightly and I can't help the slight smirk of satisfaction. He doesn't stop what he's doing so I pull my hand away and push the headphones off my head so they sit at the back of my neck.

"Maybe you didn't hear me right. Let me explain it just one more time. You are using the wrong wraps, now go get the right ones."

Again he doesn't acknowledge me and he also doesn't move to do what I ask. This kid is seriously starting to piss me off. He's actually only a few years younger than me but with his lack of confidence I swear he acts more like a nervous teenager than a peer. I've tried to tell Coach that I can't have someone like Ethan training me, the guy jumps at his own shadow and I can't take advice from someone like that, but he won't listen. When Ethan finally finds his voice it comes out as a squeaky mess and I'm not sure if it's that or his next words that nearly send me into a tailspin.

"I don't have your normal wraps, I forgot to pick them up from the training room."

I stare at the top of his head, trying to calm the inferno that's suddenly raging inside me. I'm a second away from ripping the little fucker's head off when Coach walks into the dressing room.

He must sense the tension and see that I'm one breath away from losing my shit, because he walks over and places his hand firmly on my shoulder. "What's up boys? I thought you would be finishing up by now. You don't have much time until the intros, Zeke."

I just glare at Ethan, hoping my eyes are burning holes through that thick skull of his. I don't ask him to do much, I'm pretty self-sufficient when I train. The only thing I need him to do is fucking sort all the fight prep. Is that really too much to ask?

"I would be finished, but someone forgot to bring the right equipment." I make no effort to hide the anger that seeps into my

14

tone, letting everyone within listening distance know just how pissed I am.

The hand on my shoulder tightens momentarily before letting go. "Well those look a lot like red wraps to me." I know he can see they aren't the right ones, the tone of his voice making it sound like he's trying to placate a two year old who isn't getting their own way. I know that it's a silly ritual that I've gotten into the habit of doing but I don't care. It's been working for the last ten months and I don't want to change it now. I look at Coach, clenching my jaw as I bite my tongue. I need to stay calm. I need to keep my focus for the real fight. I hold my hands out to Ethan again and let him finish his job. I'm not happy about this and it's the final straw. I don't care what Coach says; the incapable fucker will be gone after this fight if I have anything to do with it.

I feel my headphones being put back onto my ears and my nose is filled with sickly sweet perfume, alerting me to the fact that Asha has arrived. I was so intent with my glaring at Ethan, that I didn't even notice her arrival. I close my eyes, determined to block everything out until my fight is called. I start to take deep breaths, letting the hard beat of the music thrum through my blood.

I jump slightly when I feel strong hands on my shoulder and I realize it's time. I remove my headphones and hear the beat of the music from the main arena. I stand and stretch my back, feeling my spine crack as I move. I bounce lightly on my feet as adrenaline floods my body. I punch out in front of me a few times, letting my breath whoosh out as I spar with the air. I need to get into the cage. I need to hit someone. I hear Coach talking to me but he sounds distant. I know I should listen to his pep talk, but my head is filled with everything that's going on around us. The intro music is playing and the shouting from the spectators is almost deafening.

"Don't take him down in the first round, you need to give everyone the show they came for. Keep that shoulder up and don't let him get a shot in. Control the fight. You got this one in the bag."

I nod as I make my way down the dark tunnel towards the bright lights of the arena. I hear the announcer over the loud speaker and look at the opposite tunnel. Behind those doors is the guy I need to beat, the one I'm going to pummel into the ground tonight.

"Up first ... let me hear some noise for the only man brave enough to go up against the man mountain that is defending his title. Unbeaten in all his fights this year ... the guy who knows how to please the ladies."

I hear women screaming and a smile flickers over my lips. This is where I belong, this is the life I want. I hear the first few beats of my entrance song, P.O.Ds 'Boom'.

"The storm that comes to rain down the blows onto his opponents. Watch as tonight he brings that storm to our cage ... it's Zeke 'The Storm' Raaaaaaiiiiiinnnnnnneeeeeee."

The place explodes with cheers and the sound of the audience's stomping feet echoes through the arena like thunder. I think it was after my fourth win that this started. It's how I got my nickname, *The Storm*, and soon the roar of thunder started following me around every fight. I walk down the aisle, not looking at the screaming crowd around me. All my attention is on the cage in front of me. I can feel the hands of fans all over my body, rubbing over my arms and shoulders, but I don't let it distract me from my goal. I reach the cage and bounce up onto the edge around the net, ignoring the steps completely. I pace around the canvas, my energy levels rising as I focus on the door my opponent will come through.

"Let me introduce to you to the fighter who's here to defend his title of the best fighter at Rage ... let me hear some noise. Unbeaten in his last fourteen fights, he's the man you don't want to go up against unless you want chewed up and spat out. Let me hear it fooooooor ... Dwayne 'The Man-eater' Wyatt."

The arena erupts into a barrage of shouts and hollering. I can feel the floor vibrate under my feet and excitement hits me square in the chest. I watch as the spotlight finds Dwayne exiting his tunnel. He holds his hands up in victory like he's already won as he stalks towards the ring. I feel my anger rising just from looking at him. I need to wipe that smug smile off his face. We haven't met in the ring before but he's been sending me messages at the end of his previous fights, telling me that I've no chance in beating him and that he will break me. I don't do trash talk, I let my skill do the talking for me, and my unbeaten record is there for everyone to see. I've won more fights this season than Dwayne, and I think that pisses him off. When I walk away from here today wearing the championship belt, he will see who's the best.

I watch as Dwayne gets closer, and the urge to lash out as soon as he enters through the open side is the only thing I can think of. The clang of the door behind him makes my heart thump in my chest and the rest of the arena disappears. My eyes are only focused on one thing, 'The Man-eater'. I've been waiting for this day for months, praying he would win all his bouts so I could finally get here and finish him. From the moment he won his third round he's been talking shit about me, telling the world that he's going to put me in the ground. But I'm going to create a different ending for his story today, and I'm going to love every second of it.

The referee calls us together, giving us the usual rules and I only half listen to him as I size up the man in front of me.

"Let's keep this fight clean boys, give them a good show. I will let a lot go between you since it's the final, but the usual rules apply. No groin attacks, no strikes to the back of the head or the spine, no head butts. Stay away from the eyes and no fish hooking. No biting. No hair pulling, and no strikes or grabbing of the throat. Stay off the side of the cage. As I say … keep it clean." It's the usual speech and I know that Dwayne won't be listening, the guy is a dirty fighter and I need to play by his rules today. I look at him standing in front of me, flexing his muscles like he's ready to pounce any second. His body is bigger than mine and the muscles would be intimidating to most people, but not to me. I'm faster on my feet and have height on my side. My body isn't overly built but my muscles are lean and full of power. I think this is why I've won so many matches, people underestimate my strength since I'm smaller than the usual fighters.

"Right let's shake before we begin." The referee puts his hand up in front of us, expecting us to shake or at least fist bump to start the fight, but Dwayne just laughs and walks away to his side of the cage. *Come on then fucker, the sooner we start, the sooner I end you.* I don't go to my corner, choosing to stay in the center of the ring to wait for the bell. I've been told that I need to make the fight last at least two rounds but I want this over as quickly as possible. I want to knock him on his ass within the first round.

The bell rings to signal the start of the fight and I bounce on my feet as my opponent stalks towards me. His guard is down and he has a relaxed expression like he doesn't have anything to worry about. I take the chance to get a roundhouse kick to connect with his ribs, knocking him slightly off balance. Most fighters and coaches would argue against making the first move but it's my way of finding out how solid and balanced his body is. Since the kick barely shifted him I know it's going to take more than just my strength to win.

The one thing the kick does is make him put his guard up, covering his face as he moves closer to me. I need to attack quickly and get in as many hits as possible before he can adjust his large body. I start with my feet, keeping my hands up for protection in case he manages to connect with my body. I continue to kick, trying to make contact anywhere I can. I know he's thinking that I'm going to tire myself out soon but that where he's wrong, my stamina is unrivalled and I could do this for hours. The first beads of sweat drip down my face and back, igniting my body, and adrenaline rushes through me as I land each blow. I dance around the cage, bouncing from foot to foot as I alternate kicks against his mid section. He starts to back up across the canvas, his body folded over in an attempt to block my lightening feet. I follow him and carry on my assault, not giving him a second to recover. He doubles over when my shin connects with his side. I smile as I hear his breath forced from his body from my kick.

This is the moment I've been waiting for, his defences are down and I can finish this loud mouth once and for all. I throw my first punch and I'm shocked when I feel a twinge in my hand. I didn't hit him that hard, I shouldn't be feeling any pain after my first punch. I open my fingers and quickly close them, convincing myself that I just caught him incorrectly in my excitement. I'm not willing to lose the upper hand so I re-adjust my body, getting myself into a better position and punch again. My fist connects with his cheekbone and a ripping pain bursts in my hand, causing me to pull back in shock. I take a step backwards as the pain pulsates throughout my hand. One punch, one shooting pain, one moment of distraction is all it took to change my entire life. I'm so busy concentrating on my hand that I forget to guard myself against the huge guy in front of me, I realize my mistake quickly when a huge fist lands on my temple. My head flies to the side, and I swear I can see stars.

I take a few steps back, shaking my head trying to clear the fuzziness that's trying to invade my vision. A fist to the head will cause even the best fighter to falter, especially when that fist is connected to a big fucker like Dwayne. I just need a minute to recover, but I don't get a chance. Another hit followed by a kick has me losing my breath and my ribs scream out in pain, the combination making me fall to the ground. I land on one knee and try to take a second to compose myself. *Stand up you idiot, don't give him any ground.* With my injured hand wrapped around my now battered ribs I push myself up to my feet, but my victory is short lived. I'm barely on my feet when another punch is delivered to my face, my lip bursting open and spraying blood all over the canvas.

My knees give out and I collapse to the canvas. Shit. *Get up, get up now!* I repeat the words in my head but I can't get my body to comply. I feel the impact of his body on mine, winding me with his weight, my ribs crunching as he lands. I cry out, the pain too much to hold inside. Punches rain down on me and I try to hide as much of my body as I can by curling up into a ball. When that doesn't work I try to throw him from me, anything to get the upper hand again. I'm losing this fight and I can't let that happen, not when I've come so far. Working through the pain I twist, working my way onto my stomach. My plan is to use my body to throw him off me and get to my feet. I lie flat out on my front and, ignoring the punches, I start to push up with my hands. The only problem with that idea is that I forgot about my injury. I scream out again as I collapse back to the ground, pain working through my entire hand. I've never had a pain like this in my life and I start to panic.

I don't have more than a few seconds to worry about what the pain means before I'm grabbed from behind in a rear naked choke. With my uninjured hand I try to pull the arm away from my neck but it's no use, he's just too strong. I look over to Coach and see a look of worry in his face, he's trying to tell me to tap out but I hold up my hand, showing him that's not going to happen. If I'm going to lose this fight it won't be through giving up. As long as I have some fight left in me I'm going carry on. Darkness starts to invade my vision as the pressure around my throat tightens. Every attempt to get Dwayne off me fails and my strength starts to weaken as the lack of oxygen makes my body shut down. My lungs are screaming out for me to breathe but the grip on my neck is too much.

I've just wasted my one chance at the title I've been training my entire life for. This was my moment and I've thrown it all away. Those are my last thoughts as I start to lose consciousness. Before I pass out I hear the bell ring and people shouting before the pressure on my throat disappears. I collapse onto the canvas and take in a deep breath of precious oxygen. I close my eyes and try to fill my lungs. I feel hands all over my body and they cause me to moan with pain. If I could talk I would tell them to leave me here, my career is probably over so there is no point panicking over me. I can't get any words out so I drift off into a pain-induced sleep, my mind going blissfully blank.

****

20

I'm sitting on the floor of the shower, letting the hot water fall over me as I cradle my hand. I woke up not long ago in the locker room after being carried in on a stretcher. Coach has been trying to get me to go to the hospital for my hand but I'm putting off the inevitable. I know there's something seriously wrong with it, something that's possibly career ending, and finding out for certain isn't high on my 'must do' list right now. I hear footsteps on the tile floor but I don't have the energy to even raise my head to see who it is. Let them see me at my lowest point. I don't care

"Boy, we really need to get you to the hospital. You need your hand and ribs x-rayed, and your neck checked. You took a good beating out there. There may be some serious damage."

I feel anger rising in me at Coach's observation. I know I fucking lost, I'm just thankful I was passed out when Dwayne lifted the belt.

"Yeah, I'll get right on that." The water above me shuts off and I finally look up just in time to catch a towel that's thrown in my direction.

"Get your ass up off that floor and stop with the pity party. So you lost a fight, there'll be plenty more in your career that you'll win." Coach doesn't even wait for a response as he turns around, leaving me alone in the shower room.

I stand and awkwardly wrap the towel around my waist with my good hand before making my way out to the main room, praying that no one will try to talk to me out there. I grab my boxers from the shelf in my locker and struggle to get them on. In my attempt my towel falls to the floor, thankfully I'm not embarrassed about people seeing me naked. I grab my t-shirt and after another struggle I pull it down my body. The locker room is quiet, like everyone is scared to talk and I don't blame them. I'm on the verge of losing my shit, I can feel it. I have so many emotions running through me that I don't know which one to concentrate on. I'm worried, actually I'm petrified, that I've done some serious and permanent damage to my hand that will stop me fighting. I'm fucking pissed that the injury's happened, and for the first time

21

since it happened I stop and wonder why it did. My form was perfect, my hand connecting to his jaw at a perfect angle. I've also hit bigger guys than Dwayne, so his size wasn't a factor. I stop dead, my hand hovering over the shoes I was about to grab, the obvious answer finally clicking in my head. I turn slowly and look directly at the reason for all of this. Immediately I feel myself moving, walking across the room until I'm standing in front of him with nothing but a bench in between us. He looks up from the bag he's packing and a look of fear crosses his face. He knows he did this, he knows he's the reason that I may have to abandon my dream.

"Um... hi, Zeke. Are you... um... ready for the hospital?" His stuttering pisses me off even more, he fucked everything up and he has the nerve to panic. I move around the bench that's between us, crowding into his body as he moves backwards.

"You did this to me. You fucked my career up." My voice comes out calmer than I thought it would, but it's obviously louder than I think because Coach quickly tries to get in between me and Ethan.

"Come on, Zeke. Let's not do this."

My glare doesn't move from Ethan and I see him cower. I point at him, my arm reaching over Coach's shoulder, getting closer to Ethan's face.

"He fucking did this, Coach. I didn't want the fucker in the first place and now he's screwed up my hand." I can feel the anger building inside. There's nothing that I want more than to kill him.

I feel Coach push against me, using his body weight to push me away from Ethan as he talks. "Everyone makes mistakes. Let's just get you to the hospital and take it from there." If I didn't respect him as much I wouldn't listen to him, I would take all my fury out on the quivering figure in front of me but I can't. I close my eyes and take a deep breath, letting Coach move me further away from Ethan. I'm just about to turn away from him, get my shit together and leave when the stupid idiot has to make a comment.

He just couldn't keep his mouth shut for a few more minutes.

"There's always next year, I'm sure you'll win the ..." He doesn't get the chance to finish his sentence when I turn and attack him. I grab the front of his shirt and push him back against the lockers behind him. I manage to connect a few good punches to his face, despite the pain shooting through my hand and up my wrist, before I'm dragged away from him. I watch with satisfaction as he crumbles to the ground with blood pouring from his face. I try to break free from the hands that are keeping me away, I want to keep going until he isn't breathing.

"Come on, son. That's not gonna help your hand."

I don't even care how much damage it does, I just need him to suffer the way I am. I want to see him in pain. I watch as two other fighters pull Ethan from the floor, helping him from the room and out of my sight. It's safer for him that I can't see him anymore.

"He's fired, Coach."

I hear Coach's deep laugh in my ear before he replies. "Yeah, son. I worked that one out."

CHAPTER TWO

Zeke

I clench my hand and feel the tightness in the muscles start to relax a little. My cast was taken off nineteen days ago, and **after six fucking long weeks I was ecstatic.** I've been working flat out to improve the mobility since it was removed, and the hand may be getting better but my anger towards the injury hasn't. When I went to the hospital after the disastrous fight, the x-ray showed that I'd fractured three bones, which had proved my claim that my tapes were nowhere near tight enough. I pick up the tension ball again and squeeze it with all the power I can manage, imagining that it's Ethan's head in between my fingers. It worried me initially how weak my hand was, I couldn't believe I'd gone from being able to punch a bag for hours at a time to barely being able to last five minutes with this silly little ball. I'm starting to feel more confident now that I can actually feel my strength coming back and I've even managed to take a few punches at the bag, not that I've told Coach that. Even with the progress I'm making, I still need to make sure that with every day that passes I don't give in to the sense of dread that festers in my stomach. I shake my head at my own dramatics. I swear if the guys around could hear my inner thoughts, they would tie me to the punch bag and use me for boxing practice.

"Zeke, my man. How's it hanging?"

I turn towards the voice and smile at Jason, watching him as he enters the ring I'm sitting next to. I feel a pinch of jealousy as I watch him tape up his hands, ready to spar with his trainer, Angus. I haven't been in the ring since I was injured, and I miss it so fucking badly. He hits the pads Angus's holding up a few times

24

before walking towards me and leaning on the ropes next to me.

"I'm good." I look down to my hand that's still clutching onto the strength-training ball and laugh. "Okay, maybe not good but I suppose it could be worse."

He gives me a sympathetic look before pushing himself off the ropes and standing up straight. "Yeah, I suppose. It's not like you lost the biggest fight of your life and broke your hand or anything." Jason smirks, walking over to Angus and starts punching the pads again.

I drop the ball to the bench I'm sitting on and stand, stretching out my back. "Hey, Jason. You know what I can still do?" I wait until he stops sparring and looks at me. When he does I raise the middle finger of my damaged hand before turning around and walking away. His laughter follows me as I enter Coach's office.

I take a seat opposite Coach and put my feet up on his desk.

"Have you been doing the exercises you were given?" Coach doesn't even look up from the paperwork on his desk as he knocks my feet to the floor. Every. Single. Time. Not once has he let me keep my feet up there but it doesn't stop me from trying.

"Of course I did, it's all I'm allowed to do. When can I get back to fighting? I'm so over this stupid shit."

Coach glares at me over the paper in his hand. I've been riding him about fighting for the last few weeks. I need to get back in the ring and pound on someone.

"You can fight again when your coach clears you and not a second before." He looks back to the paper in his hand and I look at him in confusion. Sometimes I think he's losing his mind, maybe he's been hit one too many times.

"Then fucking clear me already. I can't believe this shit, you could have cleared me weeks ago." I can feel a touch of anger towards Coach. He's never mentioned before that he has power over my recovery. I sit forward in my seat and lean on my knees. I want to pretend that I'm relaxed, that I don't want to go and punch something but I'm pretty sure it's not looking that way.

"I said your coach can clear you, I'm not your coach. I

already told you that I'd be getting a replacement for Ethan." Not this shit again, I can't believe he's going to try and convince me to take on another trainee. The last one he sent to me made a huge mistake, and I still don't know if I will ever be able to fight again.

"And I already told you, I don't want another coach. It's you or nothing, there is no other option." I sound like a spoilt little brat having a tantrum but I don't care. I refuse to put my future in anyone's hands but his. There's no one out there who's as good as him and no one else I would trust.

He finally gives me his full attention as he puts the piece of paper he's holding on the desk and crosses his arms. "Look, Zeke. We've been through this before. I don't have the time to give you the attention you need. I have too many fighters to look after, and with your skill you need one on one training. You are gonna need someone who can focus solely on you to get you ready for the championship. You have a rematch coming up and you need to be on form in order to win."

I hate when he makes sense. I know that running the gym takes a lot of his time, that there are too many fighters now for him to deal with them all personally. There are a total of four trainers who share their time between fourteen fighters, and I will be only the second fighter in the gym's history to have their own trainer.

"Seriously? How can I tell you no when you make sense?"

He laughs before leaning back in his chair, looking more relaxed than he did a minute ago. "I'm glad you agree, he'll be here tomorrow to meet you."

It's my turn to lean back in my chair but I'm far from relaxed. A groan leaves me as I massage my temples. A part of me was hoping that after hearing about things with me and Ethan no one would be interested in the job. I go to speak but Coach holds up his hand silencing me.

"Before you start, let me just say that he's a perfect match for you. He's an ex fighter himself and knows his stuff. Maybe you won't be able to push this one around, he might be the person to kick your ass for a change."

I snort at his statement. I doubt some fighter wannabe will be able to teach me anything I don't already know. I sigh as I picture another Ethan turning up tomorrow. *Ethan.* I never liked that fucker. There was always something about him that I couldn't quite put my finger on. He seemed to be more interested in the glory of being my trainer then actually training me. The bastard even had the nerve to use my name to get freebies and perks with local businesses and the more I won the more he got. When I told Coach about it he said that Ethan was still young and training, that he would settle down, but he never did. I could overlook a lot of his shit if he had been on point with his training, but I swear that he didn't know the difference between a round house and a hook. His usual method of helping was pointing to the punch bag and telling me to do what felt natural. Forgetting my wraps and then poorly taping my hands was the last straw. No matter the outcome of the fight, Ethan was gone. I need someone who will focus on me and not my name. Forgetting my wraps at my fight was the last straw. Even if I had won he was gone.

"Yeah, I'm sure that's just what's gonna happen. I give him a week before he runs away with his tail between his legs." I get up from my chair and walk to the door. I'm just about to close the door behind me when I hear Coach shouting.

"I mean it, Zeke. I refuse to find another fucking trainer for you. If you chase this one off then you're on your own!"

I laugh as I close the door. It's not a case of if but when.

****

I'm standing under the scalding hot water in my shower at home, letting the heat soak through my tense body. I hear my cell phone ring and for about three seconds I consider answering it, but the feeling of the water on my stiff shoulders is too pleasant for me to move. Since I haven't been able to do any weights or spar I've been putting a lot of effort into cardio, and using muscles that I don't usually need. I thought lifting weights gave me the most punishing workout, especially trying to bulk up for a fight, but running apparently can be just as painful.

I move my head under the spray, and watch the water drain away. My mind is distracted by thoughts of meeting my new trainer tomorrow, finding out who Coach thinks is the perfect match for me. I hate the fact that I haven't even met him yet and he's the one with all the power. Some random guy gets to decide when I start fighting again. I think that part is what angers me more than anything. Someone who doesn't know me gets to make the most important decision in my life. I look up and let the water pour over my face before shutting the shower off.

I grab a towel from the rack next to the sink and wrap it around my waist. Walking to the sink unit, I use a hand towel to clear the steam from the fogged up mirror. I throw the towel into the dirty linen basket and look at my reflection. Thankfully all the bruising from the fight is gone. I didn't think the one around my left eye was ever going to disappear. It was like a daily reminder of how badly I'd fucked up that day. I just keep thinking I was lucky there's nothing permanent done, well nothing that's completely life changing other than my hurt pride and my damaged wrist. Hopefully I'll be able to convince this new guy that I'm ready to get going. I need to make sure I'm one hundred and ten percent ready for my rematch and that means training properly as soon as possible. I refuse to go down at the hands of Dwayne again. He will only get the best of me once.

I rub my hand over my jaw and contemplate shaving but I like the stubble. I've no plans for the next few days that require a clean look so fuck it. If this new guy doesn't approve then he can go fuck himself. I laugh to myself. I've already painted a picture of this guy, building him up to be a bastard before I've even met him. Maybe I should give him a shot, see how good he actually is before judging him. I shake my head and walk into my bedroom, grabbing a pair of boxer shorts on the way past my dresser. Dropping the towel on the floor I throw the boxers on the bed before collapsing butt naked on the mattress, too tired to even attempt to put them on. I grab my cell from the nightstand and see a missed call from Asha. I told her to call me about getting together, but I'm really not in the mood for company tonight, especially hers. Don't get me wrong, Asha is a really nice girl. She is sweet and sexy, but I just don't have the energy tonight. I want to have an early night so I can hit the gym before it opens tomorrow and get in a workout before introductions are made.

I got a text from Coach earlier telling me to be at the gym for ten o'clock, and that I better be on time. I have my meeting with Bryce at ten thirty. That's my new coach's name, Bryce Tanner. I know that he's an ex fighter, but his name has me picturing some preppy guy who has never stepped foot into the cage. Bryce Tanner, yeah, that's not the name of a guy who knows how to handle himself. I know I'm judging him and already trying to find a reason to hate him but I can't help myself. I've always found it hard to open up to people. You can't give people the power of having your secrets, to believe they won't use them against you.

I'm pulled from my thoughts when my phone rings again. I see Asha's name on the screen and I press the side button to mute the ringing. I throw the phone on the other side of the bed and get up, putting my underwear on before going through to the kitchen. I need to get something to eat before it gets too late. I hate eating late but I missed dinner earlier. I open the fridge and take a look to see what's inside. Nothing really grabs my attention and I make a mental note to drop by the grocery store tomorrow. I'm running low on eggs and milk, the two main staples in my diet. I suddenly remember that I have some chicken and rice in the freezer and I mentally pat myself on the back for cooking too much. I hunt for the Tupperware containing the food and put it in the microwave to defrost. I grab a bottle of water from the fridge and walk to the door leading outside to sit out on the back step. It's a nice night, warm and dry with a clear sky. I like this time of year; fall is one of my favorite seasons. It's not too hot and the humidity has settled, not like the height of the summer when it feels like you're breathing through syrup. Training in that weather feels like you could die, especially if you're doing it outside. I try to stick to the gym during the height of Summer, using the weights and treadmill to keep fit. Honestly the fighting itself is enough to tone my muscles and keep my stamina up but I push myself further to make myself faster, stronger. The need to win is my driving force, second place really means first loser, and that's not acceptable. The sting of losing to Dwayne is still fresh and I think it's harder to get over than my actual injury.

I sit and listen to the noises from my street, letting the sounds of the kids having fun relax me. I love living here, the buzz of the neighborhood reminds me of home. I grew up in a small town, in the type of place where everyone knew everyone else and their business. When I was a kid it was great, I used to play outside with my friends until the streetlights came on and never got into trouble, well nothing too serious. I loved high school, we spent the weekends at the drive in and partying at each other's houses, it was like the stereotypical high school movie where everyone was happy. I know it probably wasn't that experience for everyone I knew, but I was in the popular crowd so life seemed perfect. When I turned fourteen I suddenly realized that something didn't feel right, that I wasn't interested in things the other kids were. That's when the small town feeling got too much and hiding my secret became too difficult. That's when my dad decided that fighting was what I needed. According to him, I had to learn to be a man and punching another man was the perfect way to do it.

I left town soon after my eighteenth birthday, when the feeling of being constantly watched by everyone got too much. I couldn't do anything without someone being there to make sure I was moving in the direction my dad wanted me to go. So I packed a bag and jumped on a train. I ended up in the city, hungry and alone until Coach found me sleeping in the local park. He took me to the gym and gave me a sleeping bag and a space on the floor. I helped out around the gym until he saw me having a go on the punching bag after hours, and the rest as they say, is history. Once

I started winning fights, the money started coming in. Now I make my living doing the one thing I love and do best. The house I own isn't big. It has one bedroom and a patch of grass out the back that's my yard, but size doesn't matter to me. It's mine and no one can take it from me. I paid for it in cash when I won my first big tournament. I was determined to not waste the money on anything stupid, but something I could make my own.

I hear the microwave beep but even my hunger can't get me to move from my spot. I close my eyes and lean back against the doorframe, looking up towards the sky to let the sun warm my face. This is the most relaxed I've felt in a while and it's with the knowledge that tomorrow I might be able to return to the cage. The thought of being able to train again makes my heart beat a little faster and my muscles twitch with anticipation. The fighting, the cage, the burn of my muscles, I've missed every second of it. Now that I'm so close to getting it all back, I'm scared that I want it too much and karma's going to get her claws out and make me pay for all my past digressions. Maybe I need to take a different approach with this new trainer. Maybe if I act like his best friend, be accommodating and welcoming, he will clear me fit to fight. I laugh at myself, there is no way in this life that I can be that kind of guy. It's not in my nature to be Mr. Accommodating. I know that when I meet this Bryce tomorrow there is a very good chance that he will be leaving the gym without a job. Coach seems to think that we're a perfect match but I don't see how, I don't think I'm a perfect match for anyone.

My rumbling stomach finally gets me up and walking back into the kitchen. If I'm going back to training then I need to keep my strength and calories up, losing muscle mass is not part of the plan. I have eight weeks until the rematch with Dwayne. Eight weeks to train and get my strength back and then some. Eight weeks to become the fighter that I know I can be. He might have beaten me last time, but I can guarantee that will never happen again.

Dwayne Wyatt isn't invincible, and I'm going to prove it to the world.

CHAPTER THREE

Zeke

When I arrived at the gym this morning I'd already made the decision that no matter what this new coach was going to say, I was not leaving today without getting in the ring. I would be sparring before the day was out, with or without permission. I need to be able to use my fists to fight again and release the tension that kicking a strike shield just can't touch. There's nothing better than feeling your fists connecting with someone's body and then for their muscles to give way under your knuckles. You need to know how to move and place your body and how to control your own muscles, to tense them to protect yourself from impact, to create enough force to hurt. Anyone can throw a punch, but it takes great skill to control it. In a fight you want to win, but there's also great respect between fighters, so you don't want to lose control and cause serious damage. Well unless you're Dwayne. I hate that motherfucker with every bone in my body. He fights dirty and gives the sport a bad reputation. He has put more men in the hospital than any other fighter I know. That in itself would make me hate him, but he has a way of intimidating his opponents by taunting them and making them feel like they have to watch their backs outside the cage. This is a hooligan's sport fought by gentlemen, and he's dragging all our reputations into the gutter with him.

Angus is busy wrapping my wrists when I see Coach walking to the front door. I look at the clock on the gym wall and I'm surprised to see that it's nearly ten already. I'd let myself in just after eight after a shit night's sleep. I'd tossed and turned the whole night, unable to switch my brain off.

"There you go, all done. You're sure that it's okay for you to be going back in the cage? You've had the all clear, right?"

I smile at him before getting up from the bench and moving over to the punch bag. I don't want to lie to him, so ignoring the question is the best option.

"Zeke, that wasn't an actual answer," I hear him shout from behind me and I wave over my shoulder, again not answering him. I'm about to throw my first punch in months when movement from across the room catches my eye. I stop myself and hold onto the punch bag as I watch Coach talking to a guy just inside the main door. This stranger's back is to me but I can see that he has large and built shoulders which tell me that he has trained at some point in this life, unlike Ethan. Ethan was far too skinny to tell me what to do. How can someone train something they have no knowledge or experience in? I knocked him on his ass with one hit more than once. I continue to watch as Coach and who I assume is my new coach stand there, and I can't seem to get my eyes to leave the guy. I want him to turn around, I need to see him from the front. I can't explain the need to see what he looks like, all I know is that the urge nearly has me walking over and turning him around myself. I don't know how long I stare, but Coach finally points in my direction and my breath catches in my throat as the stranger turns around.

My body stills completely, my blood feels like it's frozen in my veins as I take in Bryce Tanner. He's taller than Coach and probably rivals my six foot four frame. He looks toned and muscular if the tight shirt he's wearing is anything to go by. The shirt is tucked into his pants, which highlights his thin waist and wide shoulders. On closer inspection it looks like he trains, a lot. My eyes travel up his body until they reach his face, which I realize is just as impressive as his body. His dark hair is cut into a messy style and it looks like he's spent the morning running his fingers through it. I can't see his eyes from across the gym but I can feel their piercing stare. I feel like I'm being scrutinized by eyes that see everything. He smiles at something Coach says and my heart stutters at how sexy he looks.

I shake my head violently as I listen to the thoughts going through my mind. *What the fuck's going on?* I'm not looking at some sexy woman here. This is my new coach, my new *male* coach. My reaction to him is freaking me out but I only have a few seconds to try to work out what's happening before Coach and Bryce walk over to me.

"Zeke, let me introduce you to your new coach. This is Bryce Tanner." I note that he emphasizes the words 'new coach' and his message isn't lost on me. He's already spoken to me this morning about giving Bryce a chance and I promised not to be my usual asshole self, but that's the best I could offer him. I reach out to take the hand that Bryce has offered to be polite. When my skin connects with his an electric current sparks from his hand to mine. It feels like static electricity and it makes me pull my hand away instantly. I look down expecting to see my skin red and marked, but there's nothing there. I finally meet Bryce's eyes and see a look of confusion that mirrors my own.

It takes us both a few seconds to recover and it's Bryce that manages it first. "Hi, it's a pleasure to finally meet you, Zeke." I'm shocked when I hear his voice, I was not expecting the English accent that comes out. He sounds like Daniel Craig and the effect it has on me is a little startling. I know I need to speak but my mind has stopped working and my words are stuck in my throat. I'm well aware that I'm standing here like an idiot just staring at the man in front of me.

"Why the fuck do you have wraps on? I thought I told you there would be no training until Bryce gave you the all clear?"

I look at Coach, grateful for him saving me, but pissed that he's breaking the silence by ripping me a new one. I see the corner of Bryce's mouth curl up and it takes everything in me not to punch him, to show them how well my hand works.

"Yeah you did, but I decided that maybe I knew more than the new guy." The smartass answer flies out of my mouth without a thought, but I figure the sooner Bryce knows I'm not a pushover the better. He might be here to help me get back to full fitness, but that's all he'll have control over.

"Well the *new guy* says that if you hit that bag before I check your hand, you will be on a week's suspension. That means no cage, no workouts, no gym time."

What the fuck? I just stand and stare at Bryce feeling like my ass has been handed to me. No way he just tried to lay down the law, he's only been here two fucking minutes.

I'm pulled from my staring contest when Coach lets out a hearty laugh. I look over to him to see that he's looking between both of us with an amused expression on his face.

"Well looks like you boys will get on just great so I'll leave you to it. I'll be in my office if you need me." With those parting words he walks away with his shoulders still shaking with laughter.

Fucker.

I turn back to Bryce and give him my best 'don't fuck with me' death stare, trying to let him know that I won't take any shit. I need him to know that I'm actually the boss, and he's just here to make sure I have everything I need.

"I need you to remove the wraps. I'm going to grab my bag and get changed, have them off by the time I get back." And with that he walks away leaving me standing there open mouthed as he exits the building. I'm still standing there when he returns a few minutes later with a gym bag over his shoulder. I'm shocked with his dismissal but I'm even more surprised when I find myself removing the wraps.

Bryce

I walk into the locker room and rush over to the open locker that Eddie said would be there for me. I drop my bag to the ground before I collapse onto the wooden bench in the middle of the room and lean my head in my hands. The introduction to Zeke hadn't gone anything like I imagined. When I'd been offered this job I had

35

taken time to get to know the man that the public see. I knew this wasn't going to be an easy placement and that I was going to have to fight for control, but when I saw the man I'd be training all that vanished from my head. My mouth went dry as I took in all his muscles and tattoos, but it's his eyes that took my breath away. Those eyes are something I will never forget. Like bright green beacons and in complete contrast to his almost black hair. It took all my control to look away and when we shook hands I swear it felt like someone had just handed me a live wire. The feeling of his skin against mine was like nothing I've ever experienced before. *Shit.*

When I moved to America to take this job, I'd decided that I wouldn't hook up with anyone because I needed to give this once in a lifetime opportunity my full attention. I couldn't risk the fact that I'm gay getting out, not that I'm ashamed, far from it in fact. I just know how people in this profession think, and the fact that I like guys could be a big problem. I refuse to lie about who I am, but if they didn't see me with anyone then I wouldn't need to talk about my preferences. It was a great plan and one that I had thought long and hard about, and it would have worked great apart from him. Apparently Zeke Raine is going to be a temptation I don't need. I just need to remember one thing: *the guy isn't gay.*

I take a deep breath and stand up, grabbing my workout shorts and vest from the bag at my feet, and get dressed as quickly as possible. I've been in here too long and I don't want to start our working relationship with him thinking I don't take it seriously. This is the job I've been waiting my life for and have moved to another country for so I can't do something to fuck it up. I throw my clothes in the locker, pick up my water bottle and I stretch my back before walking out of the changing room.

I need to be strong. I need to be professional. I need to be nothing but his coach.

That thought is wiped from my brain along with the breath in my lungs when I see Zeke on the running machine. He's removed his wraps like I told him to but he's also removed his t-shirt, giving me the perfect view of what he'd been hiding before. My body is toned and I'm proud of the way I look and it takes a lot of hard work, but I swear he makes me look like I sit on my arse all day. I don't think there's an ounce of fat on him and he looks like he's been carved from marble by the Gods. I shake my head and laugh. *Could I sound any more like a teenage girl?* I tear my eyes away from Zeke's glistening skin, pretending that I don't want to lick the sweat from his abs. I need to talk to him. I'm pretty sure I won't be as attracted to him when I listen to him speak. From the little interaction we've had I can tell he's a dick and that's not a quality I find attractive. Once I get my head on board, I'm pretty sure my body will follow.

"Glad to see you're warming up, but I want to check out your hand." I call out to him and wave him over to me but he just glares at me and continues to run. *Yeah, definitely a dick.* I throw my water bottle onto the stack of towels that rests on the weight bench and cross my arms over my chest, determined to wait him out. I need to assert some authority so he knows I'm not going to give into him like his last coach did. I'm here to work and I know how to do my job. The sooner he realizes this the better, he won't be chasing me off like the long list of people before me.

He must finally understand that I'm not going to give into him because he reaches out to slow the treadmill. His eyes never leave mine and I know we're entered into a pissing contest now and one that neither of us wants to lose. He stops the machine completely, jumps off and walks over to stand in front of me, grabbing a towel to wipe the sweat from his skin on his way. I try to focus on the fact that I must have been in the locker room longer than I thought for him to build up a sweat like that and not the fact that he smells better than anyone else I've ever met. There is nothing sexier than a guy who's worked up a sweat, and with Zeke, his own smell and whatever aftershave he's wearing is not helping the situation in my shorts. Yes, that's right. This annoying, headstrong guy is causing my incredibly underused dick to harden in my shorts, my extremely thin workout shorts that wouldn't hide anything under them. Not good, not good at all. I sit on the weight bench, putting some much needed distance between us to hide the bulge in my shorts, and hold out my hand to him.

"Let me see your hand. I've read over your notes but tell me in your own words what happened." I think we're going to have another standoff because he doesn't immediately move or acknowledge that I've spoken but I'm soon proven wrong as he walks over to me and holds out his injured hand.

"It's simple. I had a really shitty coach and he made a mistake. That mistake caused me my championship and almost my career." I look up at him taking in the anger in his eyes. No wonder he has a problem with me being here, he was let down by the one person who should have his back at all times. I know the story, but it was only secondhand information. I wanted to hear it from Zeke, to get his account of the events and gauge his responses. It's the best way to find out how he thinks, about how he sees what happened in the cage. Once I understand his mind I'll be able to train him. I take his hand and knead my fingers into the back of it, feeling for any trauma that might still be present.

"And your injury?" Again I've read the doctors report but I want him to tell me in his own words.

"Three fractured bones caused by lack of wrist support. I hit the other guy and his face didn't come off as bad as my hand. Shame really. I probably would have gotten away without too much damage to my hand, but I then punched the fucker that caused this and that was the source of the real damage."

I continue to press over his hand, looking for areas of tenderness but there aren't any. I think it's healed well and quicker than the ones I'd seen in my previous experience. "Does it cause you any pain now? Like when you hold or grab anything?" I feel proud that I'm managing to keep this completely professional, especially when I'm eye level with his worship worthy abs.

"No pain. I just want to get back to fighting, I have a fight coming up and I need to be better than fit for it. You, apparently, are the only one who can clear me for that." I can hear the venom in his tone and I know that it must be difficult for a guy like him to have someone else in control of his career, especially after the last coach he had.

I grab the wraps he left sitting next to his towel and get him ready to train. He watches me for a few seconds in silence but I know he's dying to talk. I can see his Adam's apple bobbing up and down in his throat as he tries to stay quiet.

Soon enough he breaks his silence. "Are we on?"

I look up at him again and nod. I'm thankful that I'm looking at him when a smile finally crosses his face. That simple act completely changes him, his eyes sparkle and I notice a dimple in his right cheek. *Note to self, don't make the hot guy smile.*

"I will let you spar with me after I work out your fitness level. I'm not going to let you go full throttle until I know it's completely healed, and I can't judge that after ten minutes and a couple of prods. I understand your frustration but damaging it further isn't going to help anyone. I'm here to do a job, one that I'm bloody good at, and that job is to make you a champion. Let me do what I came here to do and we will get on just fine."

If I'm not mistaken a look of respect crosses his features but it disappears so quickly that I can't be sure it was ever there. "Let's get this party started then." That's all he says before he walks over to the ring, leans down and enters between the ropes.

I watch him bounce on his feet and I'm impressed. For a guy that I've been assured hasn't fought for the last few months, he hasn't lost any of his grace. That's usually the first thing to go when fighters get hurt, they start to look a bit wobbly when they get back into the ring, like a toddler trying to take their first steps. Not Zeke though, he looks like he hasn't missed a day of training, he's light on his feet and fully in control. It's one of the things that I admired about his fighting when I had studied him on the flight over. He moves likes he's a featherweight fighter, but he's built like a heavyweight. That makes for an explosive combination in the ring and I can't wait to see what he can actually do.

I pick up the focus pads and put them on after climbing into the ring. Zeke's eyes are trained on me as I slowly circle him.

"I want you to hit the pads when I present them. The only rule is that you're not allowed to use your right hand. Feet, legs or your left hand … all allowed, but if you use your right hand at all, I will tie it behind your back."

Zeke raises his eyebrows at me and I can't help the flush that spreads through my body as I imagine Zeke tied up. That is the last thing I should be thinking about now. I'm risking a hard on of epic proportions with no way to hide it. To keep Zeke's attention away from my crotch, I quickly raise a pad up so my arm is out above my shoulder. Within seconds Zeke spins and hits it with his foot. His range of motion is impressive and leads to more thoughts I shouldn't be having.

After making him chase pads until he's sweating I pick up a kick pad to find out how much power he really has.

"I want you to kick this as hard as you can."

His eyes light up as he looks at the pad. His chest is heaving up and down, sweat dripping down his hard muscles to the waistband of his shorts. I try not to focus on his body but it's like showing a kid an ice cream and telling them they can't have it. I open my stance as I stand behind the mat, making sure I'm fully braced and protected. If I'm not steady I might end up on my arse. I focus my eyes back to Zeke's body as he moves around in front of me, trying to keep my thoughts on his movements, working out how he's going to attack. I can see the buildup and I know it's coming but Eddie appears behind Zeke and shouts my name at the wrong moment. I take my eye off Zeke for a fraction of a second and that's all it takes. I feel his foot connect with the soft material that's meant to protect me and I feel my feet leave the ground already aware that my landing isn't going to be graceful. I land on my back and air is pushed from my chest, leaving me lying on the floor gasping for breath.

"Shit!" I hear Zeke shouting before the pad is pulled from my arms and he leans over me on his knees. If I wasn't in so much pain right now I would take the time to enjoy this moment and the picturesque view of a sexy man above me. *Okay apparently I'm not as hurt as I thought.*

"Are you okay? I'm sorry, I thought you were ready."

I try to laugh but I'm still struggling to fill my lungs with oxygen. "Did you get the reg number of the lorry that just hit me?"

Zeke's deep laughter flows over me and the hairs on my body stand on end. It's official, I need to make sure I never make Zeke smile or laugh. The affects on me are too much and I will never be able to hide the attraction I can feel building.

"I think there's something wrong with you, I don't understand what you're saying."

This time I manage to laugh. When I first arrived I noticed that people had a problem comprehending some of the things I said, and most of the time now I remember to use words they understand.

"Don't worry about it. It takes more than a kick to scramble my brain."

I get another smile from Zeke before he stands up and bends over to help me up. I grab his offered hand and he pulls me up until I'm standing. There is a current flowing from his skin to mine, and when our eyes connect I can't seem to look away. I realize that our hands are still touching and we pull apart quickly when Eddie shouts at me, asking if I'm okay. I nod my head and smile at him before walking over to see what he wants. I focus on him and try not to think about the heat that has spread all over my body since touching Zeke's hand.

CHAPTER FOUR

Zeke

I groan as the hot water from the shower beats against my aching muscles. When I first started training with Bryce this morning, I wasn't convinced that it was going to do anything for me, but even I have to admit that my body is telling me that I've been worked hard. I lean my head to the side and feel a very satisfying crack. I've missed this, the deep down ache you feel after you've worked your body so hard. It's like a drug for me and when I couldn't have it I wasn't the nicest person to be around.

I look up when I hear the shower next to me start and see Bryce running his hands through his hair, and while he's distracted, I take the chance to look him over. His body is as built as some of the guys that I fight against, his muscles tight and well defined. His abs look like they've been cut from steel and I feel envious of his amazing eight pack. I've tried since I started fighting to get that elusive eight pack, but I've never managed it. I try to convince myself that's why I'm still looking at his body, I'm admiring his dedication to fitness and that it has absolutely nothing to do with the fact that I can't look away from him. My dick is unfortunately enjoying what it sees and I can feel myself start to harden. I turn away quickly in embarrassment even though there are half walls that separate the showers to hide me. I think about Asha, about her lush body, what it feels like when it's wrapped around my dick and that fantastic mouth that would bring any man to his knees. With those thoughts running through my head I reach down and rub along my now very obvious hard on, but I feel better now that I can tell myself that it's all for Asha. I need to make myself believe this, if I can't then I will have to think about why my body is reacting to the very naked man next to me. I would need to think about why when he's near me my mind goes fuzzy and I find myself thinking about things I shouldn't. Some of those thoughts being how amazing his lips look when he's focusing on my posture, or how his muscles flex when he moves. No I won't think about that, I'll think about Asha. Try to convince myself she's the sole reason I'm so hard right now.

"How's your hand?"

I look down to my right hand that's stroking my cock and let go quickly. I glance over at Bryce to see if he noticed what I was doing but he's washing his hair, so there is no way he could have seen anything. The timing of the question was just coincidental and actually very innocent, it's just my mind that's making it something it wasn't.

"Yeah, it feels great." I bite my lip as I answer him, enjoying my private joke.

"That's good. I think tomorrow we can increase your sparring time. I know you were pissed when I said you couldn't use that hand, but I swear there's a reason to my madness. You'll see soon enough." He puts his head under the water to rinse the shampoo from his hair and bubbles run down his chest. I swear to God I try not to let my eyes follow them, but fail miserably. My mind drifts back to when he told me I wasn't allowed to use my hand, I thought he was insane. I would've told him exactly that, but I was intrigued with the blush that had covered his cheeks when he had talked about tying my hands behind my back. When those words came out his mouth, visions had flashed through my head of Bryce tying me down, and when I raised my eyebrow at Bryce it almost looked like he'd had similar thoughts.

"Yeah, I have to admit I thought you might have lost your mind a little there, but if I'm honest, I don't think my hand could have done much."

He laughs at my comment, and I can't help but stare at his lips, wondering if they are as soft as they look. I grab my body wash from the shelf in the shower and pour a good amount into my hands before scrubbing my body. I've already washed, but I need a distraction from the direction my mind is going.

"I swear I know what I'm doing, I've done this before. We need to condition your body without putting too much strain on your hand straight away. So if you can learn to not use it as your dominant hand, then it will get the rest it needs. A few weeks of that and I promise you will be back to fighting like normal. You did well though, I didn't have to tie you up at all." The same flush as before covers his face and I can't help but wish I could hear what was going through his head. There's something about those words that cause a reaction from him, and I want to know what it is. He turns away from me and I let my eyes drift, taking in the dips and grooves of his toned back. Shit. I will not stare at his body again, and I certainly won't get hard while I do it. I turn the water temperature down, trying to get control over my raging hormones. I haven't felt like this since I was a teenager, and that never really went well. Deciding I need to get laid tonight, I come up with a plan. I don't know if it's a good plan but I run with it, maybe the distraction will help whatever is going on here.

"So, what're your plans for tonight?" I open one eye and look over to Bryce to make sure he knows I'm talking to him. He turns off the water and grabs a towel from the hook before wrapping it around his waist. I follow his lead, wrapping my own towel around me before walking over to my locker.

"I was planning on going home and making a work out plan for you. Now I've seen you I can plan better." Is he kidding me? After six hours in the gym he's going to go home to work some more. I'm a great believer in hard work, you don't get to the level I'm at without having dedication and working more hours than the average person, but everyone needs some down time.

"You're going home to work? Seriously, you don't have a hot woman you can hook up with for the night? You deserve a reward, you did a good job today." I can't help the laughter in my voice as I speak. He looks over to me and gives me the finger which makes me laugh harder. At least he knows I'm trying to fuck with him, I promised Coach I would give him a chance so that's what I'm doing. Actually if I'm truthful, Bryce seems like a good guy. I had an instant dislike for him but that was purely because of my experience with Ethan. He'd been an idiot and that has made me wary about anyone else. Bryce is completely different though. He seems to know what he's talking about, the stuff he had me doing earlier worked my muscles with the minimum of effort and it's like I can already feel myself getting stronger. He's not trying to keep me from training, he's adapting it to get me back into the cage quicker.

"I know it's hard to believe, but I don't have anyone here to occupy me. I've only been here for a few weeks. You're the first person I've really spoken to other than Eddie. Lucky me, eh?"

I laugh at his joke, happy that we are chatting like this, but take note of his words. I never really thought about him not knowing anyone, I never thought to ask how long he's been here. When I left home I spent so much time on my own, just sitting watching people walking past me on the street, not seeing me as they talked to friends and family. I spent most of my time wishing I had someone to talk to, to share my time with. I hate it when I think someone else is lonely, especially when it's someone who seems as nice as Bryce.

"What, Mr. Perfect Coach doesn't have people falling at his feet to be friends?" I turn from my locker just in time to see his towel fall to the floor as he pulls his boxer shorts up. I turn away, but not before I look down and see his naked ass. His fucking perfectly round, naked ass. I feel my dick twitch against my towel and I quickly grab my clothes. The sooner I'm dressed, the sooner I can get out of here. Being around him like this is doing something weird to my body, something I don't want to explore.

"Fuck you, Zeke. Just because the world wants to kiss your arse, doesn't mean that we all have them bowing at our feet." His words would come off harsh if he didn't have a smirk on his face.

"Yeah, it's just like that. Anyway, tonight I'm taking you out and introducing you to some people. You can't spend your whole life working. If you don't have some fun you'll become boring and I refuse to have a boring coach."

He stops buttoning his shirt and turns towards me, giving me his full attention. Standing there in tight blue jeans and a white button down, I swear I've never seen a guy look sexier. No, not sexier. More attractive, yeah that's the words I should have used. I shake my head, confused about the way my mind is fucking with me. I need to get laid tonight ... or drunk ... or both.

"So, I'm your coach?" He raises his eyebrows at me and I smile, realizing that I've resigned myself to the fact that he's here to stay.

"Yes, for now. Let's not make a big deal out of it, don't want you getting a big head. So hurry up and get dressed." I grab my own black shirt and button it up before tucking it into my trousers. I'd planned to go out tonight so I wore some good clothes to training today, and now I'm glad I did. I never invited Ethan out with us, it would have been my worst nightmare. I didn't want to spend time with him inside the gym, so outside it was a no go, but I'm glad I asked Bryce. If we can get along it would make life a lot easier, and he does seem like a good guy. So I'll take him out and show him how we like to unwind. I need to show Bryce how much trouble I can get him into, best to start as I mean to go on.

****

I grab my glass of bourbon and take a large drink. We've been at the club for about an hour now and I'm trying to pace myself. I don't want to train with a hangover tomorrow, not on my second day back to it. I look over the table towards Bryce. He's been attracting a lot of female attention but he looks uncomfortable with it and just smiles at them before taking another drink of his water. I had tried to get him to drink something alcoholic, I mean who comes to a club and drinks water? But he refused point blank. I wonder now if he wished he hadn't accepted my invitation to come out.

I feel a pair of lips brush over my neck and a hand groping my thigh, but I don't turn around. I'm used to this sort of attention when I go out, I can get any girl I want in this place and they all scramble to get my attention. I don't know who's attached to the lips or hands, but I honestly don't care. I'm not paying attention to the women in here tonight because my interest lies squarely on the guy sitting opposite me. The hand on my thigh moves higher and I reach down to stop it in its tracks.

"Oh, baby. I could make you feel so good, I know you want that." Normally having some girl talking to me like this would have my dick hard and have me craving the orgasm that had been promised to me but tonight I'm more interested in getting to know Bryce better. I stand and move past the legs of the people sitting next to me and make my way around the table to sit on the bench next to the woman who's struggling to get the button on Bryce's jeans open. He's trying to be polite and not make a big deal out of the unwanted attention, but I can see the panic in his eyes as he holds onto her wrists. I tap her on the shoulder and she instantly turns towards me, a small squeal leaving her as she sees who I am. Her arms wrap around my neck and all thought of Bryce leaves her. Unwrapping her arms from me, I lean over and talk in her ear, thankful that the booth we have is in a quieter area of the club and she can hear me clearly.

"You need to back off now. You're not wanted here, by me or the other guy." I have no idea what makes me say it, but Bryce's discomfort is pissing me off. I want him to have a good night, to be relaxed and make friends. The last thing he needs is some drunk woman pawning all over him. I turn and motion for Axl to come over. He smiles as he approaches, his eyes never leaving the girl in front of me.

I lean in again to talk to the girl, pointing towards Axl. "Now this guy here, he's the one for you. I've heard the girls talking about him and his magic cock. Not sure what it does, and I don't want to know, but I hear it makes them go cross-eyed."

I have to hold in the laugh that is dying to break free at the look on the girl's face. She doesn't even speak as she stands and grabs Axl behind the head, pulling him down towards her so she can attack his mouth. He accepts the kiss willingly and pulls her towards the dark corner of the booth. Then he holds out a closed fist to me and I bump mine against his. I let the laugh come out this time as I watch him practically dragging her to the darkness.

I turn and see that Bryce also has a smile on his face as he looks at me. "Thanks. She was a little ... forward? Are all American women like that?"

I want to tell him that they're not, but truthfully I haven't actually met any who aren't. Maybe I just attract the confident types, the ones who know what they want and are willing to go for it. I don't really meet the shy, quiet ones, the ones you can take home to Mom.

"Kinda. What kind of woman do you go for? We could try and get you a little company for the night."

I watch as he takes a long drink, his cheeks flushing with color as he does so. I wouldn't have taken him as the quiet type, but one mention of a woman and he gets all shy. I decide to give him a break and try to find a subject that won't have him feeling awkward.

"Forget it, the only women you get in here are pushy. So tell me a bit about yourself, tell me all about Bryce," I ask as I lean against the wall behind me and I watch as he visibly relaxes.

This is obviously something he's willing to talk about. "There's not much to tell really." I've always noticed that the people who say the have nothing to tell usually have the best stories, so I refuse to let him off the hook so easily. I wasn't as lucky as him, I didn't get a file with his life story like he got for me. I'm going to use tonight as my opportunity to find out about him.

"Yeah, I'm sure you're really boring, but what brings you over from England?"

He doesn't speak and simply points towards me. I point to myself, my eyes widening in shock. "Me?"

He leans forward to put his glass on the table and I can't help but watch his muscles as his sleeve slides up his forearm.

"Yeah, you. I heard there was this shit hot fighter that

couldn't keep a coach because he had a habit of punching them. Seemed like the perfect challenge. I've never been one to go with the sure thing."

I'm shocked by the laughter that bursts from me. I don't think anyone has ever spoken to me like this, like they aren't impressed by who I am. Maybe it's because he only just got here or maybe because he genuinely doesn't give a shit.

"You don't sound worried that I might take a swing at you. Maybe it's a thing I do with all my coaches?"

It's his turn to laugh now as he obviously finds my statement funny. I don't know if I should be insulted or not by his reaction.

"Trust me, Zeke. I'm not worried, I'm pretty sure I can handle anything you can throw at me." His expression is intense as he stares at me and I know I should look away but I can't. I swear I feel like I can see everything he's feeling as he sits there, and his dark eyes look heated with passion.

The moment is broken when a girl sits on my lap and kisses my cheek. This time I let the distraction pull me away from Bryce's enticing eyes. I allow the girl to move her lips to mine, opening up and taking what I want. I try to convince myself that the ass that's sitting on top of my dick, and the tongue in my mouth is why I'm hard, but if I'm honest, I know that's not the reason.

Bryce

I lean forward and grab my glass of water from the table. I don't really need a drink but I'm looking for a distraction from what's happening beside me. One minute I'm staring into Zeke's eyes and the next he has his tongue down some woman's throat. I look around awkwardly as I try to pretend that the woman isn't moaning into his mouth as he does only god knows what.

We'd been getting to know each other and it was nice having someone to chat with for a change. That's the only reason I agreed to go out tonight, I'm sick of going home to an empty apartment with only myself for company. When Zeke had invited me out I'd initially decided I was going to decline his offer. I mean how can I tell him to rest and eat well when I'm out with him partying on the first night? Thankfully, he hadn't taken no for an answer and made me come out. I had felt awkward to begin with, especially when that girl had decided that she wanted to go home with me. I didn't know how to get her off me without making a scene, and I definitely wasn't about to give in to her demands. I had absolutely no interest in her and I didn't know what to say to her. I don't want to shout about my sexuality from the rooftops, but I'm not willing to lie about who I am either.

Thankfully Zeke had come to my rescue and I thought we were getting along and getting to know each other but then I had to go and say something stupid. Why did I have to say that I could handle him? That statement had caused a hundred different images to race through my mind, making it impossible for me to look away from him. He looked like he was feeling the same thing as me and he couldn't take his eyes off me, but that changed the second he had female company.

I reach down and adjust the hard on that's pressing against my jeans, trying to hide the fact that I'm turned on. I just can't help it when I'm near Zeke. He seems to have this affect on me that I have no control over. I look over to the couple that are still making out and I see Zeke's hand disappear under the hem of her dress. That's enough to get me moving. I refuse to sit here and watch as he finger fucks this woman. I grab my mobile and write out a text, sending it to the number that Eddie gave me earlier for Zeke. Once it sends, I stand, put on my jacket and leave the nightclub.

****

I walk into my small one bedroom studio apartment and throw my jacket over the back of the sofa. I'm so fucking tired tonight. I haven't slept well since I got here, the constant noise isn't something I'm used to. I grew up in the countryside where the only noise was the sound of crickets and the occasional bird. The constant traffic outside my window now keeps me up most of the night. It just never stops. I'm hoping that tonight I will get a decent sleep since my body is tired after training with Zeke. It's the first proper work out I've had in a long time and I can feel it deep in my muscles.

I shut off all the lights as I walk to my room and close the door behind me. I get undressed before walking into my bathroom to get washed up for bed. Before I brush my teeth, I grab my supplements and swallow them down with a glass of water. I look over my body as I brush and notice my muscle tone isn't as defined as it was a few months ago. I've been doing lots of cardio in the build up to training Zeke, but I can see the effects that not using weights is having on my body. I need to get back into training properly, hopefully working with Zeke will get me back to my previous condition. Fighting at home always kept me fit and toned, but since I gave that up I've needed to work harder to keep my body the way I want. Eddie said that I had free access to the gym while I worked there, so I'm going to make good use of it. If I keep Zeke training six hours everyday and then work out for two, I will have my body back into shape in no time. I know there are probably a lot of guys who would look at my body and think I was insane for wanting to work out harder, but I'm surrounded by some of the best fighters in the country all day long. There's no way I will stand next to them with a soft body, it would be too embarrassing.

I rinse my toothbrush and put in on the side before turning off the light and climbing into bed. I pull the single sheet up my body, leaving it sitting around my waist. I'm still trying to get acclimatized to the heat here, it's so much warmer than England. I stare at the ceiling praying for sleep to come but all I can think about is Zeke. I've trained a few fighters, and been surrounded by more than that in the gyms, but I've never felt drawn to any of them like I am to Zeke. From the minute I walked into the gym this morning I've felt like I couldn't take my eyes off him. With his sexy as sin body, a body I want to run my tongue over. Even when he was chasing the pads I had been distracted by the way his muscles tensed as he got ready to punch or kick. The sweat dripping down his body had made me want to lick it off, to taste him as my tongue traced the outline of his muscles. Fuck. *This can't be happening, it shouldn't be happening.* I can't have feelings for my boss, especially when he's straight. It's like gay lesson number one. Don't have feelings for the straight guy, but I think I already do.

CHAPTER FIVE

Zeke

I groan as I reach my hand out and slap at my alarm until I hit the right button to turn it off. I bury my head in the pillow and will the world to stop turning for a few hours so I can try and sleep this hangover away.

I had no intention of getting drunk last night, training with a headache today wasn't something I wanted, but when I'd watched Bryce leave while I was kissing that girl, I had needed the alcohol to stop me from going after him. I'd started kissing her to distract myself from the intensity between Bryce and me. I don't know how or why it happened but it was there. She'd been the perfect distraction, even though I know it had been rude as fuck to Bryce. I had watched him out of the corner of my eye as I'd kissed her. He'd looked embarrassed and it had made me feel like shit, but not enough to stop what I was doing. In fact I had taken it further by slipping my hand up her dress until she moaned into my mouth. I'd closed my eyes for what felt like one second and when I opened them again, he was gone. I'd pulled apart from the girl and had gone after him, leaving her sitting completely alone without explanation, but I couldn't see him anywhere. After that, I returned to the table and drank myself into a happier place. I don't know why him leaving had pissed me off so much, it's not like I had done anything that would make him want to stay.

I hear a noise beside me and a hand lands on my back before I feel a set of lips. This gets me moving quicker than my alarm clock. I sit up quickly, only to regret it instantly when the guy with the jackhammer starts pounding away in my head. I pinch the bridge of my nose in an attempt to try and ease some of the tension in my throbbing forehead.

"Come back to bed, sexy. I'll be ready to give you a repeat of last night after a few more hours sleep."

I think back to last night, tying to remember exactly what she'll be repeating, but it's a lost cause. I don't even remember coming home let alone coming home with another person. I look down at the mass of blond hair that's lying across the pillow next to mine and the very naked body that's only half covered by a sheet.

"Who the fuck are you?" I can't keep the horror out of my voice. I never let anyone sleep in my bed. *Never*. I fight against the throbbing in my head and jump out of bed, grabbing my boxers and putting them on as I stand up. The blond sits up and lets the sheet fall around her waist as she stretches her hands up over her head. I don't know if she is clueless to what she's doing or if she's trying to entice me back into bed but it's not working.

"Baby, don't be like that. You know who I am. I'm the woman of your dreams." Her voice is husky, and a little whiney, and on a normal day I would be ready for round two but today I just want her out of here. It would be helpful if I could remember what happened last night, know what had happened in the club before I left. I can remember everything that happened before Bryce left but everything after is just a blur. I need to get her out of my bed and out of my home. Fuck, now she knows where I live and that shit's not okay. I hold my head in my hand as I try to think of how to get her out of here, I need to get to training. *Fuck, fuck, fuck.* I grab my cell phone to check the time and notice that I have a text from an unknown number. I open it, wondering who the hell has my number. I read it a few times before I realize that it's from Bryce.

'Don't get too drunk, sparring with a hangover is a bitch. I expect you in the gym at ten, for every ten minutes you're late, you will be doing ten minutes on the treadmill. Arrive ready to fight.'

I look at the time and see that it's already after nine. *Shit, I'm going to be late*. I rush to the bathroom and brush my teeth. I don't have time for a shower, and while I'm grabbing work out gear to put on I start yelling at the girl. I wish I knew her name, it would make this so much easier.

"You need to get dressed and get out." I start throwing her clothes in her direction, not caring where they land just as long as she puts them on.

"Don't be like that. I can make you feel so much better. Just come back to bed and I will blow you until you don't care anymore." She licks her lips and I wonder what I saw in her last night, I must have had more to drink than I thought.

I lean over, placing my hands the mattress and get almost nose to nose with her. "I said, get your shit and get the fuck out." I talk very slowly so she can't misinterpret what I'm trying to tell her. I don't want to be an asshole but I don't have time for this shit. This is why I never let my one night stands stay over, you can't just leave a crazy in your home.

Her eyes widen and I swear her bottom lip starts quivering. I do not have time for this. I finish getting dressed and walk to the kitchen to grab my lunch pack and four bottles of water. I look at the clock on the wall and curse when I see that I only have ten minutes to get to the gym, and it's a twenty-minute drive. If I leave now I might only have ten minutes of treadmill time, and I hope that it's only running he has planned. I stop when I realize that I'm actually worrying over the consequences for being late. When the fuck did I let him have control? Even with Ethan I was still in charge, still the boss in the equation and he did what I said. But Bryce is very different, his personality and presence has me listening to what he says after only one day. I've had sex sessions that have lasted longer than I've known him and yet he is firmly in control.

I walk to the front door and throw everything I'm holding into my hold all and grab my car keys.

"Come on …" I call out in the direction of my bedroom. *Yeah I really wish I knew her name.* "You need to leave now. You either do it on your own or I carry you out into the front yard." As I said before, I'm probably an asshole but I just don't have the time or inclination to be a nice guy this morning. I have the headache from hell, I'm now running late and I'm pretty sure that I fucked up with Bryce last night. I don't know what I'm walking into when I get to the gym. I deserve a punch for how I treated him. I was confused about what I was feeling, and needing to prove to myself that I'm not attracted to him so I did things I shouldn't have. To treat him that way, suddenly ignoring him and practically having sex on the seat next to him, well that shit's pretty fucked up.

I hear heels clicking on the wooden floor just before the woman walks around the corner. "You are a real piece of work, Zeke. How can you be so nice one minute and then throw me out the next? I thought we had a connection, you told me I was special."

The snort of laughter comes out of me before I even realize what I've done. I swear I would take it back if I could. She doesn't say anything as she walks over to me and slaps me across the face before storming out. She moves so fast that I wouldn't have even known she'd done it if it weren't for the fact that my cheek is stinging. I raise my hand and feel the heat on my skin where she struck. I guess I kind of deserved that one. I pick up my bag and rush to my car, determined not to be more than twenty minutes late.

****

I walk into the gym totally expecting Bryce to be standing just inside the door tapping his watch like my mom used to do when I was younger and would come home late. I was strangely disappointed not to see him and I look around the gym. I still don't see him, which adds to my confusion. I take my bag to the locker room and only stay long enough to get a bottle of water before returning to the gym. The place is eerily quiet this morning. There are usually half a dozen bodies working out or sparring in the ring, but it's completely empty. You know when you watch horror movies and the world has ended, you just don't know it yet? Well that's what this is like, I feel like I'm completely alone in the world.

Walking to Coach's office, I look inside to find it empty as well. This is starting to freak me out a bit and I look around warily as I walk towards the back workout room. All the equipment is on the main floor of the gym, but there is also a separate room at the back that has a few hanging bags for specific one to one training. It's rarely used because most of the guys prefer the public area. We like to train in front of each other, our egos making us work harder, work better than each other.

I can hear a noise coming from inside the room. There are slapping noises and grunts, making it sound like someone's working out. I approach quietly, not wanting to interrupt whoever is working out and I look through the door. The sight in front of me causes me to stop me in my tracks and all thought flees my mind.

There inside the room is Bryce, and I can't take my eyes off him. I would take a second to think about why I can't look away and why my heart is suddenly beating erratically in my chest but it's taking all the effort I can muster to stay standing. The guy working out in front of me is the most perfect thing I've ever seen. He's topless and is wearing red shorts that are sticking to his ass with the sweat from his workout. Every time he strikes the hanging bag he's using his muscles contract and shake under the force of the blow. It takes everything in me not to reach out and run my hand over them, I want to know what they feel like under my hand. I want to dig my fingers into them, closely followed by my teeth. He grunts with each hit and I can feel it down to my core. In a few short seconds he's given me the hardest erection I have ever had. Just looking at him has me more turned on than any woman has managed.

This is wrong. My dad's words suddenly boom in my mind. *You're not gay. There is no way in hell my son is gay, we just need to get those ideas out of your head. They're wrong and there's no fucking way you will think them.* I repeat his words in my head again and again, trying to get my body under control. I won't be attracted to a man. That just can't happen.

I turn and walk out of the room, needing to get myself under control before I speak to him. I need to get over whatever this thing is.

I take some deep breaths before shouting out, knowing that he'll hear me. "Hello! Anyone here?" I turn away from the door so when he comes out it won't look like I knew he's already here. The noise from the room stops, and I wait for him to exit the room.

"Well, well, well. Look who decided to finally turn up. Nice of you to join me."

I take another deep breath before turning to face him, hoping it will be enough to keep my thoughts away from how he looks, how he would feel. When I do finally turn around I see that he has a towel in his hand and is wiping it over his body. My eyes automatically follow the towel's path.

"I'm like ten minutes late. Are you really gonna make me apologize over ten minutes?"

I don't like the look that passes over his face as he walks past me and towards the treadmill. He presses some buttons on the machine and stands next to it, looking at me with his arms crossed, obviously waiting for me to get on. I stare him down as I walk over and get on, not giving him the satisfaction of knowing that it bothers me. I can easily do twenty minutes of running, that's not exactly pushing me to my limits. He presses the start button and watches me as I start out at a gentle pace.

"One thing I don't like is someone who wants to be the best but isn't willing to give a hundred percent commitment. How much did you drink last night?" Who the fuck does he think he is? I can feel my anger start to build as he talks to me like I'm a kid.

"I'm sorry, but who said you had any say over my life outside the gym? I'm pretty sure I hired your ass and I don't need to answer to you."

He reaches out and presses the speed button, the pace

suddenly increasing and making me need to concentrate more to keep my feet moving.

"I'm your coach, and as much as you try to fight against me, I know what I'm talking about. You've made it clear you don't want me, but Eddie hired me because I'm exactly what you need. So I'll ask you again, how much did you have to drink last night?"

I want to tell him to go fuck himself but the words don't come out. "I didn't have much, a few more once you left."

He reaches out again and increases the speed. My legs are starting to burn as he has me sprinting faster than I normally go. *Shit, he's trying to kill me.* My stamina is pretty good but I run long distances at a lower speed, this is getting difficult. I hear Bryce mutter something under his breath before looking away from me. That has my interest piqued, and even though I need to reserve my energy for the run I want to know what he said.

"Sorry, missed that. Want to repeat what you just muttered?"

He looks at me before walking away, ignoring my question. I reach out, press the stop button and jump off the machine. I follow behind him, keeping close so he knows I'm not going anywhere.

"Oh, don't go quiet now. You're normally so talkative, so spit it out."

His eyes flash to mine before walking off again. He's really pissing me off with this ignoring me thing. I catch up to him, matching his fast pace as he moves across the gym. When I get close I reach out and grab him by the arm, turning him towards me before stepping into his personal space.

"Spit it out, Bryce. Tell me what the fuck you said."

His eyes are full of fire and I honestly think he might punch me. He tries to step back but I don't let him put any space between us. He must realize that I'm not going to let it go because he leans in, anger seeping into his words as he speaks. "Fine, you want to know what it was. I said that I thought it would take more than a few drinks for you to finger fuck some woman in the middle of a club. Really fucking classy, Zeke." I'm not shocked by the anger I hear in his voice, I knew he was pissed off about me ignoring him last night.

"Fuck you. You had your own opportunity to get some action last night, it's not my fault that you're too fucking stuck up to get your dick wet." I should feel bad about the way I made him feel last night, but the anger is taking over and I can't hold my tongue. If I thought he looked ready to hit me before I had definitely underestimated him. I can now feel the anger vibrating off him and I actually brace myself ready for him to attack.

Just as I'm sure he is about to floor me, a voice echoes through the gym from behind us, saving me from having to defend myself. "Hey, sexy." Asha's voice breaks the tension between me and Bryce, making him back away from me slightly.

His eyes never leave mine, the dark anger still clear in them. "Get in the ring and ready to fight." With those words he walks away from me. I let him go this time, it's probably better to let him cool off before we fight.

After getting gloved up I enter the ring, closely watching a pacing Bryce. He looks dangerous in here, and it doesn't look like he has lost any of his anger. I notice he isn't wearing his own gloves and instantly want to remove mine but I know I can't. I usually train with just wraps, but I've been ordered to wear training gloves until my hand is strong again. I hate it. It takes the thrill out of the hit. I have a distant thought that this fight might become more real than our usual sparring, and I want to feel my hand connect with Bryce's skin without the protection of the gloves.

"I want you to show me what you can do. No holding back, I can take anything you can give me so do your worst." That's all he says before holding his fists out. I bump them before my eyes move quickly over to Asha who is standing to the side watching us. A thump to my head brings my attention back to the guy in front of me. He probably thinks I was looking at Asha to flirt with her, to make sure she was watching me, but I was actually trying to silently tell her to leave. I don't think this fight is going to end well and I don't need her running back to tell the other guys what happened here.

I bring my hands up in front of my face, protecting myself until I see how he fights. I don't want to make the first move, but apparently that doesn't bother Bryce who kicks out and catches me in the ribs. It doesn't hurt but there is enough power behind it for me to realize that he isn't playing. He bounces away from me, making sure I can't retaliate. I watch the way his body moves, trying to predict what he's about to do from the way his muscles move. I'm getting frustrated as I realize that he hides his movements well and his muscles don't contract until the second he lashes out. I'm still trying to watch him when his fist comes out and catches me on the side of my head. He's pissing me off and I think that's his plan, he wants to get me angry so I lose my concentration and it's fucking working. I throw my first punch but he easily avoids it and I end up chasing him. It's time to take control of this fight.

I fake moving left and Bryce's stance changes just enough for me to take advantage. I throw a right hook and catch him on the shoulder, knocking him off balance. As he tries to right his body I put my shoulder down and barge into his chest, taking him to the mat. His arm instantly comes out, wrapping around my neck to try and roll my body off. His power is immense and I wonder for a second why he doesn't still fight. I feel his arm tighten around my neck and I know I need to get out of the choke hold quickly. As I fight to get my arm in between his, his legs wrap around my waist and I know that I'm losing my advantage very quickly. Bryce rolls to the side and I have no option but to move with him, putting my body under his. His legs lose their hold and he moves his arm from around my neck to lean his elbow onto my throat.

He looks down at me and a shiver runs through my body. Feeling his chest on mine, skin to skin, is like a burning heat. My breathing becomes labored and I know it's not from the exertion of our activity, it's from the hot man that's lying on top of me. I feel the pressure of his arm slacken and use the freedom to gain the upper hand. I buck my hips and turn, reversing our position so I'm lying on top of him. This seemed like a good idea but now I'm lying on top of Bryce between his legs. I can feel my cock harden before my brain

61

has a chance to register how we're positioned. Bryce's eyes widen and I know he can feel how hard I am. I need to get out of here now. I push up from his body as quickly as I can, grabbing Asha as I leave the ring to hit the showers. I need to work out this frustration and she will be the perfect way to do it.

CHAPTER SIX

Bryce

I listen to the sound of his retreating feet as I continue to lie on the floor of the ring. I'm not sure what just went on but I do know that it shouldn't have happened. I let my anger get the better of me and I can't do that if I want to keep my job. I couldn't help myself though, when he walked in late, acting like he didn't have a worry in the world, it pissed me off. I had no intention of actually making him run as punishment for being late, but when he challenged me I knew I couldn't back down. He's the type of guy that if you give in once then you'll lose all control, and he will never listen to anything you say ever again. I should've stopped with the running machine and not let what happened last night bother me but no, I had to go and open my big mouth. I was just so pissed that he acted as though last night wasn't a big deal and that he had been perfectly sober. If he'd been drunk I think I could have accepted that he'd acted like an arse, but if he was as sober as he's making out then he's just a dickhead.

I run my hands down my face, not wanting to get up from my spot in the ring. I just want the ground to open up and swallow me, that way I wouldn't have to try and work out what just happened between us. I swear I was just trying to assess his skill level and see how his technique has held up during his injury. Well that's what I'm trying to convince myself now. Truthfully, I wanted to kick his arse and make sure that it hurt just a little. I let out a groan and sit up, feeling the muscles in my stomach pull in protest. My workout before Zeke arrived had clearly showed that my core is weakening so I need to work harder, make sure I get back to peak fitness. Maybe a fight with a top ranking MMA fighter wasn't the smartest move. Especially when I'm apparently insanely attracted to the guy. Being in the ring with Zeke today taught me one very important thing, if I want to keep my sanity intact I can't touch him. The first few punches were fine, but when he barged me and we fell to the floor, the feel of his whole body against mine made me feel like I was going to pass out. His body touching mine was like receiving an intense electric shock and I couldn't help my dick's reaction to it. Thankfully the way he was lying on me hid the fact that I was as hard as stone. I fought so hard against his hold in fear of him feeling my erection and firing me on the spot.

I stand and stretch my body out before exiting the ring. I look around wondering where the girl that had caught Zeke's eye when she arrived had gone. I initially thought that he was going to put on a show for her, try to impress her with his moves but now I'm not so sure. He seemed as intent as I was to do harm, to win the fight at any cost and show me he was the strongest.

My mind goes back to when he was on top of me, the memory that will be with me the rest of my life, and I realize a very important fact. Zeke had felt like he was hard and struggling with an inappropriate erection like I was. I shake my head, convinced that I got it wrong. *I mean why the hell would he get hard when he was tangled with me?* Was it knowing the woman was watching or was it something else? Was he feeling the same spark as I was? *Shit.* I could think about this for hours but the obvious reason would still be that being the center of attention turns him on, especially if the voyeur is a woman.

I sigh to myself as I make my way to the changing room, hoping that he's already left. I curse silently when I hear the shower running, I guess this is my day for bad luck. I take a deep breath and prepare myself to be ignored, the reality of what I find is very different. The woman who had been watching us fight is now pressed against the half wall in between the showers, her hands griping the towel rail on the other side. She's moaning loudly and the reason for that is the sexy as fuck naked man who's pounding into her from behind. My eyes track slowly up over Zeke's body, watching how his muscles move as he thrusts into her. His arms tighten as he holds onto her hips, keeping her in place.

Eventually I reach his face and see that he's staring right at me. As hard as I try, I can't look away. It's like his eyes are like glue, forcing me to stay locked in his stare. There is a heat in his gaze that I want to explore, but the major problem with that is where his dick is. It's inside a woman, not me, not another guy. It's pretty obvious that he likes pussy and I should walk away from this scene, but it's like when you see a car crash. You know it's going to be messy but you just can't seem to pull your eyes away from what's happening. I can hear him groaning from across the room and the sound is causing my softening dick to harden, pushing against the front of my shorts in a very obvious way. This is starting to be a constant problem around him, but this time it's even worse. I want to look away but also I want to look down and see if I can get a glimpse of what he's packing, see what's making the girl moan so much. I can't though, I just keep staring into his eyes.

There's a sheen of sweat over his forehead and his pace quickens. His breathing changes and the muscles in his neck stick out, tightening as his rhythm falters. He's getting close, and I know I can't watch him come. It'll be too much for me. But still I stand here, watching him move. I lick my lips and his eyes slowly move lower to stare at my mouth, causing my breath to catch in my throat. After what feels like a month, his eyes move back to mine as he lets out a groan and comes inside her. I'm actually panting as I watch his eyes darken in pleasure and his body shudders as release works though him. The muscles in his arms tighten as he grips onto her hips, his nipples hardening and making me want to feel them with my tongue. I can feel my balls pull up into my body, and the telltale tingle down my spine tells me that I'm close to coming. I groan as I watch and I pray that the woman is making enough noise to cover it. I reach down and grab myself in an attempt to stop what I know is about to happen but I'm too late. I release into my shorts like a twelve-year-old boy who can't control his body. I open my eyes, not realizing I had closed them. I try not to look at Zeke, but my eyes are drawn to him like a magnet. He's standing in the same spot, still inside of the woman, but his eyes are on me, a look of lust on his face that can't be mistaken. I look away, not ready to deal with this and what it means. Training is over and I will decide later what is going to happen tomorrow.

****

My feet pound the ground as I pick up my speed again, trying to outrun my thoughts. I turn up the music, trying to focus on that and not the thoughts that have been running through my head since the shower incident. I'd hoped that going for a run would clear my head and I would be able to make some sense of what happened earlier.

After coming in my pants like a teenage boy I left the gym, not even waiting long enough to clean up. I needed to get out before I embarrassed myself even more. It would take a lot for something to be more embarrassing, maybe if I was naked in public? Actually I think I would rather be naked in public than making a mess of my shorts while watching my boss fuck a woman. I hear my groan over the music as the memory assaults my brain. I pick up my pace yet again and concentrate on the burn in my muscles. I know I won't last long at this speed but exhaustion might just be what I need. I turn along the path that leads down towards the lake. I've run here before, finding the peaceful route by accident one day I got lost. The quietness appealed to me but today it's my enemy. There are no distractions, nothing to pull me out of my head.

My lungs start to burn, making it hard to catch my breath and I know I need to stop, but I don't. Instead I push myself a little further and a little harder. When I hit the softer dirt next to the lake I slow my pace down to a walk, trying to catch my breath before I pass out. I've pushed my body today and I'm surprised it hasn't given out on me yet. I've done more today than I have in the last few months, and I know when I get up tomorrow I'm going to be in a lot of pain. Pain I can do though, pain I understand. I bend over and put my hands on my knees, taking deep breaths as a set of memories flood my mind. *Not now, I have enough shit on my plate without going back there.* It's no good though, I've never been able to control the feelings that are caused by the memory of Austin. A pained sob leaves my body as my legs give out and I collapse to the ground. I grab at the dirt as I try to get control of myself. Eighteen months and it still hurts as much as it did that day. Pain rips through my heart and I feel myself struggling to breathe. I force myself to breathe through the heartache just like my therapist told me to. Once I feel like I have a little control I sit back on my knees and look out over the lake, letting the calmness of the water settle my frayed nerves. I breathe in through the nose and out through the mouth, letting my lungs fill with cleansing oxygen and exhaling the pain. I repeat the process, concentrating on the water and nothing else.

I lean against the tree that I collapsed next to, lifting my head towards the sun. I close my eyes and let the heat flow through my body. It was a warm day like this when my life changed forever.

I'd been dating Austin for nearly a year and he was my everything. We were getting ready to spend the night in the best hotel we could afford, just the two of us. We lived with another four guys in a large house close to our collage. It wasn't the most amazing place but it was cheap and had enough room for us all. Privacy was always an issue though and we never really got any time to ourselves, so tonight was going to be our chance. An entire night with just us and room service. There was only one thing I needed to do before we drove the twenty miles to the hotel. I needed to win the money to pay for it. I'd been fighting for about eight months, not legal fights, more the underground variety, and I was good. Actually I was better than good, and I hoped all the experience would get me into the official leagues. All I needed was for someone to spot me and give me a chance.

We'd been watching the fights before mine, so the night passed quickly and before we knew it my fight was next. It felt like any other night and I knew I'd be going home a winner. Just before entering the ring I pulled Austin to me and kissed him passionately, letting him know that tonight was going to be one to remember.

"Don't go anywhere. I'll be done in a few and then you're all mine, baby. I can't wait to get you alone, I'm gonna make you scream my name tonight."

I felt his chest shake against mine as he laughed and I couldn't help but smile. He was the most perfect man I'd ever met. I leaned in and claimed his lips again as my name was shouted over the speakers.

"I love you." Little did I know that those would be the last words I would ever speak to him.

I was winning my fight after quickly gaining the upper hand against my opponent. I looked over to where Austin stood and I saw someone shouting in his face. I stopped instantly to try and work out what was happening but it quickly became chaos. One minute they were standing shouting at each other and the next the guy punched Austin and knocked him to the ground. I heard screaming but it was only afterwards that I realized the sound had come from me. I tried to move but my opponent decided that this was his time to gain some ground. I watched in horror as the man who punched Austin started kicking his body. I turned and pushed the fighter away, needing to get out of the ring. I finally got out, but was met with a group of the attacker's friends who pushed me back.

"Fucking queer," I heard them say, and I instantly knew what this was about, they saw me kiss Austin. I kept forgetting that the world was filled with hate and that we couldn't be open about our relationship like other people. I couldn't believe I forgot my head and kissed him here, in front of everyone. I pushed against them but they refused to let me past. Fists flew and I didn't even know if I was hitting anyone in my desperation to get to Austin. I knew that I felt an explosion of pain in my face at some point and could feel blood dripping from my mouth but I still couldn't get to him. Time slowed as I saw his attacker pull his leg back. I pushed with all my might in another attempt to get to him, but I heard the crunch of the guy's foot connecting with Austin's face even above all the noise. Austin's head flew back and the people directly surrounding him were covered in his blood as it exploded from his face. All feeling left my body and I crumbled to my knees, the hands that had been holding me back suddenly vanishing.

"No, no, no, no!" The words came out automatically as I crawled across the dirty floor towards Austin. The crowd thinned as people realized what'd happened and didn't want to get involved. I should've been angry with them, screaming at them for not helping but all I could think was it just made it easier for me to get to him. I didn't even look to see where his attackers were, I knew they wouldn't hang around and I didn't care. I just needed to get to Austin. I picked him up gently and placed his head on my outstretched legs, cradling him against me. I looked down and I didn't recognize his face, blood and swelling covering everything that made him mine. I could see droplets falling onto his face and that's when I realized I was crying. I couldn't see his chest moving and I was too scared to check to see if he was breathing. I just needed to hold him and not let him go. I was still sat holding him fifteen minutes later when the ambulance arrived, but I knew he'd already gone.

I reach up and brush the tears from my cheek. One day I will be able to remember Austin without that memory ripping my heart out. I want to remember the good times, like how it felt to be wrapped in his arms and how his laughter made my heart fill with love. Those are the memories that I need to hold on to but they get always get shoved to the side by the last time I held him, his blood covering both our bodies. I let out a deep breath and pick up a handful of little stones before throwing them into the lake. I watch the water rippling out from where the stones disappeared under the surface. It's peaceful watching, to see that something as small and insignificant as a pebble can change something as big as a lake.

That's what Austin did, he was such a small part of my life but he changed everything and I wasn't the same after he was gone.

I drop the remaining stones when I hear my phone alerting me to a text through my headphones. Unhooking my phone from my armband, I open my messages and groan when I see that's it's from Zeke's number. I wonder if this is him telling me that I'm fired, that I ruined everything when I let my anger take control. I reluctantly open it and I'm shocked when I read what he's sent.

What's happening tomorrow? I promise not to be late.

I let a sudden laugh out, probably scaring the wildlife that's surrounding me. Of all the messages I expected him to write, this was not one of them. Every time I think I know what's happening, Zeke throws me for a loop. I smile, knowing that life will never be boring while I work with him, but at least I know I still have a job.

Zeke

Today has been one epic fuck up after another. Every time something happened I thought the day couldn't get any worse, but it was like the universe wanted to prove me wrong. Bringing home the random hookup was mistake number one and I paid for that when I got home after training. Apparently she wasn't too happy with the way we left things and threw a rock through my front window. Well, I'm not a hundred percent certain it was her, but she's the only person I pissed off today that knows where I live.

Now I'm sitting with a coffee on my back step thinking about all my other fuck ups from today. I would prefer a beer but I think that would be a very bad idea at the moment. There's a certain coach who would rip me a new one if he knew I had even thought about having a drink. With that simple thought, I'm brought back to the biggest mistake of the day, and the one I don't know how to deal with. I thought our altercation in the ring was bad enough, but getting hard when my body was flush with Bryce's wasn't where I saw the fight going. Add to that what happened in the changing room, and it cemented it into as confusing as fuck. I don't know why I watched him while I ploughed into Asha's body, and I certainly don't know why I was struggling to come until he came into the room, or why I kept my eyes on him as I filled her body with my release. Bryce staring at me pushed me over the edge into the best orgasm I've ever had. When he came, the sound he made as he threw his head back was the sexiest thing I've ever fucking heard in my life. That takes a lot for me to admit, but there is no mistaking how it made me feel, even though I know it shouldn't. I always knew I was different, that what I felt when I was younger wasn't the same as all my friends, but when I spoke to my dad about it, he told me I was confused and I needed to find a girl. According to him, once I had been with one I would know what I was meant to feel. Now I'm really confused, and I can't help wondering. *Is there more to what I'm feeling for Bryce?*

Instead of analyzing the feelings that are confusing me, I grab my cell from my pocket. I didn't get a chance to speak to him after Asha left; he had run away before I had even turned off the shower. I don't know if he's going to come back tomorrow, but I need him to. I need to find out what's happening to me. Throwing caution to the wind, I text Bryce and pray that he'll reply.

What's happening tomorrow? I promise not to be late.

I stare at my phone while I drink my coffee. For all I know he could be half way back to England by now, and who would blame him? I'm not the easiest guy to get along with on with on a normal day, so add in how fucking confused I'm feeling and I know I've been a dick to him. I can't help it, pushing people away before they see the real me is a defense mechanism. I need them to leave before they see that I'm not as happy as I make out I am. My phone vibrates in my hand and I read a reply from Bryce.

Be in the gym by 10. If you're hungover you will be running again.

I feel a smile tug at my lips, the feeling of relief is more than I imagined. I'll see him tomorrow, even though I'm not sure what the fuck will happen when I get there.

CHAPTER SEVEN

Zeke

I make sure I arrive well before ten the next morning, determined to get on Bryce's good side from the get go. My efforts weren't in vain and we've had a good day. I feel that we're getting back on track together but we haven't spoken about what happened yesterday. I don't know if leaving it hanging over our heads is a good thing, but there's been no opportunity to talk. Where yesterday there was no one here, today it feels like everyone who has ever trained here has decided to come at the same time. Even Coach decided that he needed a sit down with me and Bryce to discuss our game plan and for a guy that doesn't want to train me, he had a lot of suggestions.

Now I'm standing in the shower with memories of the last time I was in here taking up residence in my head. I can clearly visualize how Bryce had looked when he orgasmed and it's making me hard. Shit, I can't be getting hard when it's so busy in here. Every shower is taken except the one next to me, and at the moment I'm thankful for that. Or I am until I see Bryce walking into the room with a towel over his shoulder. He stops walking when his eyes settle on the empty cubicle and me. *Well this is awkward.* I can't leave now, not without making things obvious. I close my eyes and turn away from him, hoping he will just act like nothing is weird. I make sure I keep my head under the water until I hear his shower turn on, only then do I risk looking over at him. His head is leaning forward until his chin is resting on his chest, letting the hot water hit his shoulders and neck.

"Everything okay? I saw you roll your neck a lot today." *What the fuck?* Why not just admit that I couldn't take my eyes off him the whole damn day. I'm meant to play the friend card until I understand what's happening with me.

"I think I overdid it yesterday. It's been so long since I had a good workout, my body can't cope with too much anymore. I'm going soft." He laughs and rubs over his stomach.

I can't help but let my eyes move down his body, watching as his hands rub over his cut abs and down towards that perfect fucking V of his. If he thinks there's anything other than hard muscle on him he's clearly delusional. I haven't seen anyone more built than him and, as much as I don't want to admit it, his body turns me on. I feel myself harden in agreement, my dick trying to tell him just how perfect he is.

When I stay quiet he looks over to me, his eyes roaming down over my body. I see color flushing his cheeks when he sees me watching him and he quickly turns away to grab his body wash. He lathers the soap in his hands before rubbing over himself, his hands moving easily over his slippery skin. I try not to watch, there are too many men in here to witness me staring openly at a naked guy, but it's like my eyes are magnets and his body is made of iron. I start to rub over my own body and when my hands move south, the feel of my hand on my dick almost has me groaning out loud. I feel more turned on now watching Bryce rub his body, than I did when I was inside Asha. There is something wrong with me, I shouldn't be reacting to him like this, this isn't the way I should be feeling.

There have been other men in the past that I have found attractive, even though I wouldn't admit it, but none that have made me react like this. I never thought much about those passing fancies because, as I keep telling myself, I'm not gay. But with Bryce, this attraction when he's near just feels natural, primal even. I need to either stop all these thoughts, block them out like I always have, or I need to allow myself to feel everything, see where it leads. I don't know which scares me the most, but I know I'm going to need to make a decision really soon.

I'm pulled from my thoughts when a rolled up bandage

comes flying across the changing room and hits me on the side of the head. I turn and see Jason standing staring at me.

"What?"

As soon as he starts talking I wish I hadn't opened my mouth. "Look man, I know you like pussy. We're all jealous of the women you get, but who the fuck are you thinking about now? Who could possibly be hot enough to have you jacking off in front off all of us?"

I look down and find my hand wrapped around my dick as it continues to rub from root to base. I instantly drop it but I can't help the redness that spreads across my cheeks. *Shit.* Normally I would give some lame answer and just get on with my shower without worrying about what these jackasses think of me, but knowing that Bryce is standing next to me has me struggling. I look at him out of the corner of my eye and see that his cheeks are just as flushed as mine and I wonder if he's remembering yesterday. Maybe he thinks I'm thinking of Asha.

"Wouldn't you like to know? You never know, Jason, maybe it was you." I wink at him before turning away and hiding under the water. I hear Jason laugh behind me and I'm thankful that I got away with that.

"Yeah, you wish I wanted your ass. Anyway I wanted to check you were hitting Joe's with us tonight. You in?"

After going out earlier in the week I could really do with a night in, but I never turn down a night with the guys. I turn and look over my shoulder at him. "Bryce is invited, right?" The words are out without even checking to see if he wants to go. We're finally getting along and I want to use the opportunity to spend some time with him, get to know him better.

"Of course, see you at nine." He salutes me before leaving the changing room and I turn to look at Bryce. He smiles at me and I feel my heart stutter in my chest. *Shit, I need to get myself under control.*

"I'm not gonna go out tonight. I'm still trying to recover from the other night." He lifts his eyebrows at me and I know exactly

75

what he's talking about.

"How about I promise not to drink and to also not be a dick?"

He laughs and it makes me smile. "Fine. But I swear if there is any finger fucking it better be with me." And just like that I'm hard again, visions of my fingers on his body causing lust to race through my veins.

****

I'm sitting in a corner booth in Joe's watching the front door but trying not to make it obvious. Bryce knew we were aiming to get here for nine and he said he'd be here then. I look down at my watch and see that it's just turned nine-thirty. He's late and I'm starting to get impatient, worrying he's changed his mind about coming. I grab the glass of water in front of me and take a drink to distract myself, but the door opens again and my eyes zero in on it instantly. I feel my body relax when I see Bryce walking through it. He looks around the bar, presumably for us, and I wave my hand at him, making sure he doesn't miss us. *Fucking hell, Zeke, get a grip.* I'm acting like lovesick ass. Joe's isn't a big bar, so I'm pretty sure he could have easily found the large group of very noisy guys playing pool.

I resist the urge to sit on my hands as I watch him approach, but I think maybe I should when I take in what he's wearing. He has on black jeans that hug the top of his thighs that highlights the huge muscles, and a simple white t-shirt, but the way it clings to his body is making it hard as fuck for me to think coherently. In this moment I realize one very important thing, I might not be gay, but I think I want Bryce, and I don't know where I go from here. I smile as he sits next to me and our thighs brush against each other in the tight space.

"Sorry I'm late. I got a little lost and some woman took me to a place called José's. It was scary, and I don't ever want to go there ever again." His eyes widen and I can't help but burst out laughing. I don't even know the place she took him. There isn't a place called José's around here.

"How did you escape?"

He's about to answer when a waitress comes over to the table. "Hey, sexy. What can I get you to drink?" Her hands stroke Bryce's arm as she speaks to him and I can't help the feeling of jealousy that courses through me as I watch her hand. I want to reach out and remove her fingers from him to make sure she doesn't touch him again. The feeling shocks me. I've never been possessive over anyone in my life, not even with the girls I sleep with. They can touch and sleep with all of the fighters for all I care. They're just a place to warm my dick. So this feeling is strange. I have this need to take Bryce away from here and not let her look at him again.

"I'll have a water, thanks." He turns to look at what I have in front of me and I pick up my glass and shake it towards him. He smiles at me before turning back to the waitress.

"Oh, a guy like you needs something stronger than water. How about I bring you something I know you'll like?" Pushy women don't bother me, in fact the pushier the woman the more she gets my attention, but this one is starting to really annoy me.

"He said he wants a fucking water. How about you go get him one and bring me another." Her eyes widen and she walks away without saying another word.

Bryce is frowning when he turns to look at me. "Are you okay? That was rather … abrupt."

I run my hands over my face and try to get a grip of myself. "Yeah, I'm fine. It's been a long ass week and I think I'm tired." I hope he accepts my excuse, because it's definitely not one I would believe.

****

I look down at my watch and notice that I have been sitting here for nearly two straight hours talking to Bryce without realizing it. We've spoken about nothing important but it's been great just getting to know the little things about him. Yesterday still hasn't been mentioned and as much as I would love to end the night on good terms, I know we need to talk about it. I take a drink of water, wishing like fuck it was bourbon, and get ready to bring it up.

I lean forward, resting my left elbow in the table in an attempt to keep the conversation for our ears only. "I completely hate to bring this up, and I don't want it to ruin a great night. But…yesterday. I think we need to talk about it."

I feel his leg start to bounce against mine and I know he's feeling as anxious as I am about this topic. "Which part? The part where I acted like a douche, or when I caught you in the changing room with the girl?" Well there's nothing like getting straight down to it. I notice he doesn't mention anything about me getting an erection while fighting with him, or how I watched him when I came. He's totally brushed over everything I did wrong and I can't believe that he thought he was the idiot in this scenario. I know it was me, and I own it completely.

"I'm pretty sure I was the one being a dick. You were just trying to push me and I gave you nothing but attitude. That's not the bit I meant though. I meant what happened after that, when I was in the shower."

His bouncing leg speeds up and it's making me feel more nervous. "Look, Zeke. There is nothing to talk about, you were … let's just say, getting relief, and I should have left you to it."

I reach down and still his knee. I know I should remove my hand but I can't. Instead, I tighten my grip around his thigh while moving it slightly higher as I lean in and talk directly into his ear. "I was speaking more about when you came in your shorts watching me." I know that I'm taking a risk here and that there are a hundred different ways he could react but I don't expect what he does.

He shakes his head at me before jumping up from the table. "Fuck you, Zeke." With those parting words he stalks towards the exit but I'm not about to let him leave this time. He's halfway to the door when I grab him by the arm and pull him sideways into the back hall that no one uses. I push him into it and lock the door behind us. There's no way he's escaping before we sort this out. I need to tell him how I feel, and I need to know if he's feeling it too.

"What the fuck is your problem?" I can't help the anger in my voice as I speak. I start pacing in front of him, my frustration making it impossible for me to keep still.

"My problem? I thought that maybe you were a decent enough guy not to take the piss out of me for what happened. My body reacted like a teenage boy, I'm so fucking sorry. I can't help it if …" His words stop and my pacing ceases.

What the fuck was he about to say? "Don't stop there. You know, you have this really annoying habit of only saying half a sentence. If it's important enough to start it then fucking finish it."

His face contorts and he looks as if he's physically in pain. He reaches up and grabs his hair and it's his turn to start pacing. The tension he's throwing off worries me. He suddenly stops moving as he comes to stand in front of me. His eyes meet mine with an intensity that I haven't seen before. He takes a few deep breaths, obviously bracing himself.

"I was going to say, I can't help it if you turn me on like no one ever has before. That when I see you I can't help but get hard, and when you came I couldn't control my body."

I stop breathing and I'm pretty sure my heart stops beating as well. Even after everything that's happened between us I didn't imagine that he would actually be attracted to me, let alone openly admit it. I refuse to break eye contact, but I don't know what to say. *How do you reply to a confession like that?*

"Shit, I knew this was a bad idea," Bryce says as he moves to barge past me but I grab him and press him up against the wall.

"Just give me a fucking minute, Bryce. This isn't something I know anything about." I need him to slow down. I need to think. His chest rises and falls quickly, his labored breathing matching mine.

"I don't know what to do next." My confession is quiet, and I'm not sure if he can hear me over his breathing.

"What do you want to do next, Zeke?" His eyes soften as he

looks at me, almost like he's pleading with me, but I'm not sure what for.

"I want to kiss you." I lean my forehead to his and listen to the groan that leaves him.

"Zeke." My name sounds like a prayer on his lips and it breaks the control I've been trying to hold onto. I press my body harder against his knowing that he can feel how fucking hard I am because of him, but I'm past caring. I can feel his breath against my lips and his tongue swipes over them, enticing me. I finally get the courage to make the move that will change my life forever. I slowly move my lips to his, taking my time so he can stop me if he needs to. When my mouth connects with his the world stops, everything focused on the feel of his lips against mine. They feel larger, fuller, and when they move against mine I realize how much I've missed out on, the feel of his stubble against my face makes my skin tingle. I flick my tongue out, tasting his lips and I suddenly feel like I'm drowning. His tongue moves against mine, his taste exploding in my mouth as he lets me lead the way. I know he wants more, I can tell by the way he's grabbing the side of my shirt but he's letting me feel my way through this kiss. He's being gentle, like he doesn't want to scare me off. Little does he know that there is nowhere else I would rather be than here.

Bryce

I'm glad I have the wall behind me helping to hold me up. Of all the fantasies I've had of Zeke over the last few days, this is one I never pictured. Zeke is kissing me like I'm his first. I'm trying to hold back, I don't want him to feel I'm forcing this on him. I don't ever want him to think he's only doing this because I made him. This has to be all his own decision, something he wants to do. The crazy thing is, I think he really does want to do it.

When he put his hand on my thigh and whispered in my ear that he knew I had come yesterday I'd panicked. I couldn't let him

80

know how much he turned me on with his words so I ran and I certainly didn't expect him to chase after me.

Now I have his lips against mine and I'm in heaven. His timid tongue is driving me insane and I just want to pin him to the wall and show him how to kiss me properly. His hard dick rubbing against mine is driving me to distraction and I don't know if I'll ever be able to form a coherent thought again.

I pull my lips from him, gasping as I fill my lungs with much needed air. "Zeke, you need to stop rubbing on me or I'm gonna embarrass myself again." I feel his lips smile against mine as he kisses me again.

"Does it feel okay?" I can't believe he's actually asking me this, what part of my body language isn't telling him that this the best thing ever.

"If it feels any more okay, I'm gonna spontaneously combust." This comment garners a laugh from him and I can feel the hair on my arms stand on end. How can even his laugh create a reaction in my body? The deep sexy rumble moving over me like a wave.

"I really didn't imagine you being so gentle, I just thought you would be all caveman. This is a side I didn't think you had." I have no idea why I'm talking so much. It's like I'm trying to discourage him from putting his lips on me again.

"What do you want, Bryce?" His lips kiss across my jaw and my head falls back against the wall to give him complete access to my neck. He takes full advantage of this and runs his tongue across my Adam's apple, causing my dick to pulsate and him to groan.

"I want to push you against that wall and kiss you so you never forget what it feels like."

He runs his nose up my neck completely distracting me from anything and everything. When he reaches my ear, he flicks his tongue out and licks it before he speaks.

"Then do it. Show me how this works. I've never been with a guy before, show me what I'm missing." And like showing a red rag to a bull, I push against his chest, using my body weight to push him against the wall opposite us. He lets out a grunt as his back hits the wall and I use it to my advantage, attacking his mouth with mine. I kiss him with all the pent up frustration I've been feeling, with all the loneliness I've felt this last eighteen months, and with all the pain I want to leave behind. He opens to me, allowing my tongue to investigate his mouth, and to stroke over his tongue in the most erotic way.

I grind against him, feeling the outline of his hardness and desperately wanting to see and touch it, but knowing that if I did I would probably push him too far. He pushes back against me, creating a delicious friction against the zip of my jeans. The groan that leaves me is totally beyond my control, the pleasure he's giving me making me lose my sanity. Zeke's hand grabs the back of my hair, pulling my mouth closer to his as his other hand reaches down and cups my dick. If he wasn't sucking my tongue at that point I'm pretty sure I would have swallowed it. He uses my hair to pull me back from his lips and the instant we part I feel lost. *Fuck, what is this guy doing to me?*

"I don't know how far I can go. I've never done this before with a guy. I've been attracted to men before, but nothing like it is with you, nothing I've ever acted on. It's like I can't keep my body under control around you."

I take a deep breath and try to calm my racing hormones. As much as I would love to take Zeke right here, right now, I know I need to slow down and let him take this at his own speed. "I'm sorry, I'll slow down. You just … you drive me out of my mind." I try to step away from him but he grabs my dick, making my legs shake with pleasure.

"You didn't let me finish. I don't know how far I can go, but I know I want to feel you come. I want to know what it feels like to make you come." And this is the point my brain short circuits because there's no way that Zeke Raine, MMA fighter and future championship holder, is telling me he is going to make me come. I begin to believe his words when his fingers start to undo the zip on my jeans. *Fuck, I'm so close already if he touches me I'm pretty sure I'll explode.*

I still his hand, needing to control this. "As much as I want to feel your hand around my dick, and trust me, I really do. I don't want it to happen here. I don't want you to do this and then go home regretting it. Take the night and think about what you want. If we do this now and you regret it then there is a lot at risk. I like my job, I get to train this really hot fighter and I quite like to watch his arse when he runs."

He laughs at me, but I can see that he knows I'm making sense. He leans his head against mine and it takes everything in me not to just say 'fuck it' and give in to what we both want.

"That makes sense. Can you do something for me though?"

I put my hands on his face, lifting his head up until he's looking into my eyes. "Anything." And I mean it, I would do anything for this guy and it scares me. I've only known him a few days but this is more than just instant attraction. There is just something about him, something that makes me want him more than anyone else I've met.

"Can you be the one to walk away, I don't think I can."

I kiss him on the forehead before stepping back. "I'll see you tomorrow, Zeke. Don't be late." I wink at him before I unlock the door and leave the hall, and the man I want, behind.

CHAPTER EIGHT

Bryce

I'm pretty sure I've been hard for the last twenty-four hours. I've tried every possible thing to relieve it, but as soon as I think it's under control I see Zeke and I'm back to square one all over again. Today's training was like an endurance test of the hardest variety. Being so close to him but not being able to touch him or talk to him about last night is driving me insane. At one point I was actually going to claim illness just to get some time away from him to give myself a minute to breathe. He's all consuming and it's a little unnerving, I haven't been able to think of anything but him since the moment I met him.

All the guys went out again tonight but I managed to avoid them until they'd left. My head is too messed up to go and pretend that everything's okay. I need time to be by myself and think. So after they all left I locked the front door and hit the running machine. Now an hour later my body is exhausted but unfortunately, my mind isn't. I was hoping that I could make it stop thinking for a little while by focusing on my stride, but apparently I'm not destined to get peace until I sort out this thing with Zeke.

I lift my head and rinse the last of the shampoo from my hair. I wasn't going to take a shower, but I couldn't avoid it after sweating so much today. My mind has been racing all day, but since I came into the stall all I can think about is everything that's happened in here. I seem to have had most of my 'encounters' with Zeke in these fucking showers, a fact that my dick apparently remembers all too well. I turn off the water and grab a towel, wrapping it around my waist as I walk to my locker. I need to start showering at home, or at a hotel, anywhere that isn't here really. Too much has happened in this room for my mind not to go to places it really shouldn't.

I reach up to grab my deodorant from the top shelf of my locker and my towel slips from my hips a little. When I step back I meet a warm body and I let out a shocked cry. The body doesn't move and a hand moves around to my stomach, making my muscles quiver under his touch.

Warm breath meets my ear before his words do. "I haven't been able to think about anything today except what you look like naked. I want to know if you're as hard as I imagined." My breath stutters at Zeke's words, but his roaming hand has me panting like a damn dog. He runs his hand over my abs, his fingers moving and caressing the ridges. If I hadn't been hard the instant I heard his voice in my ear then this would certainly have done the trick. Just feeling his hand investigating is making me light headed.

"I swear you make me so fucking hard. I don't know what it is about you but I need you. Mmm... I'm not used to such hard bodies. I'm used to soft curves, but you are perfection. I like how you feel. Fuck, Bryce, I want you so bad." His lips move against my ear as he talks softly, making me push back into him and wish there wasn't a towel between us. His hand moves lower, his little finger moving under the edge of my towel, making it come undone slightly.

"I watched you all day, did you know that? I couldn't keep my fucking eyes off you and spent most of the day with a hard on. I thought about what happened last night, and I've come to the conclusion that I need to make you come."

The groan that leaves me should be embarrassing but I just don't care when he's talking to me like this and his hands are on me. He moves away from me slightly before tugging my towel. I feel it give way and pool around my feet. He immediately presses his body against me and his hardness pushes between my arse cheeks. I grind back, loving the feeling of him there but wanting so much more.

"Shit, you feel so good against me. I could come from just feeling you there." His words are quiet as his lips brush against my ear. I want to talk to him, tell him that he needs to touch me but I can't seem to form words. All my blood rushes to my dick, making it difficult to think, or see, or do anything other than listen and feel. My legs start to shake and I lean into him more for support. His hand slides down and wraps around my dick with his fingers rubbing gently over the length of me.

"Zeke." It's the only word I can manage and I hope it conveys everything I want to say. I want to tell him to move faster, to never stop touching me, to claim me, but I can only focus on his hand, the way it's moving on my body. I've not been touched by many people, my experience limited, but I'm sure that this might be the most erotic thing to happen to me. His palm is warm as it moves up and down my length. His thumb rubs over my head, spreading pre-cum across my pulsing cock.

"Fuck, Bryce." His words come out on a growl and my head drops back onto his shoulder, the muscles in my body melting at the sound. His hand brushes over my balls, pulling them slightly before moving up my dick and twisting his hand over the head. As he rubs, the feelings become too much. I can already feel the tingle in the base of my spine and I know I'm not going to last much longer. I need to warn him that it's going to end soon, that he feels too good against my skin and that I can't control myself, but again I can't get the words out.

"Zeke." I know I'm going to think back to this moment often, and I'm always going to wish I was able to do more, or anything, but right now I don't care.

The pressure on my dick increases and I groan as I feel my balls pull up into my body, preparing to shoot everything I have all over Zeke's hand.

"That's it, baby. I want to feel you come. Give me it." He bites down on my shoulder and I know it's over, the last little bit of control I had disappears. I close my eyes and groan, feeling my orgasm work its way through my body as I shatter. There are lights flickering behind my closed eyelids and I'm panting, trying to get some control over my body. I'm brought back from my visit to heaven by feeling soft lips on my neck. I manage to straighten my legs so I'm taking my own weight.

"Fucking perfect. And just so you know, you make me come in my pants like a twelve year old boy as well." One final kiss and he's gone, vanishing almost as quietly as he appeared.

I drop my head against the locker and try to work out what the fuck just happened. I lost all control, the need to feel Zeke overshadowing the need for common sense. He controlled my body like an expert, knowing exactly how to touch me, where to touch me. Last night I walked away, gave him a chance to think about what had happened, and he came back to me. I wanted him to make the first move, and I think he just proved that he might be a little more comfortable than I thought he would be. The one thing I know for sure about what just happened is that I have just had the best orgasm of my life.

Zeke

I pull my truck into my driveway and bang my head on the steering wheel a few times trying to knock some sense into myself. *What the fuck was I thinking going in there tonight?* I'd only wanted to talk to Bryce but when I saw him standing there with his tight body stretched to grab something from the locker, I couldn't do anything to stop myself. I had a primal need to touch him and give him pleasure like he's never had before. I laugh to myself. Bryce is obviously gay, even though he's never come out and said it to me, so I'm sure that what I just did wasn't exactly as mind blowing as I think. The guy could stop traffic with his looks and body. I'm pretty sure there were a few broken hearts when he left England. No, what I just did to him was mind blowing for me, a life altering moment that means everything, but I'm sure it was just a normal

Saturday night for Bryce. For some reason that thought makes me feel a little worthless. I want to be important to him, someone that he sees a future with. *Whoa, what the fuck am I talking about?* I think that I need to slow down and work out what this thing is between us.

I shuffle in my seat and remember that I still have a mess in my shorts I need to deal with. After making my way inside, I strip off the offending piece of clothing and throw it towards the hamper before getting under the hot water of my shower. I honestly cannot believe I came in my shorts. I've never done that before in my life. I had managed to hold myself together and not given in to the pleasure of his ass against my cock. Rubbing against his ass felt amazing, it felt like something I've been missing my whole life. His muscles were firm and my cock fit perfectly between his ass cheeks. God, even the thought of it is getting me hard. I thought I was doing well controlling the urges until he shot his load into my hand. When I felt the warm liquid hit my palm I lost it and filled my shorts with my own mind-blowing orgasm. Groaning I hit my head on the tiles and let the water hit the back of my neck. I've no idea what I'm doing and I have no idea why it feels so good. I spent all day watching him, my eyes involuntarily finding him wherever he was. The memory of his mouth from the night before made sure I was hard for the whole fucking day. I cannot begin to explain how many times I wanted to go, pin him to a wall and taste him again. If some of the looks he had given me through the day where anything to go by, I think he was feeling the same way. I don't know if it was the fact that he walked away the night before or the thrill of the unknown that had me going back to the gym tonight. I let myself in with my set of keys after sitting in the car park for nearly an hour waiting for everyone to leave, waiting for him to be alone so we could talk. I didn't know what I was going to walk into, but I had to see him.

I turn off the shower and don't even bother drying myself as I walk into my room and collapse onto my bed. I lie there, just staring at the ceiling, hoping that the answers to all my questions will suddenly appear. I list the questions that I need answers for in my head and try to rationalize the answers. *Am I attracted to Bryce?* I have never been more attracted to anyone in my life, which I'm still finding incredibly surprising. *Can I handle the fact I'm attracted to a man?* I don't know, but I do know that I can't handle walking away without seeing where this could go. And the last and probably the most important question: *am I gay or possibly bi?* I know the answer to that should be no, I had it drummed into me from a young age that wanting to be with a guy is wrong and that there is no way that I could be gay. Apparently my body didn't get the memo though, and it's finding its pleasure in the hard muscled body of Bryce. This leads to another important question, *am I attracted to men, or am I attracted to just Bryce?* This is a question I can answer easily and the answer makes me smile. It is one hundred percent Bryce.

I lift my body up and get under the sheet, suddenly needing sleep like I need my next fight. The last few days have been difficult and my mind has been constantly running at a hundred miles per hour making it nigh on impossible to sleep. Maybe now that I've made a decision I will get some rest. I've made my decision? I must have decided at some point what I was going to do. I just hadn't actually admitted it to myself. I take a deep breath and let the thought cross my mind, cementing it there so I know the truth clearly. I want Bryce Tanner and I will have him no matter what.

****

"*No son of mine is gay. There's no way that's gonna happen, I didn't produce a faggot.*"

I bolt upright in bed with sweat dripping down my body. It's been a long time since my dad's invaded my dreams and I can say with great certainty that I haven't missed him. I turn and put my feet on the floor, leaning my elbows on my knees and hold my head in my hands. Fuck, I hate it when I dream about him. He had made me feel so ashamed when I came to him for advice, and I can still feel it running through me now. I get up from my bed and grab a pair of running shorts. When the nightmares hit the best thing to do is to work out and hope that exhaustion will take the visions.

I look at the clock beside my bed and realize that I still have another couple of hours before I need to get up for training. *Fuck.* I scrub my hands over my face as my mind battles with all the thoughts running through it. I can't help but hear my dad's words repeat through my head, and I know I'm hearing them because of Bryce. I made decisions last night, one that will change everything, and I know that my mind must be freaking out. It's like a battle is raging in my head, between my dad and Bryce. The man who shaped who I am today, and the man who could shape my future.

When the noise in my head becomes too much, I use my fist to hit the side of my head in an attempt to knock everything out. I'm sick of thinking, of constantly doubting what I feel and think. I just want it all to be quiet for a while. I pull on a wife beater and grab my sneakers as I rush out of the house. I need to run, to feel my feet hit the pavement as music drowns out the world. Before I leave the house I type out a text, sending it before I have time to think about it. I throw my phone onto the couch, grab my iPod and leave.

Bryce

I check my watch again and see that Zeke is now nearly an hour late. I would be slightly worried in normal circumstances, but after what happened last night I'm even more concerned. I seem to spend a lot of time worrying about what happened the day before with Zeke. I feel like I'm constantly trying to rationalize what's between us to myself, and it's driving me insane.

I walk over to Eddie's office and pop my head through the door.

"You haven't heard from Zeke today have you?"

He looks up from the papers on his desk and shakes his

90

head. "I haven't, son. Have you lost him already?" He laughs at his own comment and I force a smile to my face. There's no way that Eddie can discover what's happening, or not happening, between Zeke and me. I'm pretty sure I would be fired before I finished my explanation. Not that I could explain something I don't understand myself.

"I don't think so, but you never know with him. I think I need to get him a new alarm clock."

He points to the chair across the desk from him and I sigh inside, knowing there's no way to say no to Eddie. I sit, trying to look as relaxed as possible.

"So how's our boy doing?" The way he says 'our boy' has my heart beating a little faster. Little does he know how much I want him to be *my* boy. I came to the decision last night, after Zeke nearly caused me heart failure with only his hands, that I was willing to do whatever he wanted. If it meant letting him explore while he came to terms with it all, then I would swallow my pride for a while and let him have me. I haven't felt a connection with anyone since Austin, and truthfully I didn't think I ever would again, so now that the opportunity is there I don't want to pass it up. I am pretty sure attraction like this doesn't come around very often, and I've been so fucking lonely. It's nice to have someone who wants me, someone that makes me feel again.

"He's doing great. There have been a few moments where I thought I might be losing the fight with him but he realized that I actually know what I'm talking about. His strength is improving and his technique hasn't suffered despite his injury."

Eddie nods his head and sits back in his chair. It's hard to have a conversation with him. He's the quiet type that doesn't give much away.

"That's good. Just thought I would check, you know, to make sure you were working well. Well I'll let you go and find the runaway." And with that he goes back to the papers on his desk, basically dismissing me.

I walk back to the changing rooms to grab my mobile phone

to call Zeke and find out where he is. When I unlock it I see a text from him and relief flows through me. The relief is short lived when I open the message.

I won't be in for a few days.

That's it? Just a few words saying he won't be in? What the fuck is that about? I press his number and try to call him but it rings out before going to his answering service. I try a total of five times to get him to answer but my calls go to voicemail every time. I have a mixture of emotions running through me. There's worry and sadness, but the most predominant one is anger. I didn't ask him to touch me yesterday, that was all on him and now he runs? He is affecting his own chances of being ready for his life changing fight and he's acting like a dick, hiding out because he did something that he's scared to admit. Does he really think that in a few days I will have forgotten about what happened? That I just need a little space to realize that he doesn't want me and then he can come waltzing back in here like nothing happened? I was willing to be his experiment and let him use me to discover if this is something he wants, but there is no fucking way he's going to treat me like shit. I will not be someone's regret, no matter how hot they are. I press reply to his text but decide against it. There is no way this is going to be sorted out over a text message. I dress quickly before slamming my locker door, allowing my anger to come out in the movement. Thankfully I have his address in the file in my car. It's time I visited Mr. Raine and sorted this out once and for all.

CHAPTER NINE

Bryce

I bang my hand on the door again. I don't know if he's out or just ignoring me, but I'm not going anywhere until I talk to him. I hear a noise from inside the house, so at least I know that he's in there, unless it's someone else. The thought sends dread through my body. It's not something I had considered when I drove over here. Maybe he has a woman in there, trying to get rid of the memory of me on his skin. I flush, suddenly embarrassed that I'm here causing problems.

I'm just about to turn and run back to my car when the door opens in front of me. Zeke stands there in shorts and a vest, his hair messed up like he's been running his hands through it for hours and, against all self-preservation, I can't help but look at him with lust flowing through me. My eyes make it to his legs before he speaks, quickly pulling my stare back to his face.

"Did you not get my text? I need a few days off." He tries to close the door on me but I put my foot in between it and the doorframe, halting its movement.

"Yeah, I got your text. Did you not hear me calling?"

I get a grunt of response but that's not going to work with me now. I need to get a few things off my chest and there's no better time than right now.

"Was that an actual answer, because I'm pretty sure all I heard was a grunt?"

He doesn't even respond as he turns and walks away, leaving the door open behind him. Apparently I'm meant to follow him, and if I wasn't as determined to have this out with him, I would piss him off by leaving but I'm not sure that would piss him off today.

I walk into his house, following the noise he's making until I'm in the kitchen. I watch as he grabs a bottle of beer from the fridge and puts it on the table in front of the chair across from where he's sitting. He takes a swig from his own bottle and I really want to tell him he shouldn't be drinking but I refrain. There are more important things to talk about at the moment. I sit across from him and take the bottle that's obviously meant for me, deciding to have a drink to calm my racing nerves. It doesn't bode well that he thinks we need alcohol to get through this conversation.

"So you want to tell me why you're not at the gym? It doesn't look like you're missing a limb, and that's pretty much the only excuse I'll accept."

His eyes meet with mine as he takes another drink, his look intense and filled with something I can't quite put my finger on.

"Are you gay?" Okay, not where I thought this conversation was going, and really not an answer to what I was asking.

"I thought it was obvious but if you're looking for confirmation then yes, Zeke, I'm gay."

He nods, finishes his bottle of beer and grabs another one from the fridge. Sitting again, he starts ripping the label from the bottle. "I'm not gay."

I want to tell him that he felt pretty gay last night and that most straight men don't give other men hand jobs, but I don't think this is the time for that. Instead I sit quietly and let him lead the conversation.

"I thought I was once, when I was a teenager. I told my dad but it's okay, he showed me the error of my ways." He laughs but I can't hear an ounce of humor in it. He looks so sad sitting there and it's taking everything in me not to wrap my arms around him and tell him that everything is going to be fine, but I just sit here. I don't know what demons he's battling but I need him to let me in so I know what I'm fighting against. He obviously has a past, and one that isn't happy. I sit patiently and let him work out what's going on in his head.

94

"How did you come out? How did your parents react?"

My head is getting a bit confused with the sudden changes in subject, every time I think I know what the conversation is about he throws something else at me.

"Wow, well that was a few years ago now. It went well, I told them that I wasn't attracted to women. They were very supportive, but maybe I was lucky because I have a big brother and sister who are both straight, so they know they're gonna get grandkids from them." I smile when I remember my mum crying, telling me that I was always special so she should have known I would be different. My dad was a bit shocked I think by the fact I was so into what he considered masculine pastimes. He had preconceived ideas about gay men, and my love of fighting and cars didn't fit with what he thought he knew. He supported me the whole way though, he never thought any less of me or was embarrassed by my life.

"It must have been nice, having all that love and support around you." He finishes another bottle of beer and stands. Walking to a cupboard, he pulls out a bottle of Jack Daniels. He grabs two shot glasses before sitting down at the table again. I watch as he fills the glasses before pushing one in my direction. I don't drink the one in front of me, I just watch him as he downs his.

He starts to speak as he refills his glass. "I was nearly fifteen when I told my dad that I had feelings for guys. That the girls I knew didn't get me excited but seeing the guys in shower after gym made me hard. Fuck, you would have thought I told him I wanted to murder babies the way he exploded. He told me that no son of his was a faggot, that I just needed to be with a girl and get over my crazy thoughts." He downs the drink and fills the glass again, I want to take it away from him but at least it's getting him to talk. I can't believe that his own dad treated him like that, especially when he had been brave enough to speak out.

"What happened after that?" I want him to get this out, maybe it will help him process what he's feeling.

"Life changed after that, like, seriously changed. I'd had a great life before that, but speaking those simple words made things

95

quickly go to hell. That's how I got into fighting. My dad thought it was important that I had 'manly' pursuits, that maybe if I acted more like a man I would become one. I had to learn fast how to protect myself because my dad soon started to organize fights for me, most of them against his friends. For the first few months I was in constant pain. I had broken ribs, bruises and my face was always a mass of cuts. I was a quick learner though, and it wasn't long until I was kicking their asses and enjoying it."

I stare at him in horror. He's talking as though all this is normal, that fighting against grown men is the usual way to start your fighting career. But that wasn't even his dad's plan, who was pretty much trying to beat the gay out of him.

"Oh, don't look like that. He was making a man out of me, and look at me now. There isn't a man out there that can beat me in the ring." I see him clench his hand, before downing his drink. I can tell him being beat in the championship is still eating at him, still making him angrier than it should. "Dwayne never would have beat me if Ethan hadn't fucked everything up. It was all his fault. He knew I needed the right equipment to win the fight. I could put that motherfucker in a grave."

I make a mental note to work on the fact that he's blaming someone else for him losing the fight. He needs to be able to alter his technique when something goes wrong, to dig deep and use all his skill. To be the best and to win at all costs. This is where Ethan was actually at fault with his training. He spent too much time worrying about Zeke's strength and brute force instead of his actual technique.

The silence is broken by Zeke, but when it is I wish he'd stayed quiet. His voice is lightly slurred now as the alcohol starts to have an affect on him. "I remember the day that my dad proved I wasn't gay. That's an experience I'll never forget. He got one of his female friends to show me what it was like to be with a woman, and hey, I got hard so it must have proved I wasn't gay. Fuck it was *horrible*. I just lay there while she used my body. And afterwards my dad patted me on the back and told me that he knew I liked women." He doesn't even fill his glass this time and drinks straight from the bottle. I listen in absolute horror as he speaks. I grab the shot glass and down the contents, needing something to ease the shock.

"She raped you." The words come out on barely a whisper but I know he hears me when his head turns sharply towards me.

"She didn't rape me. Didn't you hear me? I got hard so I obviously wanted it." The words he says are full of anger but I know this isn't Zeke speaking, he's repeating the words that he's listened to all his life. I want to make him see sense but I know with the alcohol in his system this isn't the time to make an issue of it. Hopefully we can return to this conversation in the future when he's sober, I need him to see that he wasn't the one who was wrong. He was treated badly by the people who should have protected him, and I need him to see this, I need his demons to stop having control over him.

"Then we need to disagree about that, Zeke. Because I think she took advantage of a very young and confused boy."

He huffs before taking another drink. He puts the bottle down and I reach over the table, grab the bottle and hide it under my chair. He glares at me but he doesn't say anything. I stare into his eyes, watching as the mask of anger slips, showing me the pain that he usually keeps hidden. He looks lost, like the teenage boy I imagine he was, just looking for someone to love him, someone to accept him for who he is. I can feel tears burn my eyes as I watch him, desperate to reach out and touch him but I don't think he would want that. He would think I thought he was weak, when I think he might just be the strongest person I've ever met.

"Want to tell me why you weren't in today?" I want to change the subject to something safer. I think he needs a break from his pain and I'm hoping this will help.

"I'm so fucking tired, Bryce. I'm sick of being confused about everything. Just when I think I know what I want, my mind screws me over again."

I hate that I've come into his life and caused all this shit for him. I swear I'm thinking I should walk away and leave him in the capable hands of Eddie. "Would it be easier if I left? I'm sure Eddie can get you another coach, one that suits you better."

He looks at me with panic in his eyes. "Please don't go." His voice is soft and full of emotion. I feel my throat thicken with my need to cry. I never imagined that under Zeke's tough exterior there would be such a damaged man. It's like he's never had anyone that accepted him for who he is.

I swallow, trying to clear my throat before I speak. "I don't want to hurt you any more."

He puts his hands on the flat surface of the table and slowly moves them towards my clenched ones. "It's not you that's hurting me. I just need some time to work out … shit, I don't know, but please don't go." He looks pleadingly at me and I move my hands closer, being careful not to touch his. He needs to make the final move himself and close the distance between us if that's what he wants.

"Are you sure? I've been in your life for less than a week and look at all the shit I'm causing."

His hand touches mine and he entwines our fingers together. "I'm sure. It's been a long time since I felt anything and, Bryce, you make me feel."

I tighten my hold on his hand, not wanting to ever let him go.

Zeke

I turn my head and look at Bryce who's lying next to me on the sun loungers that we dragged into the back yard from the garage. The sun went down over an hour ago and we've just been lying here talking. I stopped drinking a while ago, after telling Bryce about my past I thought it was the safer option. I've never told anyone how I lost my virginity and I became so defensive about it because I know it was wrong. Even as it was happening I knew I shouldn't have been there, so I'd closed my eyes and prayed for it

98

to end. The amount I drank tonight made me talk about things I shouldn't have, and it hurt more than I thought it would when I was telling him about it. The pain from my dad treating me like he did, the way he thought it was more acceptable for his friends to beat me than for me to have feelings for men, it tore my heart out. To see Bryce's face when he listened, to know that he could see how wrong it was but my own dad didn't, that made it feel worse. But I'm actually glad I told him, for some reason I feel a lighter now, like there is less pressure pushing down on my shoulders.

"So you're telling me that you've never had biscuits and gravy?"

He laughs, probably finding my horror a bit dramatic. *But shit, how the hell could he have lived in America for more than a week and not tasted the best thing in the world?*

"I repeat, I have never had biscuits and gravy. I was in a café and saw them serving it up and I have to say it didn't look appetizing. How the hell can you eat that crap?"

My mouth hangs open, shocked that he dares dis one of my favorite meals. "I swear, if I could be bothered to move, you would be in so much trouble."

I hear an even bigger laugh and I can't help but smile. The last few hours have been the most comfortable I've experienced in a long time. I don't often just get to be myself around someone without anything being expected of me. When I go out with the guys it's great, but I always feel as though I have to be Zeke 'The Storm' Raine instead of just Zeke. It's completely different with Bryce, I can show him the side that I usually hide, and he hasn't run away yet.

"I think we may need to start a diet sheet as well. I seriously thought you would know the basics but now I'm beginning to wonder." He shakes his head at me, looking like the perfect disappointed coach, except any coach I've ever had hasn't been as hot as him.

"Bryce?"

He raises his eyebrows and waits for me to continue.

"Fucking bite me."

His eyes soften as he takes in my words, and when his expression changes and his eyes heat with passion, I realize what I've just said. The look Bryce gives me, the one that says he's only too willing to have his mouth on me, makes my shorts suddenly feel too tight. He closes his eyes and takes a deep breath before opening them again. I'm not sure if he's meant to look less turned on now, but it's failing.

"I have so many answers to that, and none of them are suitable or remotely clean." He shakes his head, making a show of sucking his lips into his mouth.

I sit up, placing my legs in the space between our loungers and lean forward with my elbows resting on my knees. "Are you cold?" I ask as Bryce follows me, mimicking my position and his leg brushes against mine.

"Are you kidding, it's so fucking hot here I don't think I'll ever be cold again."

I laugh at his answer and his body shifts slightly until we're both leaning towards each other. "You get used to it. You won't even notice it soon." I have no idea why I'm talking about the weather but if it keeps us moving closer to each other then I'm willing to talk about the fucking precipitation levels in the air. I can feel his breath against my lips and I think I might pass out. I might be confused about what to do about Bryce, but when he's this close I know I'm not confused about my feelings. It's like an attraction but on a deeper level, like it's something written deep in our DNA. I would laugh at myself, about the fact that I'm talking like a chick, but when Bryce's breath brushes over my lips I lose all ability to do anything but feel.

"Can I please kiss you, Zeke? But just so we're clear, if you don't want me to I need to leave right now."

I don't bother answering him as I lean forward until our lips meet. Immediately a sense of peace flows through my body and I finally feel like I'm home. I don't know if I would class myself as gay, but I know I need to hand over my man card to Bryce since he has me thinking like a love sick girl.

Our lips tangle together gently, both of us happy to take our time. This is different than in the corridor at Joe's. I'm pretty sure it's because we both feel a little more certain about things, and Bryce must feel happier now I've had his dick in my hand. I know that first night he was worried he was pushing me into something I didn't want, well now I've shown him that I'm exactly where I want to be. Bryce's hand moves up and works its way into the back of my hair, pulling on it as he presses harder against my lips. I groan into his mouth as he pushes slowly back down on the lounger with his body before coming to lie on top of me. He presses into me and I notice that our bodies line up perfectly like we were made for each other. I've only ever known the softness of a woman's body and even though this feels very different, I know it feels very right. His body matches mine: hard muscle and chiseled lines and it makes me achingly hard. I'm panting when he pulls back, his hand cupping my cheek as he looks deep into my eyes.

"I should have asked, is this okay for you? I just needed to feel you."

I answer his question by lifting my hips and rubbing my cock along his, our matching hardness causing a delicious friction between us. His head drops to my shoulder as his body shudders on top of mine. I've never dreamed that rubbing against another cock would give me so much pleasure, but I know that I don't want it to stop. My entire focus is on our cocks, nothing else is important. That is until I feel his hand touching my stomach. His hands caress my abs and it's my turn to shiver as I feel his fingers moving over my muscles, digging in slightly as he explores me.

I lift my torso off the lounger and pull my t-shirt over my head. He's seen me topless before, hell he's seen me naked, but knowing this time there's more to it is exciting. His eyes roam over me and it feels like he's touching me.

"You are the most perfect thing I've ever seen." A look of sadness crosses his face and he pulls his hand away.

I reach up to cup his jaw, running my thumb along his cheek.

"Hey, where did you go?"

He blinks a few times before his eyes come back into focus. He smiles down at me, but it no longer reaches his eyes. "I'm here with you. I don't want to be anywhere else." I don't know what he was just thinking about but I know the moment is gone. He looks so sad and I want to know why, I want to ask him what happened in his past but I respect his privacy. I understand the need to keep secrets and if he wants to share them he will when he's ready.

He pushes himself off me and returns to his lounger again, rubbing his hands over his face as he does. "I'm sorry, I completely killed the moment. Maybe I should go?"

I sit up and grab his hands, pulling them into my lap. He looks at me and I feel a smile touch my lips.

"Will you stay with me tonight?" I don't know what makes me ask, but all I can think about is how amazing it would be to wake up with him in my arms in the morning. I've never wanted to hold someone as much as I do him and I'm hoping he agrees. He raises his eyebrows at me and I look at him in confusion.

I repeat the question in my head and it hits me how suggestive it might sound to him. "Shit, I didn't mean it like that. As stupid as it sounds, and I can't believe I'm admitting this. I'm a fighter dammit, I never do this." I make sure I'm looking him in the eye as I speak, letting him know that I mean every single word. "But I want you to spend the night and I want to hold you while you sleep."

The sexiest blush covers Bryce's cheeks. Fuck, he is so attractive, I have no idea what he sees in me. I'm new to this and I'm going to make so many mistakes, but I'm planning on holding onto him as long as I can. I brush my hand over his cheek, feeling the heat under my fingers and I realize I need to man up and show him that I am all Alpha, and I will, tomorrow, after I hold him.

"I think I'd like that. One question though, who's spooning who?" He winks and I laugh as I stand and grab his hand, pulling him up behind me.

"You're a funny man, Mr. Tanner, a funny, funny man."

His laughter follows me as I drag him down the hall to my room.

CHAPTER TEN

Bryce

I wake in the morning surrounded by heat. It feels amazing and I don't want to move but there is a rather large dick pushing into my arse. That causes a smile to appear on my face and I push my arse back to meet it. A groan meets my ear with a breeze of warm breath. My dick instantly goes from semi hard to fully erect in the blink of an eye.

"I'm pretty sure I could wake up like this every morning. Your ass feels amazing." The words are whispered in my ear just before his lips brush over my neck.

Fuck, I could wake up like this every morning as well, I'm pretty sure this is the best wake up call I've ever had. I grind against him again, lingering slightly to make sure he doesn't mistake what I'm doing. Teeth meet my shoulder before the body behind me moves away, leaving cool air moving over my overheated skin.

"Behave. I'm going to start breakfast. There is an extra toothbrush in the bathroom if you want it. See you in the kitchen."

I roll onto my back and contemplate opening my eyes but I think that not looking at Zeke is the best option at the moment. I'm already at bursting point and I haven't even seen him in his sleepy hotness yet. If I look at him I don't know if I will be able to control the urge I have to pin him to the bed and show him how good we could be together.

"Are you trying to tell me I have morning breath?"

The bed dips beside my hip and he kisses my lips gently before brushing his nose over mine. "I tried to be subtle, but I seriously suggest you brush your teeth." I hear the humor in his voice and laugh as I feel him leave the bed.

Once he leaves the room I brave opening my eyes and look around to see Zeke's room in the daylight. Last night we'd only put on a small lamp as we lay in bed and talked some more. It was nice, being wrapped in his arms while we spoke about… well pretty much about everything and nothing. Our favorite foods, sports and then we spent a strange ten minutes talking about feminine hygiene products. I laugh as I get up from the bed, and I try to remember how that conversation came up but draw a blank.

I run my hand through my hair and walk in to the hall, trying to get my bearings so I can find the bathroom. I used it last night but everything looks different in the light and it takes me opening a few doors to finally find it. Locking the bathroom door behind me I stand in front of the mirror. I can't help but notice that my eyes are shining with happiness, the kind of happiness that I thought I would never see again after Austin. *Austin*, my smile falters as I remember him. He's the reason I stopped kissing Zeke last night out in the garden and almost ran from the house. It's the stupidest thing ever, and I don't want to spend my life comparing them, but last night I did. When I told Zeke last night that he was the most perfect thing I'd ever seen there wasn't an ounce of lie in those words. I truly haven't seen anyone like him before and that caused a lot of guilt to stir inside of me. I loved Austin, I will always love him, but there's just something about Zeke that makes my heart beat faster. I don't think I ever looked at Austin and felt my body react the same way it does with Zeke, and I'm having a hard time coping with the feelings. I've been alone for the last eighteen months because I felt that I didn't deserve to be with anyone when I couldn't protect Austin. It's my fault that he's gone. When I first laid eyes on Zeke all thoughts of being alone vanished from my head. Actually, I had no thoughts of Austin at all.

Maybe this is the universe's way of telling me I've been mourning for long enough and it put Zeke Raine in my path for a reason. I'm hoping the reason is the one I want it to be. I want to be with Zeke and I pray to god I'm not fooling myself.

After brushing my teeth I walk towards the kitchen where I hear dishes being moved and music playing. I follow the noise and enter the kitchen where I stop just inside the entrance, my feet suddenly becoming cemented to the floor. *Fuck, this guy is so sexy.* He's standing by the sink with his back to me. His pajama shorts hang low on his hips and I want to run over and lick the dimples on his lower back. No one should look this hot in tartan shorts, but my mouth is watering from watching him and my dick is painfully hard. He's washing up some pots and pans and I can see the muscles in his shoulders flexing. I love hard bodies, but my favorite thing on a guy is a sexy back. I walk over to him quietly, pressing my naked chest to his back and enjoy his body shivering against mine. I lick up the side of his neck and the taste of his skin makes me moan in pleasure. God, how I want to devour this man.

"Is it my turn to make you come?" I tease him with my words as I wrap my arms around his waist, tickling his skin just above the top of his shorts with my fingers. His head drops back and he pushes his arse against me.

"Can I taste you? If you don't want it just say no, but fuck, Zeke, I want you in my mouth."

His stuttered breath gives me confidence that he wants this and I move my hand under the elastic of his shorts. "You can tell me to stop at any time and I will, but I need to do this. For my own sanity, I need to do this." I barely recognize the husky voice that comes out of me as I finally wrap my hand around his dick.

"Holy fuck, Bryce." His body jumps like I've given him an electric shock and I know how he feels. My hand feels like it's on fire as I rub over his soft skin. He's everything I imagined he would be: hard and smooth, hot and thick. I tighten my hand around him, loving the way he fills my hand with his size. It's not enough, I want my mouth around him when he comes.

I carefully pull his shorts over his erection and let them to fall to his ankles. I step back, making sure that Zeke can stand on his own before I drop to my knees, and work myself between his body and the kitchen unit. I make sure I don't touch him as I settle on my knees and just look up at him, waiting for him to give me the go ahead. His dick is mere inches from my mouth and I can't help but lick my lips as it twitches. I can see Zeke's hands clutching the edge of the sink, his knuckles white from the pressure of his grasp and his eyes wide as he looks down at me. God, he looks fucking sexy when he's turned on. I look up at him, heat passing between us as we look into each other's eyes. I can feel my body vibrate with need and I give in to the urge to taste him. I flick my tongue out, lightly caressing his head and we both moan when I make contact. He tilts his hips, giving the approval I have been so desperate for. I lick my lips before taking the end of his dick into my mouth. His taste explodes over my taste buds and I moan, pressing my tongue into his slit to try and get more.

"Oh fuck." I hear the words from above me but I'm too focused on the feeling of him in my mouth. I want to take it slow for him and let him see how good it is when a man blows you. This is his first experience and I want the memory to last forever. I momentarily look up at him as I take him deep into the back of my throat, but I need to close my eyes. The look of sheer pleasure I saw on his face will have me coming in my own shorts if I'd carried on, and I've done that too many times already with this man. Instead I concentrate on taking him deep, sucking on all the areas that I like and hope he likes it too. When I run my tongue behind the head of his dick and gently tease it with little flicks, he pulls down on my chin and I open my mouth for him. He places his dick on my tongue and slides in deep as I try to relax my throat, letting him set the pace he wants.

I reach out and gently cup his balls, pulling on them slightly as he takes full control. His dick hits the back of my throat as he pumps into my mouth making me gag slightly, but I refuse to pull away. Wet hands wrap themselves into my hair and he tugs it as he holds on. I moan, loving the burning sensation that runs through my scalp and makes my skin tingle. It's been so long since I gave head that I forgot how fucking good it feels doing it. My own dick is like rock and is so close to coming that it's becoming painful. Zeke's thrusts falter and he pulls my head back.

"I'm going to come if you don't stop."

Why on earth would I stop? I want to taste him when he explodes on my tongue and to show him what I want, I put my hands on his arse and pull him back into my mouth. I hear a cry from him as I suck, my cheeks hollowing out with the pressure.

"Fuck, Bryce, baby. I'm gonna come."

I bob my head quicker, working up his length to encourage him to let go. The grip on my hair tightens and I'm sure I feel some being pulled out, but I don't care as drops of pre-cum hit the back of my throat. *Fuck he tastes so good and I want more.* An almost animalistic cry sounds from above me as the first spurts of cum hit my throat. I suck him even harder, moaning as he thrusts his orgasm into my mouth.

When he's given me everything, I let his dick slip from between my lips and he drops to his knees in front of me. He grabs my face and pulls my lips to his, kissing me with such a passion. I know he has to taste himself on my tongue and it makes me even harder, which I didn't think was possible at this point. His hands fight with the tie on the front of my shorts until he manages to tug them down enough to have has access to my dick. With an almost desperate feeling, he grabs me and immediately begins to run his fist along my length. My eyes roll into my head with pleasure and I grab his shoulders, needing the support to keep myself upright. Embarrassingly it only takes a couple of strokes before I'm coming in his hands for the second time. I lean my body against his, wrapping my arms around him partly because I physically cannot hold my own body up, and partly because I don't want to give him the chance to run this time.

"Are you okay?" I'm impressed I managed to get any words out let alone ones that actually make sense. My brain is still a little fuzzy from my orgasm.

He kisses my ear before responding. "I have never been fucking better, babe."

I smile as he calls me babe again, loving the way it sounds coming from his lips.

Zeke

I'm struggling to function properly. I'm pretty sure I just shot my brain down Bryce's throat. *Shit, even the thought of it has my dick stirring again.* Neither of us has moved, so I'm currently kneeling on the floor with my shorts around my ankles and Bryce's cock and cum in my hand, and the thing is, I've never felt happier in my life. I hear Bryce's voice, it's slightly muffled by my neck but his words make me laugh.

"I think I need to go have a shower before your hand dries to my dick. Not that I'm complaining, I rather like your hand there but it might be a bit hard to fight like that."

Even though I know he's right we both stay as we are for a few more minutes. It's Bryce that makes the first move and I pull back, looking at his face to make sure there's no regret there. I know I don't regret one second of what just happened, and that actually shocks me a little. I like getting head, I would actually say that it's my favorite, I just didn't realize how good it would be from a guy. Looking down and seeing my dick disappear into Bryce's mouth was something above and beyond erotic. He knew exactly when to increase pressure, when to ease back, and then he just knelt there and let me fuck his mouth.

God, I need to stop thinking about it before I'm rock hard again. This guy is doing something to my body. I've never done so little with someone but gotten so much pleasure from it. It makes me wonder how far I'm willing to let this thing between us go. As I look into Bryce's eyes I realize that I'm willing to give him, or at least try, anything he wants. I want to see where this goes, as long as he's the one showing me the way.

I lean forward and kiss him gently on the lips, loving the smile he gives me in return.

"Go and grab a shower. I'll finish breakfast and have it waiting for you." It takes me a few attempts to stand as the feeing slowly returns to my legs. When I'm finally up I reach out and take his hand to help him up as well.

"When you get out I think we need to talk and work out what the hell is happening here." It might be a little early for this conversation but I think it's important to get it over and done with. We work together so there is more at stake here than just our feelings, we need to make sure that this wouldn't affect his job if this doesn't work out between us. I need him to know that even if this stops today his job is safe, and that I will hold nothing against him. A look of worry passes over Bryce's face and I can't help but laugh.

"Don't look so scared, it's not that bad. Go grab a shower, babe." I kiss him again before leaving him standing in the middle of the kitchen. Just as I reach the sink I hear him call my name, I turn to look at him and see that he's looking down at my hands and laughing.

"Do me a favor? Wash your hands before you cook." He winks at me and leaves me looking at my still messy hands.

I'm sitting at the small table in my kitchen when Bryce walks out of my bedroom wearing the jeans he arrived in yesterday. He's rubbing his still damp hair with a towel and I can't take my eyes off him. He's fucking gorgeous. It's still a bit of a shock that I'm finding a guy so attractive, but I can't deny it any longer. I know he's not the first guy I've looked at in this way but he's the first that I've admitted to myself. When my dad told me that my feelings were wrong, that I shouldn't be thinking like I was, I became an expert in denying them. I can hear the distant voice of my dad in my head but I'm determined not to listen this time. I've listened to his advice all my life and it's gotten me nowhere, maybe it's time to let the real me out.

"Do you have a spare top I can borrow? My t-shirt is crushed to hell and it's not smelling too great." He stands in front of me but I just point to the seat across from me. He sits with a smirk on his face and his dimple shows on his right cheek. It's not the first time I've seen it, but now I can freely admit how sexy it makes him.

"I like what you're wearing. I'll get you something after you eat, I like the scenery at the moment."

He laughs as he picks up his mug of coffee and takes a drink. "Wow, you make good coffee. Maybe I should get you to make it for me more often." He looks at me over the top of his mug as he takes another mouthful.

"Maybe you should." I pick up the bowl of eggs and pile them onto his plate while thinking how to start this conversation.

"As much as I love eggs, I don't think I will manage the whole bowl."

I look down and see that I've nearly filled his entire plate with scrambled eggs. "Shit. Sorry, let me sort that."

Bryce reaches out and stops my hand before it grabs the eggs. "Calm down. You're the one who told me not to worry, so how about you take your own advice. Tell me what's bothering you." He lets go of me and I look at the table, unable to meet his eyes just yet.

"See that's the thing, nothing's bothering me." I look up and see a confused look on Bryce's face. *Yeah, I would look like that too if I was him.* I continue, trying to make some sort of sense. "This thing between us, it's not bothering me. I think it should, and I thought it would, but it doesn't. The way I'm feeling about you doesn't feel wrong, it feels like I'm meant to be with you."

I hear a loud sigh from Bryce and see his shoulders visibly relax. "Thank fuck you said that. I was beginning to think that I was the only one feeling… whatever this is."

I shake my head, my own relief working its way through my body as Bryce speaks. "No, not just you. Man, this shouldn't be so hard, but I swear I feel so out of my depth here, Bryce. I don't do relationships, actually I don't do anything more than a one night stand. With you though, I want to get to know and be with you.

That's a new thing for me, wanting something more."

He leans over and grabs my hand, entwining our fingers together. "I know this is all new to you, especially with me being a guy, so I'm letting you decide what you want. I can be anything you want, the only thing I won't budge on is being faithful. If you're with me Zeke, then you're with me. I don't share, I never have and I won't start that for anyone."

I squeeze his hand, trying to decide what exactly I want. I just need to be honest with him and hope he understands. "I hear you. And I don't know what I want exactly, but I do know that I want to see where this might go. I won't be able to be with you openly in public until I'm sure, and that's something you need to decide if you're happy with. I'm not in a sport where I can come out until I'm sure that's who I am, but yes, I want to find that out with you and only you. So if you are happy to be with me, behind closed doors, then I'll try to give you everything." I finish and look at him expectantly.

He seems to think about what I've said for a few minutes, and I start to worry that he's going to leave. Maybe I shouldn't have said I couldn't be public with him, maybe it was too soon, but I can't lie to him. I do want this with him but I'm not willing to chance ruining my career for something that might not go anywhere.

"Okay, I can accept that to begin with, but know that if we go somewhere I won't be your secret." That's the best I can ask for, a little time to see if this is what I want.

"Thank you, babe. I think we need to keep this very separate from the gym and fighting. I want you to know that no matter what happens, your job is safe. I'm not that kind of guy. I know I hated Ethan, but that's not because I was fucking him."

Bryce's cheeks flush when I mention fucking and my stomach tenses at the thought. The thing is, I don't know if it's tensing in fear or anticipation. There are so many things to consider but I think that's enough for the day so I push his plate towards him.

"Eat. We can work it all out as we go along." A funny thought comes to mind, which makes me laugh as I put some food into my mouth.

"Do I even want to know what's making you laugh?"

I take a few minutes to calm myself down, the thought makes me laugh more than it probably should. It's really not that funny, but now that it's stuck in my head I just can't stop. "It's not even that funny. I just realized that by the end of this I might have a boyfriend, or even a husband." Saying it out loud makes it seem even funnier. Bryce laughs at me and thankfully doesn't seem to be taking offence.

"Only if you're really lucky." He winks at me and I feel a heat spread in my chest, I'm not sure what it is but if someone asked me to put a name to it, I would probably say I was happy. It's been a long time since I felt truly happy and it feels strange.

We eat in silence for a few minutes, but its comfortable, like we're happy just being together.

"I know that you've come out to your family, so have you ever had a boyfriend?" I didn't think it was such a bad question to ask, but the color drains from Bryce's face and he quickly puts his fork down. He won't meet my eyes and I wonder what I've done wrong. I didn't mean to upset him but I obviously have. I reach for his hand and tug him towards me, turning him in his seat before moving my chair so I'm sitting in front of him.

Cupping his face in my hands, I kiss his lips gently before speaking. "I'm sorry. Whatever I said to upset you just forget it, I was being stupid."

I feel him exhale against my lips before he speaks, his voice quiet. "It's not you, it's me. It's just hard for me to think about what happened back home."

My mind is racing with all of the possibilities of what might have happened in his past, and I want him to tell me but at the same time I really don't want to know.

"I had a boyfriend, Austin. He was the first guy I'd had a proper relationship with. We were young and in love, thinking that we would be together forever. We were at a fight one night, I was in the ring when some guys started hassling Austin."

I remember Coach mentioning his fighting history but I never thought to ask about it. I want to know more and I go to ask him about it but he kisses me, effectively stopping me from talking.

"It's a long story, one for another time. I'll tell you about my limited experience one day, but it's very limited."

I lean forward and kiss him, letting him continue his story without interruption. I don't think this story is going to have a lovely happy ending, but I think I need to hear it.

"So they were hassling him, pushing him around, getting quite rough. Things got out of hand and they really started pounding him, calling him a queer and a bender." I hear his breathing become labored as his eyes fill with tears.

"I couldn't get to him, his attacker's friends held me back. It was my fault, I kissed him before the fight and they saw. It was my fault and I couldn't save him. They killed him and I couldn't do a thing to stop it." His body shudders as he loses the fight against his tears. I swear it's like I can see his heart break right in front of me. I pull him into my arms, wanting to take away all his pain but I can't, so I let him cry as I try to hold him together.

We sit like this for a while, I don't know how long and I don't care. His crying stops and his breathing is almost back to normal. He pulls back from me looking a little embarrassed. I run my finger over his cheek and remove the last of his tears. He stares into my eyes for a couple of seconds before speaking again.

"When you said you didn't want to come out because of the fighting, I fully understand. I know this sport isn't the best place to be gay, I've been there and lived it. So yes, I will keep us a secret until you decide if it's what you want. I will do anything to keep you safe, Zeke."

My heart breaks a little, knowing that Bryce would put his happiness aside for me and my career. I just hope that I will never have to choose between the two.

CHAPTER ELEVEN

Bryce

The past few weeks with Zeke have been amazing, spending nearly all our time together. Inside the gym we're nothing but professional, well actually that's a lie, we try to be professional but sometimes the attraction just gets too much. I've found myself on my knees in the changing room a few times, with Zeke returning the favor more than once. The first time Zeke gave me head was a life altering moment. It wasn't at the gym, it was at my place as I was trying to convince him that we needed to get to work. We'd been running late after my alarm didn't go off and Zeke needed to leave first so we could arrive at different times. He wasn't making it easy for me to rush him out the door though. After an incredibly passionate kiss he made us late in a very memorable way. He was awkward to begin with but was soon giving me the best blowjob of my life, and making me explode in a very embarrassingly short amount of time.

I'm watching him now as he fights with Santo. I can't help the way my eyes roam over his body. I know that I'm not meant to show my feelings publicly, but I'm hard and there's only one way that problem's going to be solved. I make my way into the ring, watching as both men stop to look at me. Thankful that I have a long t-shirt on today I walk up behind Zeke and stand close behind him. I feel him tense slightly, probably wondering what I'm doing.

"You're dropping your right shoulder. You need to keep yourself level or you're gonna tell your opponent what your next move is." I purposely grind my hard dick into his arse and hear a gasp leave him. I pull his shoulders back with the pretense that I'm helping him, but I just want his body close to mine. He smells amazing, the mixture of his shower gel and him is the most intoxicating scent ever.

"Wow, you're good, man. I was just standing here thinking how perfect Zeke's stance was. I didn't even notice that he was dropping. You need to teach me all you know," Lewie, Santo's trainer yells over to me as I readjust Zeke again, still grinding into him. I contain my laughter, knowing that he's right, Zeke's form was perfect but I'm not planning on telling him that. I back up, leaving Zeke looking over his shoulder with darkening eyes, and I know that I will pay for that move later. A shudder runs through my body as I imagine what he might do.

"Right try again, keep your shoulders level." I exit the ring, my eyes looking at Zeke's body as he moves. He's hard like I knew he'd be, so he's hunched over pretending that he's blocking punches that aren't actually coming. He's going to be mad, but it's not like he's never done this to me before. I think the worst time was when I was lifting weights with a few of the fighters. I was bench pressing with Zeke spotting me when he started talking to me quietly, telling me everything that he planned to do to me that night and all the different ways he was going to make me come. It took about four seconds for my dick to be as hard as the weights I was lifting, and the way I was lying made it glaringly obvious. My shorts were tenting enough to allow an entire family to camp under there. I was going to stop and sit up when Zeke announced to the room that I had another set to do. I could've killed him, not only did I have to lie there for another six count, but everyone turned around to see why he was so loud. I don't know if they noticed my hard on, but if they did, they were kind enough not to mention it.

I'm finding that the more time I spend with Zeke, the more I'm falling for him. He's nothing like I imagined, I expected a very alpha man who would grunt a lot and beat his chest a little. What I got is a really caring guy who actually thought deeply about things and he's smarter than I think anyone gives him credit for. I swear, some of the things he comes out with leave me in shock. He always wanted to study to be a pilot, but he never got the chance. After his

116

dad had pushed him into fighting, leaving his body in pain on a daily basis, he lost all passion for school. He dropped out as soon as he was able to and ran as far away from his family as he could. It's a shame really, I would totally have loved to see Zeke dressed as a pilot. I mean, who doesn't love a man in uniform? I have a feeling he would have worn it really fucking well.

I'm brought back to my senses when Santo hits the ground and I watch Zeke as he helps him get to his feet.

"Good fight, Santo, but I think I'm gonna head out. There's something at home that needs my attention." He starts unwrapping his hands as Santo throws his gloves to Lewie.

"Got some hot date waiting, do ya'?"

Zeke turns to look at me as he speaks. "Something like that, there's just someone that needs taught a lesson or two."

I don't even wait to hear what his next words are. I know I need to get out of here right now. If there's one thing that we have discovered together it's that we both love the chase. This game of cat and mouse is becoming one of our favorite things. I rush to the locker room, grabbing my bag without even checking if everything is in it before rushing out the front door. I knew it would end like this. I poked the bear and now he's going to charge. I need to get home before he catches me, he won't care if we are behind closed doors or not. When he gets in this mood he'll take me wherever I am. I know this after a hand job in the changing room of a local sports store. I had spent the day touching him, stroking his arm or brushing my hand over his arse. It took less than two hours for him to pin me up against the changing room wall and take his frustration out on me. I smile as I remember that day and my dick hardens as I imagine what he's going to do to me today.

****

I pull into my driveway and jump out of my car quickly. I don't know if Zeke would have hung around at the gym to grab a shower, but if he did I will have a little longer to get prepared. I enter the

117

house, leaving the door unlocked behind me for Zeke and throw my bag into the closet by the front door. Rushing down the hall to my bedroom, I strip out of my clothes as I move. I turn on my shower and climb in before it heats up, the sting of the cold water making my skin tingle but it's soon replaced by a warm caress. I'm rinsing my hair when a hard body presses against my back and pushes me up against the tiles.

"Is this what you had in mind when you were teasing me? Is this what you wanted to feel?" He grinds his rock hard dick into my arse and I groan. My own dick hardens immediately, the pressure of it against the tiles making me go cross-eyed with the intensity.

"Does that feel good, baby?"

I lean my head back onto his shoulders as I moan in agreement. He bends his knees, pushing his dick between my cheeks, and my legs nearly give out.

I hear Zeke's groan in my ear as he moves his lips to my ear. "I think I'm ready." Four words and my whole world stops turning. My mind is finding it difficult to focus and I hear him repeating the words again. *He's ready? Is he sure?* I need him to be sure, but I also need to feel him more than anything. We've done a lot of things, had many orgasms in many different ways but we haven't taken that final step yet.

"Are you sure? How do you want it?" My voice is shaky. I should sound more in control but it's just impossible.

"I'm sure, but I'm not ready for me. Can I have you?" He sounds hesitant, like he's worried that I'm not going to agree to him taking me. Little does he know that I want him inside me as much as I want inside him. My arse cheeks clench as I imagine him slipping inside my body and slowly filling me. I reach out and turn off the water. I want this to mean something, and there's no way it's going to happen in a shower. I push back against his chest and he moves, letting me turn around. I kiss him, trying to show him how much I want this to happen. He pulls away, takes my hands and pulls me slowly out of the bathroom and through to my room. Standing next to the bed he captures my lips again as his hard dick

118

brushes against mine.

"This is new territory for me, baby. You're gonna have to show me what to do." I smile at his words. I really love it when he calls me baby. I don't think he realizes he's saying it, it's just something that seems to come naturally to him.

"Just take your time, the rest we'll work out." I push against his chest until he's lying on the bed. He scoots himself backwards on his elbows and I follow him closely, kneeling above his prone body. I claim his mouth while making sure my body doesn't come into contact with his. I want him to just feel my lips and let the anticipation build. My lips leave his as they brush over his jaw, down his neck and over his chest where I take his nipple into my mouth and bite it gently, earning me a breathy gasp. I don't get to torture him very long as he wraps his legs around me and flips me onto my back before positioning himself above me. When he moves away, I start to panic that's he's leaving but I hear the bedside drawer open and I know what he's doing. He throws the lube and condom next to me on the bed and my muscles clench in anticipation. Leaning down he kisses me. It's lazy but full of passion, making my blood hum under my skin. I could lie here all night and kiss him like this, but I need to feel him inside of me now. I reach out, grabbing the lube that's beside me and open it. I drip it onto my own dick, making sure that there's enough to spread between us both. I rub it over myself and the back of my fingers brush over Zeke's dick, making him groan.

"If you keep doing that I won't last long enough to get inside you." Even though he says the words, his body never stops moving against me, and I open my fist taking both of us in my grip. I love it when we move together like this. Zeke's dick is slightly longer than mine and I love the way it looks when it moves between my fingers. He thrusts a few times, his eyes closing as I increase the pressure and our lips never part.

All too soon he pulls away, sitting back on his knees and looking down at me. He looks worried, like he's unsure what to do next and I decide to help him out. I sit up slightly, the bottle of lube

119

in my hand and I pour some into Zeke's hand before curling his fingers around my dick. He stokes his hand over me, spreading the slickness and making my eyes roll with the blissful caress. I jolt when I feel his mouth connect with me, his tongue licking the underside of my erection all the way down to my balls. Sucking in a breath, I concentrate on just feeling what's he's doing, a groan leaving me as he sucks one of my balls into my mouth.

I'm so turned on, barely able to control my hold onto my orgasm. I can feel it building already, tingles shooting through my body from deep in my balls. I think knowing that tonight we will be taking that extra step is making every touch more important, more intense. We've done a lot of exploring so far, I've blown him while fingering him and even tongue fucked his arse, but tonight I will get everything. I will admit that I can't fucking wait until he gives me his whole body, but tonight I'll be more than happy to feel him inside me. I'm brought out of my thoughts by his finger slipping between my arse cheeks and I suck in a breath as he presses over my hole. *Fucking hell, that feels amazing.* He rubs around it gently, and I want nothing more than for him to push inside me. What I don't expect is for him to move to the side of me. I look up at him in confusion and see Zeke smile down at me as he taps my hip.

"I'm sorry, sexy. But I want you on your stomach. I don't know what I'm doing so I want to do this the easy way to start with." He leans down and kisses me. "I promise that next time I will look you in the eye when I take you."

Fuck, his words make my dick twitch. I roll over onto my stomach, keeping my arse tilted up so I don't put pressure on my already aching cock. His fingers knead my cheeks when I feel his body move up behind me. I keep my head down, knowing that if I turn to see his face I may lose it completely.

The cool drops of lube between my crack have me gripping the sheets and biting my lip until I can taste blood. I hear the ripping of the condom wrapper and I never realized how erotic that sound was before. The quietness after has my body vibrating where I lie. My skin feels like it's fully charged and ready to leave

120

my body.

My heart starts to race as his finger comes back and meets with my skin, the pressure against my hole making my eyes cross. He pushes inside me, easing in gently with one finger. After a few strokes he adds another finger, scissoring them inside me. He brushes over that spot inside me that has my body shooting up of the bed.

"Did I hurt you?" Zeke asks as he rubs his free hand up my spine, soothing me back down onto the bed.

"No, baby. It's just so good, better than good. It's fucking perfection." I give myself a mental pat on the back, proud I managed to get some words out when my entire brain is focused on what his fingers are doing inside me.

"Am I doing okay? I don't want to hurt you, but I want you ready to take me." I suddenly work it all out. If he's trying to give me a heart attack by just speaking to me he's doing a bloody good job of it.

I can't take much more. I need him inside before my part in this is over. "Do it, Zeke. For the love of fucking god, get inside me."

I hear his chuckle from behind me and it makes the hair on the back of my neck stand on end. *Yeah, he's definitely trying to kill me.*

I feel warmth against my hole as he presses the tip of his dick to it. *Fucking hell.* It's like it's scorching me through the condom and I'm not sure if I'll survive what's about to happen. He pushes against me, slipping past the tight ring and making my breath catch in my chest. I feel tears building in my eyes, but it's not from discomfort, it's because with every inch he pushes inside me I feel myself fall in love with him. When he's fully inside me I know without hesitation that I am deeply in love with Zeke Raine.

His movements still, but I need him to move, I need that feeling of completion.

"Zeke, please. You need to move."

I can hear him panting behind me as his fingers dig into my

hips. "Don't move. I swear if you do then we're both gonna be really disappointed." Even through his pleading words my body clenches around him. I don't meant to do it but I can feel his control slip and his fingers dig deeper. I'm sure that I'll be sporting bruises in the morning, but I can't seem to find it in myself to care.

"Fuck it, Bryce. Please don't. I've never felt anything as tight as you and it's taking everything I have not to come right now."

I relax around him, letting him take control and move when he's ready. I lie there, trying not to give in to the urge I have to rock back onto his body, making him move inside me until I come. After what feels like a year, he starts to leave my body and I hold my breath, releasing it when he pushes back inside.

He builds a rhythm, increasing the pace and strength with each thrust. I can hear him behind me muttering to himself and I wish I could hear what he's saying but my brain is a mushy mess of arousal. I can only think about the feelings he's causing inside me, the feeling of his fingers digging deep into my muscles, and how I need to try and calm down. Zeke puts his hands on my shoulders, pulling me backwards until my back is flush with his chest. He wraps his arm around me and grabs my dick. The combination of him thrusting into my arse and his hands stroking me is too much. I can barely breathe and I think I might pass out before I can come.

"You need to hurry, baby. I'm barely holding on and I want you to come with me." A tingle rushes down my spine and my balls pull up into my body.

Zeke groans behind me as my body starts to tighten, putting more pressure on his dick. "Bryce, fuck. God, oh *god*." His breath on my neck is what finally sends me over the edge and I come hard in his hand. I feel him tense before his dick pulsates inside me. I smile knowing that he's just experienced having sex with a man for the first time, and I got to be the one he did it with. His arms tighten around me and I feel worn out but content. I just pray that he doesn't run, I don't think my heart could take it.

122

Zeke

I'm holding onto Bryce's body tightly as I try to breathe. I feel like I've just had the first orgasm of my life. It might not have been my first but everything before this pales in comparison. I slip out of Bryce's body, pull off the condom and walk to the bathroom.

After cleaning up I go back to the bedroom and climb into bed. I lie for a few moments before pulling Bryce to my side. He didn't look like he was going to move to me and there's no way I'm not holding him after what we just did. If I didn't realize it before I certainly know it now, I like Bryce, actually it's more than just like. What I just did to him, with him, just cemented the fact that I'm happy with Bryce, with what we're doing together. I never thought I would be happy with a guy but now I think that maybe this is who I was meant to be with all along.

I was nervous before entering him, it was new territory for me and it felt like losing my virginity all over again. I was so scared I would hurt him, push too hard and cause some damage, so I took my time with him. I couldn't concentrate on anything except my cock and how it felt as I pushed into his tight ass. I wasn't even sure I would get all the way in before I exploded. I think I lasted quite well all things considered. I think nerves helped me hold out, allowed me to try and make it good for him, when everything was pushing me closer to release. I mean the guy is gorgeous and tight. What a dangerous combination.

I rest my nose to the top of Bryce's head and inhale his scent. Add that to the list of things I like about the man in my arms. He always smells so fucking good, even after a workout. I honestly want to bottle his smell and keep it. I laugh out loud as I realize how fucking creepy I sound right now. I'm one step away from giving him lotion and telling him to rub it into his body.

"What's so funny?" I feel his lips move against my chest as he speaks and it sends goose bumps all over. I'm still laughing when I answer him, not able to resist repeating the line from the movie.

"Nothing really, I was just thinking about saying 'it puts the lotion on its skin.'"

Bryce lifts his head up, resting his chin on his hands. He raises his eyebrows at me and a little smirk appears on his face. "You planning on skinning me so you can wear me? I know I'm hot but come on, you're not *that* bad looking."

I can't resist kissing him. I love the fact he knows what I'm talking about, that he gets the connection between my comment and 'Silence of The Lambs'. This right here is everything that I want: someone that gets my jokes, who can do the things to my body that I crave, and more importantly, someone I can be myself with.

I pull him closer to me, feeling his body snuggle against mine as we get ready to sleep.

"Well this *not that bad* guy wants to sleep, and he wants to do it with a sexy guy in his arms."

I feel Bryce getting comfortable against me, his hand resting against my stomach and his head on my shoulder. "Thank you for tonight, Zeke."

I kiss his head and close my eyes. "It should be me saying thanks, baby. It was fucking perfect."

Chapter Twelve

Bryce

I can't keep my eyes off Zeke as he sits across from me in the café we decided to go to for breakfast. We haven't really spoken this morning, content to just be in each other's company. I hadn't meant to fall asleep so quickly last night but being in Zeke's arms had felt so good that I couldn't help it. I had wanted to talk to him about how he felt after what we did and whether he was comfortable with it, but then he pulled me into his arms and sleep stole me.

When I woke from the nap we took this morning, I was determined to talk to him, to make sure he hadn't panicked about taking our relationship to another level. I needed to make sure he felt comfortable. I don't really want to label what we have together, but we spend all our time together and we have sex, so yes, to me this is a relationship. I know about his past, about how he lost his virginity and I'm scared of making him feel pressured. I would hate for our first time together to be because he felt forced, so I need to check that he wanted it as much as I did. The plan had changed quickly when I woke up with a mouth around my dick, making it officially the best wake up call ever. I thought there was no way to make the morning better, but I was wrong, so very, very wrong. When he kissed his way up my body to my ear, he whispered that he couldn't wait for me to take him and that he was nearly ready for it. With my eyes crossed and my fingers digging into his skin, I felt like the luckiest person in the world.

"How are you feeling?" This is probably the tenth time I've asked him this, but I need to keep checking. I have this need to make sure he isn't regretting anything, so I might be going slightly overboard.

"Again, I'm fine. I will tell you if I'm not. Will you stop stressing over it? We're good, I'm good." He winks at me and I smile. I love the way he's trying to make me feel better when he's the one who pretty much lost his virginity all over again. I know he's slept with a lot of women, but last night I popped his gay cherry. This thought makes me laugh, and it's one of those laughs that the more you try to control it the worse it gets. He puts his fork down and stares at me blankly which causes me to laugh harder. I try to take deep breaths and close my eyes to block him out so I calm down.

I manage to get it under control when Zeke speaks and I nearly lose it again. "Now I need to know what's so funny. What's just gone through that sexy little head of yours?"

I take a few more deep breaths, trying to control the laughter. "I was just thinking. Not many men can say they lost their virginity at twenty eight." It's not until the words are out my mouth that I realize that I'm talking really loudly. The waitress serving the next table turns to look at us, a shocked look on her face as her eyes rake over Zeke's body. I don't think I've ever seen Zeke blush so this moment will go down in history.

He leans in close, making sure that I will be able to hear him as he whispers across to me. "I didn't lose my virginity, well not fully. I will class myself as a virgin until you push that hard cock into my ass."

My mouth drops open at his words, and it's my turn to turn bright red. I can't believe he just said that in the middle of a café. Thankfully he kept his voice down.

I'm saved from the conversation when my phone rings in my pocket. It's unusual for someone to call me so early, but I see Eddie's name and I answer straight away. I've been waiting on some news from him and I'm hoping it's good.

"Hey, Eddie. How's things?"

Zeke goes back to eating his breakfast but his eyes never leave mine. I can see him trying to work out why Eddie's calling but I've kept this from him until I knew for sure.

"He's in."

And just like that he hangs up the phone. One thing I know for sure is that no one could ever accuse Eddie of wasting time with small talk. I throw my phone on the table and pick up my fork, ignoring Zeke's stare as I focus on my plate.

"You're just doing that to piss me off."

I nod, still not taking my eyes off my plate. "Yuuuuuup." I feel something hit my head and a slice of toast lands on my plate. I look up with surprise on my face. "Did you just throw a bit of toast at me?" I can't believe he did that, no actually I can, and I'm just happy it wasn't his fork.

"What did Eddie want?"

I have two options here. Do I come out and tell him, or do I drag it out until it drives him insane? Well there's no real question here, second option it is. "He was just letting me know that we need to change your training schedule."

I can see the muscle in his jaw twitch as he resists the urge to throw something else at me. "And why does my training schedule need to change?" His words are clipped, his frustration clearly showing.

I decide to be kind and tell him before he does actually hurt me. "You have a fight."

Immediately he stills and his mouth drops open as he stares at me.

"Say something, Zeke."

He sits there for a few more seconds before he manages to talk. "Are you fucking with me?" This is why I hadn't mentioned the fight before I knew for sure. I didn't want him to get his hopes up and then not be able to get a place. I cleared him to fight about a week ago and I've just been trying to find the right tournament for him. There's one coming up in two weeks' time, a big one that will get his name back out there, and Eddie used some of his connections to get him onto the fight sheet.

"You have two weeks to get fight ready. The hard work begins now."

I can see his hands twitch on the table, like he wants to reach out and touch me but knows he can't.

"I could fucking kiss you right now. I want to reach across there and grab you so badly." His eyes darken and he licks his lips, looking down to mine.

And just like that my dick hardens to an almost unbearable level. I clear my throat before speaking, the arousal flooding through me making my voice sound husky. "As much as I would love that, we need to get to the gym. I'm not lying about only having two weeks to get you ready to fight."

Zeke puts his napkin on the table and stands, throwing some dollars on the table to cover the bill. "Well what are you waiting for? Let's get the fuck out of here."

I follow him out the café, watching how excited he is. *I wonder if he will be just as excited once I show him how much harder his training is about to get?*

Zeke

My muscles are screaming in agony as I push myself to do another round of speed bag work. I'm pretty sure I won't be able to put my clothes on once I'm finished but I make my arms work even harder. I thought the sessions Bryce had me doing before were hard but they were nothing compared to what he's putting me through today. I just want to get through this relatively unhurt and go home so I can relax until I need to do it all again tomorrow.

"Concentrate, Zeke. You can go faster. Keep your elbows up."

He's lucky I *like* him because if I didn't I would use the last of my energy to punch him square in the face. I know he's only doing his job, but I kind of hate him right now and I'm sure in the morning I will hate him even more.

"Right, now drop and give me three sets of eight press ups."

I stop punching and let my arms fall to my side like lead. I can't feel my arms and he wants me to hold my body up on them. *Good fucking luck with that.* "Fuck off, Bryce. That's not happening anytime soon." We've been working out for five hours straight, alternating between cardio and strength work, and I'm done. I have nothing left in my reserves to give. I need to eat and I need to rest.

"Let's call it a day then. I was going to call it a day about an hour ago but I thought I would see how far you would actually go. You did a lot more than I thought you would."

What the fuck? I stand staring at him, and he's lucky I have no energy to kill him just now. "Are you kidding me? You mean I've just about killed myself and I didn't need to?" I would be angrier with him but he looks impressed with what I just did, how much of myself I gave.

"I wanted you to push yourself and find that place inside you where you feel comfortable, and then push harder. And you did it. You kept going until you had nothing left to give. Now let's get home and I'll cook you dinner." Listening to him, I realize that what he did was actually perfect. He gave me the control to see how far I could go. I pushed myself like a motherfucker and I needed to find that determination again so I can keep going, even after I think I'm done. I gave up in my fight with Dwayne, even though I thought at the time I was giving it my all. As soon as my hand went I lost my focus and I need to be able to maintain it, no matter what happens. I think this is why Coach hired Bryce. He's just what I need, someone who won't let me give up, who will force me to go longer, hit harder, push deeper. For the first time ever I'm actually really fucking happy with Coach's decision to hire Bryce, and not just because I'm fucking him.

****

129

"Zeke!"

I groan as I hear Bryce shout down the hall to me. I'm lying on the couch, finally comfortable, and I don't want to move. When we arrived at my house the only thing that got me moving was food. Bryce understood that my first day of hardcore training would be an uphill battle so he's been looking after me. I've had a protein shake and the meal he made, and now I pretty much just want to go to sleep. I close my eyes, praying he'll forget that I'm here but I'm not that lucky. I feel him pulling on my arm, making me get up from the couch.

"Babe, please. I just want to sleep. Look I don't even have the energy to open my eyes. See? Eyes closed."

He doesn't stop pulling me and I decide I do have the energy to open my eyes, especially if it stops me walking into a wall.

"Come on, I have a surprise for you."

I follow behind him because fighting against him isn't something I want or have the energy to do. "It better not be some kinky shit, unless I don't have to be awake for it."

Bryce laughs and I can't help my smile. His laugh is so damn sexy and it makes that little dimple on his cheek make an appearance.

"What kind of kinky stuff can you do in your sleep, Zeke? Are you holding out on me, do I need to see these mad skills?"

We stop just inside the bathroom and I look around in surprise. The lights are off and every surface is covered with candles. Soft music is playing and the bath is nearly overflowing with bubbles. I look at Bryce and see that he's looking awkward, as if he's not sure if he's done the right thing or not.

I reach out and cup his face, pulling him towards me so I can claim his lips. "You did this for me?"

He nods, his eyes softening as I speak.

"Thank you. No one has ever done something like this for me before."

His hand reaches out, grabs the bottom of my t-shirt and pulls it over my head. "Have you ever let anyone?" He asks the question as he pulls my shorts down my legs.

I didn't even have the energy to take a shower at the gym, promising myself I would do it as soon as I got home but the couch called out to me instead. I think about his question for a second. *Have I let anyone get close to me before?* I think the only one who knows a little about me is Asha, but she's more of a friend with benefits than anything romantic. What he's done here is the most caring thing I've ever experienced.

He doesn't wait for an answer before removing his own clothes and climbing into the tub. He motions for me to join him and I follow him in, settling between his open legs. The hot water feels incredible against my skin and I can feel it loosening my tight muscles. I lean back, resting against Bryce's chest as his arms wrap around me.

We sit in silence for a while, just listening to the music playing softly. I didn't think I could feel so content just being with someone, not even having to talk. It's like we can just be together and relax knowing we are safe in each other's arms.

"Feeling better?" Bryce reaches over and grabs my body wash before pouring some into his hand. He adds a little water and lathers it up before he rubs into my shoulders. I groan as his hands knead the knots that have built in my muscles.

"I'll take that as a yes?"

I just groan again, hoping he will take that as some form of answer. My muscles are starting to feel like putty and I'm not sure if I'll be able to get out of the bath when he's finished. "I hope you're not wanting to get lucky tonight, Bryce, I don't think I could get a boner if I tried." It's a complete lie. Feeling his hands on me has me hard but he can't see under the bubbles.

His lips move to my ear, licking over the outside before speaking. "That's a shame, but I'm sure I can go a night without jumping you." His hands leave my body and warm water pours over my hair before fingers knead my scalp. I don't think anyone has ever washed my hair before. I don't even remember my mom doing it for me when I was a kid. Thinking about her makes me miss her a lot but not enough to go home and visit. Seeing her would mean seeing him, and I couldn't cope with that.

"What are you thinking about? Your body just tensed."

I don't think there is a minute that Bryce isn't fully aware of my mood and it's a little strange having someone so in tune with me. As much as I don't like talking about this subject, I don't want to lie to him. "I was just thinking about my mom and how much I miss her sometimes."

He doesn't stop massaging my head as I speak, and for the first time ever, I feel ready to tell another person everything.

"When was the last time you saw her?"

I think about it and am shocked when I realize it's been about four years. "It was the day after my twenty third birthday. I'd gone home to see her because I thought my dad was away on business. I always timed my visits for when he wouldn't be there and usually she was happy with that. She knew that I didn't want to see him but she never asked why, which I'm grateful for. I didn't know how to tell her that the only reason I started fighting was because she was married to a homophobe who would rather have his child beaten than love him for who he is." I take a deep breath, trying to calm the tension that's building inside. This always happens when I think of him. I know that I like to make out the way he treated me doesn't affect me, that I don't think about what he put me through but I do. I remember feeling so lost when I was a teen, just wanting my dad to hug me and tell me it would be okay. Instead I had him organizing for me to fight against his friends and to have sex with a much older woman, sex that was forced on me without my consent. Yes Bryce was right, what that woman did to me was basically rape, but what guy speaks out about something that embarrassing? After it happened my dad patted me on the back and told me he was proud of me and as fucked up as it sounds, I felt happy. For once my dad was proud. Even through school when my grades were great and I made the football team it was never enough, he always wanted more from me. When I finally left I swore I would never feel useless again, and not seeing my dad was the best way to do that.

"Anyway, she knew I didn't like to see him so on this occasion, she lied to me. She told me that he would be gone even though she knew he'd be there. A huge fight broke out between us with him calling me some pretty graphic names until I punched him. Knocked him out completely and she went running to him, screaming at me to get out. So I did. Haven't been back to see her since."

Bryce rinses the shampoo out of my hair, his hands still gently massaging my scalp. "Have you thought about going to see her?"

I sigh, knowing that I'm about to sound like a child. "She chose him over me that day, so no, I haven't thought about going back. She heard what he was saying to me and she still chose him. What sort of mother does that?" I feel his hands leave my head and wrap around me. I relax back immediately in his hold.

"I'm sorry you were treated like that, you don't deserve it."

And just like that, a little piece of my heart is claimed by the man who's holding me. It's then that I realize that I'm going to have to be careful, there's a real possibility that I could fall for this guy and I'm not sure how to deal with that. I knew I wanted to be with him, but I didn't honestly think I would fall for him as much as I have. He's the full package. He's smart, sexy and as funny as fuck. He's everything I didn't realize I was looking for. I never would have dreamt that I would be lying here having one of the most romantic experiences of my life with a guy. I wonder how he feels about me, whether he has any real feelings for me or if this is just a little bit of fun to pass the time while he's over here? It's something I would love to ask him, but I'm shit scared of rushing us and making things awkward. We just need to go with the flow and see what happens.

"I think we should get out before you turn into a prune. Come on, let me put you to bed." He kisses my head and I force myself to move. The only thing that could get me moving is the thought of me wrapping myself in Bryce's arms as I fall asleep.

CHAPTER THIRTEEN

Zeke

I try to keep my knee still but it won't stop bouncing as my nerves about the upcoming fight showing rear their ugly head. I need to win. If I don't then I won't be scheduled for any future fights. It's not a headline fight but I've been told that there's a lot of buzz surrounding it and that it's being billed as my big comeback.

I look down and watch as the ref wraps my hands. I smile when I see that Bryce has brought my red wraps, I suppose he would after me reminding him about a thousand times. He laughed at me when I first told him that they were first on my preparation list, made sure he understood I needed them and that's why I lost the last time. I know it's a stupid superstition but it felt like not having the right ones had started a chain reaction of bad luck in my last fight. This time I wasn't taking any chances. When he realized that I wasn't kidding he went out and bought dozens of pairs, telling me that I would need them for all my fights so it was better to stock pile them now.

I see Bryce pacing behind the ref, and I want to tell him to stop before he wears a hole in the changing room floor. I know something's bothering him but I haven't been able to find out what. I'm sharing a changing room with the other fighters, only the headliners get their own room, so I can't ask him and I hate not being able to go to him and hold him until he settles. I don't know what he's so stressed about. He knows I'm stronger than I've ever been thanks to him.

I hear a loud voice from behind me and I tense up, all my muscles twitch with the need to hurt the owner. The ref finishes my tapes and pats me on the shoulder as he tells me that I will get called just before my fight. I fist bump him and he walks away, leaving me trying to control my anger.

"Well, well, well, look who it is. I heard a rumor that you were back. Didn't I break you enough last time? Did you really need to come back to let me finish you off?"

I close my eyes, trying to reign in my rage, but his words rattle around in my head and I want to lash out and hurt him. I feel a hand on my shoulder and I immediately calm, the warmth from Bryce's hand relaxing me.

He leans down and talks quietly in my ear. "Don't let him get to you. He wants a reaction. He knows that if he gets you to fight outside the ring you'll be disqualified and then he will never have to fight you. He knows he won't win again, so he's trying to get you to make a mistake." His words make sense and I let them drown out Dwayne's words as I put my headphones on, pretending not to listen. I don't play the music when I see him approach and stand in front of Bryce. Call me a glutton for punishment but I want to know what he's planning on saying. He looks Bryce up and down, and I want to poke his eyes out, then rip his arm off and hit him with it.

"So, you're loser boy's new coach? Word on the street is that you're pretty impressive. Why you settling for second best when I could use you in my squad? How about you come work for a winner?"

I'm about to get up into Dwayne's face when Bryce calmly talks to him.

"You're right, I do want to work with a winner. That's why I'm working with Zeke. I have a way of seeing true winners out there, so, we will see you in the final where I will watch him pound you into the ground."

I have never seen Dwayne stuck for words but that's what he is right now as I watch his face redden and he storms away. I can't help but laugh when Bryce sits next to me on the bench. I want to kiss him so badly but I know I can't so I make a note to myself to kiss the fuck out of him later.

"That guy's a bellend, just thought you should know."

I look at him in confusion. *What the fuck is a bellend?* I can usually understand most of what Bryce says, but this is one of his British things that I don't get. I think the last time he had me confused and then rolling on the floor laughing was when he asked me to get him a jumper from his closet. I just stood there in utter confusion, convinced I was going to find a kangaroo type animal in there.

"Nope, I'm lost. You need to explain that one to me. It's like the whole pants thing all over again."

He laughs at me and I smile, waiting patiently on an explanation. "A bellend is like… a wanker."

I look on, still in confusion, waiting on him using a word I understand but all that comes out are a lot of words that sound great but don't make any sense.

"You know tosser, knobhead, wankstain… shit… let me say it in a way you understand. Asshole." By this point Bryce is laughing so hard I think he's going to fall off the bench and I can't help but laugh with him.

"Yeah, he's an asshole." I smile at him, seeing his body relax as he laughs. "It's nice to see you relax, what's been bothering you?"

He takes a deep breath and lets it out slowly. I don't what's about to come next but I'm thinking that I might not like it.

"I just need to tell you something and I don't know how to say it." He gets up from the bench and starts pacing again.

Yeah, I'm pretty sure this is going to be bad. An ocean of thoughts flood my mind as I try to think what it could be. He's leaving, he's seeing someone else, he doesn't want with me anymore? All of these things have me panicking. Maybe he wants to leave after the fight and he's warning me that he won't be here.

I'm pulled from my thoughts when Bryce comes to a stop in front of me, looking down at his sneakers. "It's just… I'm so sorry, Zeke. I can't go out there with you. I can't watch you fight, it will bring back too many memories and I don't think I could handle it. I'm getting Jesse to tape it so we can go over the fight after. I'm so sorry, I feel like such a shit coach for not standing with you." His voice is soft and I know that this is really bothering him.

I look around and see that the section of changing room that we're in is empty so I stand and go to him. I keep walking when I reach him, forcing him to back up until he's pressed against the wall behind him. I crowd him, getting as close to him as possible and I feel him take a shaky breath that makes me smile. I love being able to get this reaction from him, knowing that I can make him feel so turned on by just being near him.

I lean in until my nose is brushing over his. "I understand. I can't believe that this is what was bothering you. I would never make you do anything that would make you uncomfortable. Never."

I feel him relax against my chest and I struggle with the need to wrap my arms around him. I move closer until there is no space between our bodies, and I lean in, just about to kiss him when I hear a voice behind me that makes my body freeze.

"Well maybe it isn't my name that should be 'man eater'. Is this why you won't come work for me, Bryce? Getting special benefits from your current boss?"

Panic seizes my body and I start to breathe heavily. *This can't be happening*. I can't be caught with Bryce like this, especially by that fucker. I turn to Dwayne, planning on telling him that he has the wrong idea, but the look on his face tells me he won't believe a word I say. I hear Bryce talk but I can't make out his words, there's a ringing in my ears that I can't get rid of. I need to get out of here. I can't be in here. I can't breathe.

I start walking, shoulder barging past Dwayne who's still standing with a shit-eating grin on his face. I walk to the corridor that will lead me to the arena. I don't care that it's not my time to fight; I'll wait cage side until I'm needed. I can't stay in this room with Dwayne's eyes on me, judging me already. All I can think is how much did he see? How did it look from the outside? *Shit! This can't be happening. What if he starts telling people I'm gay?* For once the universe is working in my favor and I hear my name come over the loud speaker, calling me for my fight. I walk towards the cage, determined to work out this anger.

I need to sort this shit out, and sooner rather than later.

Bryce

I pace the changing room, waiting for Zeke to come back. I heard his name being called and the place erupted into a deafening roar. I also heard his name come over the loud speaker as the winner, a knockout in the first round. As proud as I am, I know that he won through anger. The way he ran out of here when Dwayne caught us, I knew that there was no way he would lose. I see the other fighter's team enter the room with their arms wrapped around their guy as they help him drag his broken body to a bench. My eyes make their way to the door, waiting patiently for Zeke to enter, but as the minutes tick by I start to worry. I'm just about to suck up my fear of going out into the crowd when Eddie walks through the door.

I rush over to him, worrying that something has happened. "Where's Zeke?"

Eddie looks confused and that makes my heart race. "He's not in here? He left the ring and I thought he was coming here."

My heart drops to my stomach when I realize he's left. He's run from me the first time someone thought there might be something going on between us. I never expected him to confirm it, to suddenly come out of the closet because someone saw us together, but I didn't think he would run. I thought he would stay and talk to me, let us sort it all out together. Instead I don't know where he is and I'm standing here alone and in the dark. I feel tears building in my eyes and I blink them away, knowing I can't show any emotion or I will make Eddie wonder what's going on.

"I must have missed him. I'm sure he wanted to get out of here as quickly as possible. I'll catch up with him later."

He doesn't look convinced with my answer and I'm sure there will be a lot of questions coming my way.

I grab my bag from the floor, not even checking that everything has been replaced and walk past Eddie out of the door. I need to get out of here before I lose it. I make my way through the venue, pushing past bodies to get out the main door. I race to my car, wanting to get inside before the emotions take over. I slam the door behind me and let it all go. I start punching the steering wheel as tears run down my cheeks. Anger and pain rages through my body and I don't stop hitting the wheel until my body is heaving with my painful sobs. I can't believe that I gave him my heart, I should have known better. I *did* know better. I knew that there was a fucking huge chance he would leave, and still I did it. Like a stupid fucker I went and fell in love with Zeke, and now he's gone and broken my heart.

****

I'm sitting in the driveway of Zeke's house waiting for him to come home. I've been here about two hours now, and I'll sit here all night if I have to. His truck isn't here so I know he's not inside but I figure he has to come home at some point. When he does, I'll be waiting right here for the inevitable showdown.

I pick up my mobile and dial his number again, listening as his answering message plays in my ear. I haven't heard it ring once, it's gone straight to voicemail every time so his phone must be off. I'm trying not to let my mind wander but it's hard not to think where he might be. If he's at a club or bar, or even if he's just hiding from me that won't worry me as much, but some of the places I picture him are making my heart hurt. I can picture him in bed with a woman trying to prove to himself that he isn't gay, that he had a little blip on his scorecard but he's back on track now. That's the thought that hurts the most, knowing that he's probably regretting our time together. I thought what we had is special, but now I think I'm the only one who thought so.

Anger flares inside me again and I start the car, peeling out of the driveway as fast as I can. I refuse to wait around for him. He knows where I live and he's the one who ran. He can come and find me when he's ready to talk. I refuse to be used and to be ignored until he decides to grace me with his presence. Why should I be the one doing the chasing? He fucked up here, he needs to do the groveling. I drive, letting the anger chase away the hurt that this is causing. As I put distance between me and his house, I try to tell myself that I can't feel my heart breaking in my chest, that my body isn't aching with the loss of Zeke.

I pull into my own drive, exiting my car without taking anything with me. I'll get my bags tomorrow, or when I can be bothered. I need a drink, something to take away the memory of watching Zeke walk away. I close the front door behind me, kicking my shoes across the room as I walk to the kitchen. I walk past the fridge where the beer is and open the cupboard above my sink. Inside is a bottle of Bourbon that Zeke brought over when he came for dinner. It's never been opened since I don't drink hard liquor, but tonight that's going to change. I grab the bottle and unscrew the lid before taking a huge mouthful. I walk through my house, collapsing on the couch as I take another drink from the bottle. I think back to Zeke's face when Dwayne caught us. I really shouldn't be surprised by the look of panic that was clear for all to see. He always told me that he couldn't come out, but I was stupid enough to think I could make him change his mind, that I would be everything he needed and he would realize that it didn't matter what anybody else thought. Talk about being big headed, like I'm the type of person that someone would change their life for. I snort at myself and take another big gulp of bourbon, enjoying the burn as it makes its way into my stomach. I can feel the fuzziness in my head already and I'm thankful that I don't drink much. It will make getting drunk a lot easier.

****

I wake up lying on the couch and the darkened room around

me tells me that I've been asleep for a while. I don't remember falling asleep but then I drank a lot. I sit up and the room spins. As I hold my head I remember why I don't drink, that feeling of not quite drunk anymore and not quite sober is the worst. I slowly stand, taking a few moments to gain my balance before walking down the hall towards my room. I pull my t-shirt off over my head, hitting the doorframe as I lose my balance, and throw it on the floor. I collapse on my bed, not even thinking about attempting to take my trousers off. I close my eyes trying to settle the feeling of nausea that flows through my body. I'm going to feel so bad in the morning if I don't get up and get a drink of water, but I just can't get my body to listen to me. All I want is sleep, actually no that's a lie, all I want is Zeke. I lost my anger after the first quarter bottle of bourbon as it took me deep into the sadness I've been trying to avoid.

Since that first night together we haven't spent a night apart, and I don't know if I can fall asleep without him. It's funny that he's become my everything without me being aware of it. I've had some of the best times of my life with him. He makes me laugh like no one else can. I remember the time we went to the cinema to see some cult horror movie he wanted to see and even after everything it still brings a smile to my face.

I've never heard of the film before but Zeke's been raving about it for days so I finally gave in and came with him. It's the midnight showing and when we turned up there were only another four people here, which doesn't give me much faith that it's going to be any good. He's undeterred, buying popcorn for us to share while he speaks nonstop about what I'm about to watch. It's about a doll that's possessed, only waking up at Halloween. I just nod a lot while listening, not really wanting to hurt his feelings by telling him that it sounds awful. We sit towards the back, Zeke joking that it's so we can make out. When the screen goes dark I feel Zeke moving around next to me before putting his arm around my shoulder, pulling me close. He offers me popcorn a few times as we watch the incredibly bad film, but I say no because I don't really like sweet popcorn. After about the sixth time of me turning him down he leans over and growls in my ear for me to 'take some fucking popcorn'. I look him in the eye before reaching down and digging my hand into the large tub. He's eaten about a quarter of the popcorn so I have to put my hand in further to get some. When I grab a handful and try to take it out, something in my hand won't move, so I open my fist, dropping the popcorn and grabbing again. This time I get less sweet treat and more dick. I cry out in shock, making Zeke cover my mouth with his hand while giggling. He'd made a hole in the bottom of the tub and fed his fucking cock into it, waiting for me to grab it. We had such a laugh about it, but that soon led to groaning as I gave him what he craved right in the middle of the movie. He said it was the best visit to the cinema he'd ever had.

He did lots of things like that, always trying to put a smile on my face. No matter my mood he would be there with a joke or just that gorgeous smile he would give me when no one else was looking. I think that's what I'll miss the most. His smile, it could light up a room without him ever trying. I'm also going to miss talking to him, just spending the time with a friend and being able to talk about anything.

Why am I lying to myself? I'm going to miss everything about him.

As I fall asleep I already know that I've lost him because if he wanted me he would be with me now, no matter who found out. I knew his job was important to him but I thought given time, he would accept that he's a gay man, or at least admit he was bi. I suppose it's better that I find out now that what people think will always be more important than me.

CHAPTER FOURTEEN

Bryce

I feel like I'm dying. My hangover is in full flow as I stand leaning against the running machine. I grab my water and down it, hoping that maybe this will clear my head. I was surprised that I managed to make it in on time this morning, but I shouldn't have worried since Zeke is now an hour late. I wonder if he's going to show or hide from me again. I throw my empty bottle towards the bin, groaning when it misses completely. It means I'll need to bend down and pick it up.

I drag myself across to the bottle, moving slowly to grab it and throw it in the bin, silently cheering to myself when it goes in this time. Just as I turn to walk back to the running machine I see Zeke coming through the front door and my heart crashes to my feet. I knew I'd see him today. I'd braced myself for it, knowing that I would need to suck it up and get on with my job, but I didn't expect this. The scene in front of me makes me want to run away this time. Asha's giggle reaches me as she snuggles into Zeke's side, her head burrowing into his neck as he kisses the top of her head. They have their arms wrapped around each other looking like the picture perfect couple. At least now I can stop worrying that he's drank himself into a coma or ended up in a ditch. Apparently while I spent the night worrying about him, he was proving to himself and the world that he was straight by being between Asha's legs. I turn away, unable to watch them anymore but the universe apparently wants to make me suffer today.

"Hey, Bryce!" Asha shouts across the gym and I lock a smile in place before I turn around. She looks really happy but Zeke won't meet my eyes.

Fucking coward.

"Afternoon, Asha. How are you today?" I'm determined to be polite. It's not her fault that Zeke's acting this way and using her to prove a point to himself. I actually feel sorry for her. He'll go back to being the closed off person he was before, who hides a huge part of himself from everyone, eventually.

She giggles before she answers, pulling Zeke closer to her. "I'm so good. I've had the best few hours." She looks up at Zeke shyly and then back to me. "I don't know if I'm meant to tell you, but Zeke and me are now an official couple."

And just like that my world collapses around me. I stare at Zeke, daring him to look at me but he leans down and whispers something into Asha's ear. She gives me a little wave before walking off towards the locker room. I turn and start to walk away but he grabs my arm, stopping me.

I don't even turn to him as I talk, trying to keep my voice low and even. "Get the fuck off me."

He doesn't listen, moving closer behind me. "Bryce, please."

I pull my arm out of his hold, refusing to listen to anything he has to say. I hear him call after me as I leave the gym. My only thought is of escape, I need to get away from Zeke before I do something I regret.

I wanted to cover Asha's mouth the minute she started talking to Bryce. The last thing I wanted was for her to go blabbing about what we'd done together. I knew he would find out, but I was hoping that when he did I wouldn't be there to see the look of utter devastation on his face. When she spoke he looked like he was in physical pain, as if something was tearing apart inside him. I wasn't planning on talking to him today but when he was leaving, I reached for him out of instinct. Touching him had brought me peace but I can't think about that anymore. I can't think how Bryce makes my past feel less important, that everything I went through doesn't need to influence who I am today, or how he settles my racing mind with just being near me. He has this ability to make me feel that I'm enough, that maybe I could be loved. That doesn't matter now. My feelings don't come into account. I need to move on with my life and be the person they all expect.

That's why I ended up at Asha's house last night. I needed to feel like I did before Bryce arrived. She opened her front door and even though I felt how wrong it was, feeling it deep in my bones, I went inside and fucked her. I think I needed to prove something to myself, but now that I've seen Bryce I'm not even sure what it was. After having sex with her I got straight in the shower, needing time to myself to sort out what I was feeling and to wash away the memory of her touch. The whole thing felt wrong, like I was cheating on Bryce, and I suppose I was. I swore to him that I wouldn't be with anyone else while we were together, then at the first sign of trouble and I run from him straight into someone else's arms.

"Fuck!" I turn to go after Bryce but Asha comes back from the locker room with the gloves I asked her to get for me. I don't really need them, but I needed to get her to leave in case Bryce said something. Deep down I knew he wouldn't, even though I've been a bastard to him he wouldn't ever say anything that would affect my career or me.

"Here you go, baby." She runs her empty hand over my back and it takes everything in me not to shudder under her touch.

I turn and kiss her head like a good boyfriend would do. "Thanks. I need to go and do something. Can you get yourself home?" I drove her here, and I won't abandon her if she can't get another way home.

"Is everything okay?"

I force a fake smile, not wanting her to see that I'm getting closer to falling apart. I feel like my nerves are buzzing and I need

145

to move, need to go after Bryce and sort this out. "Yeah, it's all good. I just need to rush off and sort something out, something that can't wait."

She gets a funny look on her face before she smiles, but it doesn't reach her eyes. "I can get a lift home with Jenny. Will I see you later?"

I lean forward and give her a kiss on the lips. "Of course. I'll be at your place for dinner." I turn and leave, not even looking back as I follow the man who has my heart. I need to talk to him, try to explain why I'm doing this. I just hope he's willing to listen to me.

****

I bang on his door again, planning on making as much noise as possible until he answers. I know he's in there, his car's in the driveway and it hasn't moved because I blocked it in with my truck. I had visions of him sneaking out the back door and driving away as I knocked.

"I know you're in there, Bryce. I'm not leaving until you talk to me." I hear movement from inside but the door still doesn't open. "Please let me in, I need to talk to you."

I hear a thump on the other side of the door before I hear him. "The time to talk was last night, Zeke. Where were you then?"

I lean my head against the door, making the same noise he made a few moments before and I wonder if we are mirroring each other's positions. "Please, I don't want to do this through a door."

There's silence and I think he's gone and left me standing here on my own. I'm about to start banging again when I hear the lock click, the sound making me both excited and scared. I know that we need to talk and clear the air but I'm scared shitless about what I can actually say to explain.

I open the door just a little since I'm worried that something might be thrown at my head. The hall is empty with no sign of Bryce at all. I would shout out to him but I'm pretty sure he won't

146

reply. I walk through his living room and see that it's also empty, so I continue on to the kitchen. There's no point checking his bedroom, I know there's no chance he'll be in there. I walk into the kitchen and see him leaning up against the kitchen unit, his arms crossed against his chest. He might have looked hurt earlier in the gym but there's no trace of that now on his face. All I see is anger glaring out of his eyes.

I lean on the unit across from him, I know I need to start the conversation but I'm not sure how to go about. Maybe I should start with the obvious. "I'm sorry, Bryce."

He gives a humorless laugh at my words and I know this isn't going to be as easy as I hoped. "What are you sorry about? Running, pretending I don't exist, having me worry all night about where you were… or for fucking someone else?"

I flinch at his words, feeling them deep in my gut. I didn't let myself think of how he was feeling last night, that he might be worried about me. I just thought about losing myself inside Asha's body.

"I got scared. Dwayne saw us, he fucking saw us." I can feel the same panic as yesterday start to build. It's crawling under my skin making me feel like I need to scrub myself clean.

"He saw what, Zeke? And even if he saw you bending me over and fucking me, you could have talked to me and told me how you were feeling. Instead you went and sunk yourself into the first female body you could find. Tell me, have you been fucking her the whole time you've been with me?"

I can't believe he's asking me this. Does he really think I would cheat on him? Okay, technically I did but who the fuck does he think he is to doubt me? One night of second thoughts doesn't mean the whole thing was a lie.

I stand from the unit, moving towards him. "How the fuck can you ask me that? Everything I've done over the past few months has been centered around you, and now you doubt me? I know I said I didn't want to label what we have, but that doesn't mean I wasn't trying, our relationship is important."

He stands, mimicking my stance as he gets in my face, anger seeping out his pores. "How was Asha last night?"

I feel my face heat with embarrassment. I can't deny I spent the night with her, he saw it pretty much first hand earlier.

"What, you can't remember or you don't want to tell me? Then tell me this, can she please you the way I do? Scratch the itches you don't like to admit you have?"

He has a right to be angry. I keep trying to tell myself that as he shouts abuse at me. Shame floods through my body knowing how much I've hurt him. I can see the pain on his face, hear it seeping through his angry tone. I've done the one thing I promised I wouldn't and now I'm arguing with him like I think it's his fault.

"I know you're angry. I didn't mean to hurt you, I just think that we need to take a break. I need to focus on training and winning the tournament. I think that's the only thing I should be thinking about right now."

He flinches like I've just hit him. I want to erase the look of pain on his face and never see it there again. It's tearing me apart to say all this to him, to pretend that what we have isn't important to me, when in reality it's the best thing that's ever happened. I just know it can't go anywhere, that there's no way I can be gay in the world of MMA. Half the fighters would refuse to go up against me and I would be pushed out. I have worked my whole life for the chance to be the best and I won't ruin it, not for anyone. I've lived my life so far denying who I am, now I just have to become a master at it.

"You'd throw me away just like that? After months of getting to know each other, all the fun we had together, all of the times we made love together, and I'm gone as easily as that. *Fuck*, I actually thought we might be going somewhere. I'm such a fucking idiot, you were using me to fulfill some urge you have, and now you've done that I'm gone. Does it even matter to you how I feel? That maybe I get a say in what happens?"

I want to reach out to him and tell him that it's for the best but I know I don't have the right. Everything he's saying makes complete sense to me, I'm making the decision for both of us and, as unfair as it is, it's the way it needs to be. If I make the decision now it won't hurt as much in the long run.

"This is for the best, Bryce. It never would've gone anywhere."

I feel my heart shatter in my chest when tears swarm his eyes. His shoulders fall and I can almost feel all the fight leave his body. "After everything we've done together, I can't believe you don't want me. You're the first person I've let in since Austin, the only one I let in when I was sure I should spend my life alone."

I instinctively move closer to him, needing to make him feel better. I know it doesn't make any sense but I need him stop hurting because when I see him like this it creates an ache in my heart, making it hard to keep my distance. I reach out and cup his face, feeling the warmth of his cheek as he leans into my hand.

He opens his eyes and looks up at me with pleading eyes. "Why are you doing this? If you don't want me then why are you touching me? Why make me feel like this is still something you want. What do you want, Zeke?"

I need to be honest with him. Maybe if I tell him how I feel he will understand. I need him to understand that this is hard for me, and if I could walk away from him without hurting him I would.

"Do I want to touch you? Yes. Do I want to taste you? More than anything. But I can't, it's not who I am. Why can't you understand? Being with you is not that simple."

He pulls away from my touch and I miss him instantly. He looks deep into my eyes as he speaks. "That's the thing, Zeke. It really is *that* simple." He goes to walk past me and I grab him again.

"Don't fucking walk away, I'm not done yet." I don't even register what's happening until it's too late. His fist moves quicker than I could have ever imagined and hits me square on the cheek. The power behind it is surprising and it makes me stagger backwards. I hold my face, taking a few seconds to clear my vision before I can look at him. *Fuck, this guy can hit.*

"Get out my fucking house." It's the only thing he says before disappearing into the hall. A few seconds later his bedroom door slams shut and with it goes any chance I had of keeping the man of my dreams.

Bryce

I pace across my bedroom floor until I hear my front door slam. *I hit him.* I can't believe I actually hit him. I didn't mean to, he was just throwing so many mixed messages at me. One minute he didn't want me, and then the next he did but couldn't be with me. I needed to get away from him and clear my head but then he tried to stop me and I just reacted. It was a reflex to his tone of voice he used from my fighting days. I haven't hit anyone properly since my last fight. I've sparred but that's not what this was, I wanted to hurt him as much as he'd hurt me. I wanted to smash his face in and hope that Asha wouldn't want Mr. Pretty Boy anymore.

I collapse onto my bed and stare at the ceiling while I decide what's going to happen. Zeke was always going to be a flight risk. I should have known better and then there's the added problem of him being my boss. *Shit, I'm going to need to find a new place to work.* Maybe I should take Dwayne up on his offer to work with him, if that's even on the table anymore. The only problem with that is that I don't want to work with him, I want to work with Zeke. He's an amazing fighter and I want to be part of the team even if it will hurt to look at him everyday. Luckily, Eddie doesn't know about our relationship and even though Zeke technically employs me, my contract says that only Eddie can fire me. So unless Zeke wants to go to him with a reason to get rid of me, I still have a job. I don't plan on quitting that's for sure. No way am I going to make it easy for Zeke. I'm going to stay right where I am and make him look at my face every single day. Make him live with what he did to me. I just hope that it'll make him suffer. I don't want to be the only one in pain.

Feeling determined, I get up off the bed and get changed into my running gear. I refuse to drown my sorrows in another bottle of alcohol. I refuse to give him that power over me. I will work out, run until my body is exhausted and then I'll sleep. Tomorrow when I get up, I will go to work and be professional. There will be nothing between us other than me being his coach. Exiting my house, I push my earphones into my ears and take off up the street. My feet pound the pavement in time with the music and I feel light. Exercise always makes me feel better, it clears my mind like nothing else, well other than sex but that's the last thing on my mind just now. I need to get back into this. I missed a lot of running recently, preferring to spend time with Zeke. I just need to get my routine organized and spend more time on myself again. Maybe I should Google for gay bars around here and look for a little fun of my own. I'm not usually into one-night stands but maybe it's just the thing I need to get me over Zeke. My chest hurts to even think about being with someone other than him, but I need to move on. It's time to be Bryce again, whoever he may be.

CHAPTER FIFTEEN

Zeke

I flinch as Jason's glove catches me on the side of the face again. I swear this black eye will take a month to go away if people don't quit hitting it.

"Where's your form, Zeke? Come on. Pretend you know how to fight."

I turn and glare at Bryce, wanting nothing more than to return the favor and blacken his eye. He's been pissing me off for the last week. Actually it's been since the day after I went to his house. I was worried about training the morning after, not sure how we would be with each other, but Bryce turned up with a smile and acted like nothing had happened. I think it's pissing me off that he doesn't look like this is affecting him at all. I'm tired and completely off my game, but he looks as amazing as always. I don't know if it's my imagination or not, but he looks more toned now than he had when we were together, and he's changed his hair. He's wearing it shorter at the sides and it looks as sexy as fuck. All I can think about is how he might have someone new in his life, someone special. I know I can't say anything since I'm with Asha, but I don't want Bryce with anyone but me. This is what's upsetting me the most. I didn't think he would get on with his life so quickly without me. I was the one who'd left. I was the one who wasn't meant to hurt.

I see Asha walking towards the ring and I go back to trying to get my shit together. I've been struggling to get my head sorted for so long now that I'm beginning to worry that I'll lose my next fight. I have just over a week to get my head out my ass, and I'm hoping that when I do what I have planned tonight, that my mind will be able to concentrate. There will be no going back after it's done. I will just need to live with the consequences. Another punch to the ribs steals my breath and I hear Bryce shouting from behind me. Something needs to happen before I lose everything.

****

I pull at the collar of my shirt, feeling like it's trying to strangle me. I never thought I would be in this situation, doing this has never been in my life plan. I feel my leg shake under the table and I try to hold it still, hoping that if I manage that then my nerves will go away.

I look over to Asha as she eats her dessert. It's nice in here, a little too fancy for my liking but I needed to make tonight special. If I'm going to live a lie with her I need to give her everything she could want. I'll love her the best I can and give her the life she wants, the one she deserves. I take a deep breath and slip from my seat, getting down on one knee in front of Asha. I have given this a lot of thought and even though I don't love her, I'm sure she likes me enough to become my wife. I need a good cover just in case Dwayne tells someone what he saw, and I know he will if I make it to the final with him again. This is the most logical thing to do: marry a woman that I like. I know I'll never love her, but who really falls in love these days? You find someone you're compatible with and do the best with that. I think I'll be happy with Asha. She makes me smile and has been a good friend for a long time. I'm pretty sure I was always her end game, even if she slept with the other fighters it was always me she came back to.

She lets out a little squeal as she watches me take the ring out of my pocket. I've practiced my little speech quite a lot to try and get it to sound remotely believable.

"Asha, you've been my friend for so long. I think we could make a great couple, and I'm wondering if you would do me the honor of marrying me?" I can't even bring myself to say that I love her. Maybe one day I'll be able to do it, but today I just can't.

She squeals again as she throws her arms around me, kissing all over my face and repeating 'yes' over and over again. I push her back slightly and place the large diamond ring on her finger. She has tears in her eyes and looks so happy. I hope I can keep making her happy like this. We both return to our chairs and she reaches over and takes my hand.

"Thank you for asking me, Zeke. I love you so much, but I honestly didn't think you saw me that way. I've dreamed of this moment for so long."

I've only been in an 'official' relationship with her for a few weeks now, but I would try anything to get my life back on track. Maybe if I settle down, commit to someone that I can take out in public with me, I'll be able to organize everything else. I'm pretty sure my mum married my dad because she had to. I never once saw them being affectionate with each other. This will just be like that. We can be companions.

"I hope you don't mind that it's quick. I was always told if you believe in something then why wait? And I do believe we can be good together."

She looks down at the ring on her finger, sucking her lip into her mouth. "Do you love me, Zeke?" It was the last thing I expected her to ask and I don't know how to answer it. Starting an engagement admitting I'm not in love with her might not be the best route. I try to avoid answering, hoping she won't notice.

I lean down and kiss the ring on her finger. "I would do anything for you, baby." The name gets stuck in my throat, it feels wrong saying it to anyone but Bryce. I don't even know when I started calling him baby, but I know that now I can't call him it, it hurts.

She smiles at me, obviously accepting my answer and I'm relieved. I really do want to make this work and have some semblance of a happy life with her. I just need to get over the pain of leaving Bryce and I will be able to live my life somewhat happy. *Please let it happen soon.*

****

Asha leans over me, kissing down my neck and bites my shoulder. I keep my eyes on my bedroom ceiling, trying to get in the mood.

"Baby, you're so sexy." Her hand brushes down over my chest and lands on my very limp cock. I haven't had enough to drink to fake this with her. I close my eyes and focus on the feeling of her hand on me, the stroking that should be getting me hard. Thankfully, I feel my cock twitch to life.

"I didn't think this was alive." She giggles and I can feel myself going soft again. *Shit, she needs to stop talking or it isn't going to happen.* Her fingers wrap around my balls and she sucks my cock into her mouth. I groan in pleasure, instantly going rock hard. She's always been great at blowjobs and she can suck like no other woman I know. Most try to be gentle, but not Asha, she likes to let you know she's there. She hums around me, causing a shiver to run through my whole body.

Fuck that feels really good.

I grab her hair, pushing her further down onto me. My mind starts to drift, imagining shorter hair, rough stubbled cheeks. I push her harder until I can feel my tip hit the back of her throat. I want to clear the thoughts that are trying to invade my mind, the thoughts of a certain guy's lips around my cock, the thoughts that are threatening to make me explode in her mouth. Asha is pretty relaxed when it comes to oral. You can fuck her mouth as rough as you want but you can't come inside, that's her limit and I want to respect it. I try not to think of watching my cum hitting Bryce's tongue, of him sucking every last drop from me as I struggled to breathe. I pull on Asha's hair, pulling her mouth off me as I explode on her chest. I reach down and stroke myself through my orgasm, the strength of my release making my muscles quiver.

I collapse back onto my pillow and stare at the ceiling. That was close. It crept up on me without any warning. Just the thought of Bryce made me lose control. I have to remind myself that I can't think of him while I'm with Asha. It's not fair on her and apparently it's too much for me to cope with. I feel Asha move up my body and I feel bad, I finished without giving her anything in return and that's not the way I do things.

When she's level with me, I roll her over so I'm on top. I kiss her as I slip my fingers inside her, scissoring them so they rub over her g-spot. Her back rises off the bed and I know I'm hitting it. I use my thumb to rub over her clit, pressing just enough to make her squeal. I'm happy when it doesn't take long until she's coming around my fingers. Every time I'm with her it feels wrong. I thought it would get easier, that I would eventually get over the feeling that this isn't who I'm meant to be with but it doesn't, it just gets worse. I kiss her shoulder and collapse back to the bed, feeling a little awkward. It's always like this for me once I've been with her, and I have to resist the urge to rush to the bathroom to shower. I need to get myself under control, I can't have her feeling that something's wrong.

I feel her get off the bed and hear her walk into the bathroom for a few minutes before climbing back into bed, lying close to me but not touching.

"Is everything okay? You seem a little … distant."

I turn my head to look at her. She looks so innocent lying there with her head resting on her hand. How can a girl who does such naughty things look so fucking innocent?

"I think I'm just tired, I haven't been sleeping well. Maybe I was nervous about asking you tonight?"

She smiles at me, her eyes looking dreamy. I need to try harder with her, to make her feel as important as she should.

"Go to sleep now." I kiss her forehead before turning away. I spend the next few hours trying to fall asleep, all the while wishing there was another set of arms around me.

Bryce

I watch Zeke as he punches the bag in front of him. His timing is off and I have to admit that he looks like shit. His technique has been suffering recently and he needs to get it under control before next week. It's an important fight, one that will get him a place in the semi-final for the belt. He needs to win this or he's done for the year and if that happens, I'm not sure if he can come back from it. The crowd has his back after his injury, but I'm not sure they will hang around for him if he loses. We have been building up the anticipation of a rematch with Dwayne, but he still needs to earn his spot in the final.

"What the fuck is up with you? Your fighting hasn't been worth shit for a while now. Get it together for fuck's sake." I can't help but raise my voice when I talk to him. He needs to get his head out his arse. He starts punching harder, his anger showing. Good. I want him to get angry, I want him to feed off it so that he pushes himself harder, fights cleaner, does what he's been training for years for. The sweat starts pouring down his back and he suddenly stops, grabbing the bag and resting his head against it.

I walk over to him, getting as close to him as I feel comfortable. "What is it?"

He knocks his head against the bag a few times before tilting his head to look at me. "I don't know if I can do this."

Every athlete gets a moment when they doubt their abilities, when they don't think they're good enough to win. Maybe this is what he's struggling with. *Is he seriously doubting himself?*

"You can do this. You've been training for months and your last match was over in minutes." I cringe as I think about his last fight, the last day I was allowed to kiss and touch him. I close my eyes and take a deep breath before continuing. "You just need to get your focus back. I have full faith in you, you can do it."

He keeps looking at me and sadness appears in his eyes. "That's not what I meant."

Now he has me really confused. It's like he's talking in riddles that I can't work out. "Zeke, what's wrong?" I can't help him if he doesn't tell me what's bothering him. I need to know what's going on in his head in order to get him over it.

"I miss you."

Time stops and I'm sure that my heart skips dozens of beats. How can he say that to me? *He misses me.* I step back from him, putting some much needed distance between us. I've been masking my feelings so well for the last few weeks, making it appear that life is just fantastic. No one would know that I spend most of my evenings working out, doing anything to make myself sleep.

"Zeke, don't."

He stands up straight and turns towards me. "I know, but that's how I'm feeling. Things are going to change now, but I needed you to know that no matter what, I miss you."

I'm about to ask him what he means when I hear Asha shouting his name. He turns and walks away without a glance at me. I see her talking to some of the other fighters as Zeke disappears into the locker room. I start to clean up the equipment we were using when Asha's words drift over to me.

"And then he got down on one knee and proposed. Can you believe it? I'm going to be Mrs. Zeke Raine. I'm so fucking excited."

I drop everything I'm holding as my fingers suddenly feel numb. My legs give out from below me and I collapse onto the bench behind me. *He's getting married.* He's going to prove to the world that he's straight by marrying a woman. I can still hear the murmur of voices but the words aren't making it through the ringing in my ears.

I don't know how long I sit there but when I look around the gym is empty. I make a decision and I get up from the bench before walking into the locker room. I stop by my locker and begin packing up everything I've accumulated in there during my time here. I leave nothing, closing the door quietly behind me when I leave.

I make my way to Eddie's office, knocking on the door before entering. "Can I have a word Eddie?"

He looks up from the paperwork in front of him and nods. I don't think I've ever seen him not doing some kind of paperwork. He seems to spend his whole day in here trapped under mountains of letters and printouts.

"What's up?"

I take a seat across from him, putting my bag at my feet. His eyes move down to it before he looks back at me. I haven't had a chance to think about what I'm going to say to him, I just know I need to do it. "I'm sorry to have to do this, Eddie. But I need to leave."

He scrunches up his eyebrows, a confused look crossing his face. "No one stopping you, son."

Shit, he doesn't get what I'm trying to say. I need to make myself really clear so I can get out of here. "No, I mean I quit. I'm sorry to leave you without any notice, but I can't work here anymore."

He leans forward and rests his arms on his desk. "Can I ask why?"

I shake my head, knowing there's no way that I can tell him about Zeke and me. No matter how much I've come to hate him, I will never give away his secret. "You can ask, but I don't have an answer for you. Let's just say that circumstances say I need to go. It's better for everyone that I go now before my work suffers."

He sits in silence for a few moments before leaning back, steepling his hands in front of his face. "Fair enough. Is there anything I can do to make you stay? I'd hate to lose you, you are one of the best coaches we've had."

I stand from my seat, reaching my hand over the desk to give to Eddie who stands and shakes it.

"I wish I could stay, I wanted to see Zeke win this tournament, but I just can't. You have my mobile number, call me if you need anything, I'll still be in the area for a while." I smile at him

159

before I leave his office, taking one final look around the gym that's become my home.

****

I stand at the bar and look out over the dance floor. After finding out about Zeke's impending nuptials, I decided that I needed to move on once and for all. He's never coming back to me so I need to find some nice guy to get to know, either for the night or for longer. This is the first gay bar I've been to since coming to America and it feels very different from at home. The club looks similar, but there's a more relaxed welcoming feeling. I take another drink as my eyes work their way along the hot bodies that are lined up against the railing surrounding the dance floor. They stop moving when they land on a young blonde guy with a really nice arse. I'm thinking of making my move when a body moves close to mine, too close to be an accident. I turn to see another sexy blonde standing smiling at me. His eyes drop to my lips as I lick over them. He has nice eyes, blue and intense, like they could see right through to your soul.

He leans in, talking loudly so I can hear him. "Hi, you're new here."

I nod my head at him, not even attempting to speak over the music.

"My name's Brent. Do you want to go somewhere a little more quiet?" *Do I?* I think I need to try this and clear my memories of Zeke, to erase the feeling of his body against mine. I nod and follow him as he makes his way across the club. We exit through the main door and I follow him down the street a little. He disappears up an alley, making me stop for a second before I follow.

He's standing leaning against the wall, watching me as I approach. "Are you gonna tell me your name?"

I'm pretty sure that this is going nowhere after tonight, so names aren't needed. I shake my head, walking over to him and

160

kissing him. His lips are soft and he tastes like apples when I suck on his tongue but it just feels wrong. I don't have time to think as he pushes me back, his hands on my chest, until my back hits the opposite wall. Without hesitation Brent crouches in front of me and undoes my zip. I feel myself harden as he pulls my dick from my trousers, licking up the underside before sucking the tip into his mouth. I've never done this before, the abrupt and impersonal nature of it takes me by surprise. I was used to the build up with Zeke, the way he teased my body before he took me to heaven, but not this guy.

He sucks me deep into his throat and I grab his hair to keep myself standing. What he's doing is almost too much for me to handle, and I'm torn between enjoying this for what it is and stopping what he's doing. I don't know what he'll expect from me after this. *Do I need to return the favor?* Firm hands cup my balls and I cry out, the noise echoing through the alley. My head drops back to the wall until I'm looking at the sky. The feeling of his tongue running over my balls has pleasure rocketing through my body. I didn't know if I would get into this, now I don't know if I will be able to hold on. My hips start to thrust of their own accord, hitting Brent's throat as I set a punishing pace. The only thing on my mind is my impending orgasm, to be able to come in his mouth and purge this feeling from inside me.

I want this.

I need this.

I picture Zeke's face, the little grin he gives me when he's turned on. I thrust a few more times into Brent's mouth, my balls pulling against my body before emptying into his throat. He pulls back, wiping a hand over his lips as he smiles up at me. He stands and brushes the creases from the knees of his jeans before walking away.

I struggle to zip myself up, calling after him and making him stop. "Don't I need to… return the favor?"

He laughs and he shakes his head, his blonde hair moving over his forehead. "No that's okay, I like to give." He winks at me and I stand there in the alley, feeling more alone than ever.

CHAPTER SIXTEEN

Zeke

"What the fuck do you mean he left?" I've never shouted at Coach, but today I just can't help it. I don't know what he expected to happen when he told me that Bryce had gone. There's no way he could've thought I would be okay with it.

"Like I said, he told me that he had his reasons and it was better if he didn't work here anymore. Did you two have an argument? Were you a fucking dick to him?"

I was a dick, but that had been weeks ago and he still stayed. What made him leave now? I need to find him and get him back. I grab the back of the chair that's in front of me, trying desperately not to throw it across Coach's office.

"No, I wasn't a dick, well no more than normal. He seriously didn't say anything? Doesn't he have a contract? Can we make him come back?" I start to pace again, my hands working through my hair, grabbing the strands and tugging. I probably look like a mad man but I have more important things to worry about. Did he leave because I told him that I missed him? Was I being unfair by admitting it?

"He had a rolling contract. I thought it was safer after what happened with Ethan. You don't have the best track record when it comes to coaches, Zeke. I can't afford to be sued."

I walk around the front of the chair and collapse into it. I bury my head in my hands, feeling completely defeated.

"So do you want to tell me what happened between you two? I'm not stupid, Zeke, I know there was something there. Is there anything you need to tell me?"

I'm so confused right now. I don't know what to do. Should I tell Coach about us, that I completely messed up the relationship between Bryce and me, both personal and professional? I'm about to open up and finally lay it all out, risk his ridicule, when I hear Asha's voice from outside the office door.

"Saved by the fiancée, Zeke."

My head jerks up to meet his face. I never told anyone I was engaged, and I wasn't planning on doing so any time soon. "Who told you I was engaged?" My voice has taken on a menacing tone that makes Coach's eyes widen a little in shock.

"Asha was shouting it to anyone who would listen yesterday. I heard her through the closed door."

If she had been yelling it yesterday then Bryce must have heard her. *Shit. Fuck!* I was going to tell him first and make sure he would only find out from me. Fucking hell, no wonder he left, I tell him I miss him and then a few minutes later he's told I'm engaged. How to fuck with the guy's head.

I get up from the chair with rage flooding my body. I throw open the door and see Asha talking to a few of the guys, holding her hand out and showing the ring to whoever will look. I storm over to her and, grabbing her by the elbow, I pull her towards the locker room. She struggles a little but follows after me, it's not really I'm really giving her a choice. When the door closes behind us I turn and glare at her. She shrinks a little under my intense stare.

"Did you tell Bryce we were engaged?"

She looks confused at my angry tone, and I know I need to calm down. I never told her not to tell anyone and she's excited about it so of course she's going to tell people, but Bryce is gone and that's all I can think about right now.

"Um … yeah … maybe. I don't know, I told a few of the guys yesterday. Why, what's wrong?"

I don't answer her as I turn and walk towards the steel lockers. I place my hands against them and lower my head, taking deep, calming breaths. I try to swallow my anger but it's not working and I can feel it tugging at my brain, telling me to lash out.

Asha walks up behind me and rubs her hand down my back. The feeling makes my anger double. She's the reason he's gone, she's the reason I won't ever see him again. I finally give in to the urges inside me and punch the locker in front of me, causing Asha to scream. The pain in my knuckles clears my head a little so I do it again, and again. When the punching isn't doing enough I start to kick them, feeling my feet start to ache as I continue my assault. I know I'm going to damage my hands but I can't seem to stop, and my anger doesn't feel like it's fading. The world has faded away and my focus is on the pounding of my hands.

Several strong hands pull me away from the lockers and drag me across the room until I'm pushed against the wall.

"Fucking stop, man. What the hell has gotten into you? You're scaring Asha."

I slap the hands off me, glaring at Jason as he speaks. I need to get out of here so I can clear my head before I do something I regret. I push off the wall and walk through the crowd that's gathered around me. I come face to face with Coach, neither of us speaking as we stare at each other. Moments tick by and the silence becomes thick. He still doesn't talk as he moves to the side and lets me past him.

As I'm level with him, he reaches out and puts his hand on my shoulder, stopping me in his tracks and makes me look at him. "Don't do anything stupid, boy. Don't ruin everything you've worked for."

I nod at him, understanding what he's trying to tell me before I walk out the gym door. I have no idea where I'm going, but I know that I can't be here right now.

****

I slam my front door behind me, making the windows vibrate. The anger I felt earlier only intensified once I got to Bryce's house and saw that his car was missing. I don't know how long I sat outside his house before I went to the grocery store for a bottle of Bourbon. If I was going to have to wait on him, then I would do it while getting so drunk that I wouldn't hurt any more. I knew I would be disappointed when he didn't come home, but that didn't stop me from waiting there. While I was sitting there, taking large mouthfuls of alcohol, I wondered if this is how Bryce felt the night after my fight, the night I ran from him. I know it must have been, and knowing where I'd been and what I was doing, made me drink even more.

I waited for hours, my bottle of Bourbon finished and thrown into the back of my truck. I knew I had to leave, but I was struggling to get my feet to move. I knew I couldn't drive with all the alcohol in my system, but I couldn't make myself walk away. It felt like I was giving up if I left. I needed to stay in case he came home, that way he would see me waiting and would know I wanted him.

I eventually moved when the sky went dark and I started getting strange looks from Bryce's neighbors. I didn't want to spend the night in a cell so I left, walking slowly along the sidewalk towards home. Now I'm here I don't know what to do. I feel so lost. I don't know why it's hit me like this all of a sudden. I haven't been with Bryce for a few weeks now, so this shouldn't feel any different. I think it's because I know he's not out there and won't be at the gym in the morning. He won't be around for me to look at. Even though we weren't together I always knew he was there, that I would see him every day since the gym and my training brought him back to me. I don't have that safety net of his job to keep him tied to me any more.

I walk through to my room, trying desperately to walk in a straight line. I strip off my t-shirt and throw it across the room. I feel wrong, like my skin's too tight, and I need to do something to ease the discomfort. I need to shower, maybe if I scrub my body it will make these feelings go away. This is why I don't fall for anyone. I keep things simple because when someone leaves me it doesn't usually hurt like this does. If I'm honest I've never felt like this before, the pain is almost too much for me to take. I undo the fly on my jeans as I move across my room, before suddenly changing my mind about a shower. I need to run, I need to work this frustration and pain from my body. I visualize my feet pounding the sidewalk and music filling my head as I let the world around me fade away.

My mind is set and I only have one focus; that is until my eyes find the t-shirt that's sitting on my bed. The one that Bryce left the last time he was here. I found it the day after my last fight, and never returned it. I just couldn't hand it back to him. It would've been like giving back the last part of him that I had. At least this way, I could always keep a part of him with me, even if it's not the part that I wanted. Tonight it sits on my bed mocking me, reminding me that I'll never have him again. He's gone and is never coming back. Anger fills my chest, pushing out the pain, and I embrace it, preferring that to the crushing ache. I turn away from the t-shirt, putting my hands on the top of my drawers and letting my head drop. I concentrate on my breathing to let the feelings flow out as I exhale. I open my eyes but the anger's still there. I'm angry at myself for losing the guy I want, I'm angry at Bryce for leaving me, and I'm even angry at Asha for not being Bryce.

I let my frustration take over, picking up the photo frame from the chest of drawers and throwing it against the wall. The feeling of satisfaction as it smashes is welcomed and it's the catalyst for what happens next. I grab anything that's close to hand and throw it, knock it over, basically destroying everything in my frustration. I stand in the middle of the room with my chest rising and falling quickly as I take in the mess around me. I'm not out of breath, but I can feel myself breaking. Now that my anger's spent, all that's left is the ripping feeling in my chest. It feels like I can't catch my breath, that I can't fill my lungs enough to survive. My heart is pounding against my rib cage and I don't know how that's possible, because I know that it's not there. My heart is wherever Bryce is. He has it and I pray to god he never gives it back. I let out a strangled sob, walking backwards until my back hits a wall. I let my legs give out and I crumble to the floor. I drop my head and for the first time ever, and let the pain come out in tears. My heartache streams down my cheeks for the world to see.

I don't know how long I sit there crying. It could be minutes, hours or even days, but I startle when arms wrap around me.

"Baby, what's wrong? Oh my god, what happened?"

I look up into Asha's worried eyes. I didn't hear her arrive but as she holds me I'm glad she's here. Maybe she can tell me what to do and how to make this pain stop.

"He left me." I don't have to say anything else; I have a feeling she knows who and what I'm talking about. She pulls me close to her and strokes my hair gently, the tenderness making the words flow. I know that if I was sober I would never talk to anyone like this, but, with the alcoholic courage, I say the words I've needed to say for a while. "He was everything and he left. I can't believe he's gone. What am I meant to do without him?" Tears are still falling as I lean against her chest. Her arms around me give me comfort and I suddenly feel tired. All the emotion has drained my energy from me, and all I want to do is sleep. As I let the darkness take me, trying to outrun my misery, the last thought I have is of Bryce. He has that smile he would get when he looked across the room at me.

A smile that I will never see again.

****

Holy fuck. What train hit me? I turn in bed and I regret it instantly when my stomach rolls and vomit fills my throat. I throw the bed sheets off me and run towards the bathroom, barely making it before I lose the contents of my stomach. When I'm finally finished I lie on the floor, enjoying the feel of the cool tiles against my overheated body. I close my eyes and try to concentrate on my breathing. I think if I manage to just keep breathing all day, it will be an achievement. I contemplate lying here all day but know that the pounding in my head is going to make me move. I need to get medication for it but even the thought of putting something, even water, in my stomach has it churning again.

168

I hear soft footsteps walking up beside me before a cool cloth is placed over my head. I sigh in appreciation of the angel that's helping me.

"Are we feeling a little rough?" Asha's voice has a tinge of humor to it and I wonder what I look like and what the fuck I did last night. I remember being at Bryce's house, waiting for him to come home. I pray that I didn't attempt to drive.

"What happened?" My voice is rough, making me sound like I've been asleep a week… or have the worst hangover of my life.

"That I would love to know, but I think only you can answer that." I would wonder what she meant by that, but thinking is making my head throb.

I feel her grab my hand and I groan as she pulls, trying to get me to sit up. "Let's get you off the cold floor. I've put a bottle of water and some Tylenol next to your bed for you."

It takes me longer than it should to get to my feet, and every movement makes me want to die. "You know, I didn't realize you had such an evil side to you." My words are met with laughter but she never stops her insistent pulling until I walk into my room. As soon as I'm through the door I come to a complete stop and look around. My room is complete chaos. There isn't a flat surface that has anything left on it. The objects that should be there are scattered around the room, most smashed or damaged beyond repair. There are also cracks in some of the furniture and several holes in the wall.

"What the fuck happened in here?" I'm hoping Asha will tell me I came home to find a frat party that got out of hand, because if it wasn't that then I don't think I want to know the real reason.

"That's another thing you will have to try and remember. I came in to find the place like this."

I look around in shock at the mess. I don't remember anything no matter how much I try. "Where was I when you got here?"

A strange look crosses her face before she smiles, but the smile is too big, too bright. She starts picking up things from the floor and I'm sure it's so she doesn't have to look at me. *What did I do last night?* I'm going to have to try really hard to figure out what happened by myself, because by the look on Asha's face there's something she's not telling me.

"You were asleep on the floor, I managed to get you into bed and then I tidied up a little. I didn't think it was a good idea to leave you with the mess you were in, so I slept in the bed next to you. Something obviously had you upset." She still won't look at me and now I'm actually happy about that. I don't want to have to lie to her. I might not know what I did last night, but I know what caused it. I didn't know how to cope with Bryce leaving, all my emotions finally catching up with me. The alcohol had helped me block everything out for a little while, but now in the cold light of day, all the feelings come flooding back. The pain from last night seeps into my bones and I just want to start drinking again but I don't know how I would explain that behavior to Asha. She's the woman I'm going to marry, but she's also the person I have the most secrets from.

I watch as she moves around the room, cleaning up the mess that I've caused, and I wish that I could love her like she deserves. She's such a nice girl and she would make an amazing wife. Standing there in my underwear, surrounded by what's left of my bedroom, I realize one important thing, and something that makes me rethink everything I'm doing. *I'm taking away Asha's chance to find someone who truly loves her, someone who wants to give her the world.* There's someone out there who will be her everything but she won't look for him if she thinks I love her.

I close my eyes, making the decision that I need to leave her and let her get on with her life. "Asha." I say her name softly, and she stands slowly.

"Not today, Zeke. We'll talk soon." She walks towards me, still looking at the ground. When she's standing next to me, she reaches up and kisses me on the cheek. "No matter what, I love you, I always have." She walks away from me, leaving me standing in the same spot.

I finally walk over to the bed and collapse on top of it. *When did my life become such a clusterfuck?* A year ago I thought I had life sorted out. That I had everything that I ever wanted. I was working towards my first championship, I was at the top of my game, and I was fucking any woman I wanted. But now? Now I'm hurting people by using them to make my life easier. I hate this. I hate what I've become and I can't go on like this. I can't keep letting them get as hurt as I am. Why should their lives become harder just so mine can look picture perfect from the outside? It's time to stop being selfish, even if it's too late for my happy ever after. I threw away my one chance at true love when I ran from him, and I'll never get him back.

CHAPTER SEVENTEEN

Zeke

I bounce in place watching my opponent walk towards the cage. This is the final obstacle standing between me and my showdown with Dwayne. Just this fight to win and I'll be in the final. I can finally show the world that I'm the best, and believe me when I say I won't be stop until someone drags me from his fallen body.

I look over to where Asha's standing and see her smiling widely as she watches me. Things have been strained ever since I decided we needed to end things a few weeks ago. I think she knew what I was going to do. Her expression told me that she could tell there was something bad coming, and I haven't seen her much since then. She's dropped into the gym a few times, since that's where I've been practically living in the build up to tonight, but I refuse to talk to her with an audience. What we have to sort out isn't the sort of thing you want to do in front of others. I have more respect for her than that. I've decided that it will be sorted tomorrow. I will win this fight tonight, getting my professional life back to where it should be, and then I will get my personal life back on track by telling Asha it's over. I just pray that she can understand my reasons, and that one day she might forgive me because hurting her is the last thing I ever wanted.

My attention is pulled back to my opponent when he walks up in front of me with a cocky look on his face. Little does he know that he is about to get his ass kicked. The skills that Bryce taught me have been invaluable. He knows how to fight and showed me it all. I clear my mind, knowing that if I spend too long thinking about Bryce it will affect my concentration and that's the last thing I need right now. I fist bump with my opponent before backing up into my corner to wait for the bell. I start to bounce again, the energy inside me starting to build so much that I can't keep it inside. I just want to get this fight over with so I can concentrate on training for the final. My only goal is to get there and kill Dwayne. Okay, not actually kill him but hurt him... a lot.

The bell goes and I instantly go into attack mode. Coach told me I had to make this fight last, to let the guy get a few hits in before I floored him but I'm not planning on that happening. I have watched DVDs of this guy's fights, and to say that he's here by pure luck alone is no exaggeration. He couldn't fight himself out of a paper bag, and I'm pretty sure some other contenders had been paid to throw fights against him. If I let him connect a punch with my skin then people think I'm not as good as I am, and if I pretend that he's winning at any point I may as well just go home. Even now, he's bouncing about like he's fucking Tigger and I'm not sure what to do with him. He doesn't stay still long enough for me to hit. Out of nowhere his fist flies and hits me across the cheek. The fucker just managed to punch me and I'm not happy about it. Another fist strikes across my jaw and I feel my lip burst under the pressure. This guy is really annoying me now. He's moving so much that I can't plan my attack, so I decide to just let him wear himself out, there's no way he can keep this up for too long.

Movement catches my eye and I look away from the bouncing idiot in front of me. I don't know what makes me look; there are so many people in the place that movement in an aisle shouldn't distract me but there is something that pulls me. Walking up the aisle is a guy in jeans and a shirt, his hair cut close at the back. My heart starts beating faster in my chest as I watch him walk away from me. I recognize the way his body moves and I have to stop myself from running to him. I don't know if he can feel my stare on his skin or if he just happened to look back, but he turns and my breath is stolen when our eyes meet for the first time in weeks. The world around me fades away as I stand and look at the man I didn't think I would ever see again. I didn't think it was possible but he looks even sexier now than I remember with his hair styled and his body bigger.

A sudden punch to the ribs brings my attention back to what I'm meant to be doing. I turn my head as I hear coach shouting at me to get my head out of my ass but all I can think about is Bryce. I need to finish this now so I can go after him. I need to talk to him and ask him why he left. Thankfully my opponent has stopped jumping like an irritating frog and I throw a perfectly practiced punch. I smile as it connects under his chin and I watch his head as it's thrown backwards and his eyes roll back into his head. I see him start to fall towards the ground and I know there will be no more fighting for this guy tonight. He is out like a light so I've won the fight. I wait for a moment to hear the referees call it and as soon as I hear my name being announced as the winner I jump from the cage. I barely take time to land properly before I take off up the aisle towards where I last saw Bryce.

I push through the doors, shouting his name even before I enter the hall on the other side. I look around, panic starting to rise in me when I can't see him. I run blindly, my only thought is to find him. I want to know why he's here and where he's been. I want to tell him that I can't stop thinking about him and my heart is breaking into smaller pieces the longer I'm without him. I don't think I'll be able to tell him any of this but just to see him close up, to make sure he's okay will be enough. I'm worried about him, the last time I went by his apartment it was empty. I don't know when he moved out or where he's gone, and that has me worrying. I know that he moved here not long before he started working for me, so now he's jobless and living fuck knows where. I heard rumors about him working for Dwayne but I know he wouldn't do that, or at least I hope he wouldn't. He knows what I went through at his hands, and he's also the reason I acted like a fucking fool, so I'm sure that Bryce wouldn't want anything to do with him. I need to make sure though and this might be my only chance.

After searching for far too long I realize he's gone. He must have left while I was still fighting. I hear Coach shouting down the

174

corridor to me, telling me to get my ass into the changing room. I barrel into the room, slamming the door into the wall behind it. All heads turn towards me and I don't know what they see in my face but they all step back, putting a lot of space between them and me. I'm glad they do because the way I'm feeling just now, if someone said one wrong thing there's a chance that I will put my fist through their face. I unwrap my hands, throwing my bandages across the room. I can't believe that I finally had him in my sights and I let him get away. I don't know when I'll ever see him again and I missed my one fucking chance. Damn it!

I lean over slightly with my hands on my knees, concentrating on taking deep breaths. I realize that since I met Bryce I've spent more time controlling my emotions than at any other time. Everything was simple before him. I spent my days training and my nights fucking. Any nameless woman would do since there was no attachment or emotions, but then Bryce ruined it all. He made me feel, he made me want something I'd never had or needed before and now I want more. But when faced with telling the world who I really was I got scared and went back into the little box I'd tried to fit so neatly into. No wonder Bryce wanted nothing to do with me. I couldn't even admit who I was, so what chance did I have being the man that Bryce deserved.

When I stand up I realize that the room has emptied and I'm alone with Coach. He's sitting on the massage table watching me very closely, a look of worry on his face. "Do I need to worry about you? Are you going to do something stupid to ruin your chance at the final?" His questions are simple ones, ones I should be able to answer in a heartbeat but I can't.

I stand and look at him, thinking how to answer him. I know that when it comes to my fight with Dwayne there're no problems. I could win that fucker in my sleep, but I don't think that's what he's asking. Then it suddenly hits me and even though I shouldn't be surprised, I am. I didn't think anyone had noticed what was happening between Bryce and me.

"How did you find out?" I try not to confirm anything until I find out how much he knows. I hope he'd support me no matter what I did with my personal life. He's known me longer than anyone, but there's still the fact that the MMA world is not ready for a gay fighter.

"Was it meant to be a secret? If it was you really need to work on that."

I can physically feel the color drain from my face and sweat starts to bead over my forehead. *Did everyone in the gym know? Had they known there was something between us?*

"Shit, I'm kidding. You look like you're gonna have a heart attack. I came back one night after the place had been closed up and saw you both in the shower. And let me tell you, that shit I won't ever unsee."

The color that drained a moment ago is back, making my cheeks burn. "Shit Coach, I'm sorry."

He waves his hand, dismissing my apology. I walk over and collapse onto the bench, lowering my head until my chin is resting on my chest. I can't believe that he actually caught us doing... whatever it was. I have no plans to ask him what we were doing, but all of my memories of the shower room tell me that it wasn't anything that he should have seen.

"Like it's the first time I've seen you fucking someone in the shower. Though I have to say, I was surprised when I saw it was a guy. Actually, I was more shocked that it was your coach."

I don't even know what to say to him. No one is more shocked than me that I've fallen for a man. My life was all about pussy; the more I got the better. Now even Asha can't seem to get me hard.

"But you know what surprised me more? The fact that you put a ring on Asha's finger. I didn't see that one coming at all."

I rub my hands over my face, bracing myself to tell Coach everything. I haven't had anyone to confide in about all this, and maybe if I tell him how I'm feeling I'll be able to work out what to do.

"Yeah, that kinda shocked me too. What I had with Bryce was... complicated. There was just something about him that I couldn't resist, not that I tried very hard. I didn't know what was going to happen between us and there's no way I could have gone public about it. Then someone saw us. We weren't doing anything, just talking, but I panicked and ran to Asha. I thought that if I settled down with her I would stop feeling anything for Bryce."

Coach nods his head as I talk, listening closely to what I'm saying. He doesn't interrupt and when I'm finished he doesn't seem put out by my confession. "So, how's that working out for you?"

I laugh at his question, my head falling back as I let my laughter flow through my body. It's been a long time since I found something funny and it takes a few minutes to compose myself.

"It's not. I have a fiancée that I don't love and who hasn't spoken to me in weeks, and a coach that's left his job and home to escape me. So life pretty much fucking sucks just now."

Coach gets up from the table and grabs his bag as he walks towards the door to leave. He turns around when his hand touches the handle. "Well I suggest you get a shower because you stink."

I smile as I stand, grabbing my towel and heading for the shower. Just as I'm about to walk into the cubicle, Coach shouts my name. I turn and look at him over my shoulder. "He might have left where he lived, but I'm pretty sure his number is still the same." He says nothing else as he leaves the room.

I walk under the spray of hot water and think about what just happened. Coach has known all along about my relationship with Bryce and never said anything, never judged me. Instead he's pretty much told me to call him. I wonder if it really would be that easy and whether he would answer my call this time.

****

I'm lying in my bed wearing nothing by my boxer shorts, surrounded by darkness. I've been here since I got home from my fight. I had wondered if Asha would hang around and wait for me

177

but I couldn't find her after my shower. I seem to have spent the whole day losing people. When I got to my car, I picked up my cell ready to call to see where she was, but I couldn't press the call button. I didn't really want to talk to her and I knew if I did then I would have to spend the night with her, which isn't something I wanted. I would feel guilty about this if I wasn't planning on ending it tomorrow, this has gone on long enough and I need to let her go. I can't risk dragging her down with me so I need to do one good thing in my life.

I've spent the last few weeks trying to forget everything by focusing on my training, but I don't think I went an hour without thinking about Bryce. It didn't seem to matter how hard I trained or how much I pushed myself, the emptiness I felt never left. I didn't think it would hurt this much, but it feels like my heart is ripping apart every day. Seeing Bryce tonight just brought everything crashing down on me all at once. I try to convince myself that I don't want him, I don't need him, I don't love him. Except I know I do. It took me a while to realize it but I know I love him. He was why I got up in the morning, the main reason I smiled. But I don't know if I will ever be able to admit my feelings to anyone. The thought of going public scares me, and I would never keep him as my dirty secret, not that he would let me do that anyway.

I think back to our time together, the times that I made love to him and when we just … *were*. I've never felt so accepted by anyone before. He was with me for who I was, not for what my name could give him. He spent time getting to know the real me and I shared with him things that I wouldn't have shared with anyone else. I told him about my past with my dad, about how he had reacted when I tried to come out and received no judgment. I haven't told anyone about that before, not even Coach, so when I heard the words coming out my mouth I was in shock. That's what it was like with Bryce though, easy, comfortable, everything I've ever wanted.

I pick up my cell for probably the tenth time and unlock the screen. I look at Bryce's contact details, my finger hovering over the call button. I've wanted to call him since I collapsed on my bed, but I haven't built up the courage to go through with it yet. I don't know if I'm more worried about him potentially ignoring my call or him actually answering and me needing to be man enough to talk to him. I lower the phone to my naked chest, and it must brush over the button because I quickly hear ringing over the line. I panic and press the end call button. *Shit! It's going to show as a missed call on his cell, fuck.* My heart races in my chest as I try to work out what to do. I'm concentrating so much on what to do, that when my cell rings it flies out of my hand and I let out a very unmanly scream. I rub my hand over the mattress until it comes into contact with my cell. I take a deep breath, trying to calm my heart rate, when I see Bryce's number flash on the screen. I press the connect button and put the phone to my ear. There's a few minutes silence between us and I wonder if I should say something, anything to get us talking, but before I do I hear the voice that's haunted my dreams.

"Why did you call, Zeke?"

I close my eyes and listen as he says my name and it's like that single word heals a little part of my heart. "You came to my fight, but you left. Why?" There's more silence between us and I try to imagine what he's doing.

"It was too hard to stay. I thought I could watch you fight but I couldn't." I don't know if he means the memories of Austin that still haunts him or if being around me is too much for him.

"I'm sorry, Bryce."

He lets out a very audible sigh and I feel this conversation is about to go off the rails. "I wish you were, Zeke. Is that all you called for?"

I panic, suddenly needing to keep him on the call for as long as I can. Hearing his voice makes me feel the most at ease I've felt in a long time. "I *am* sorry. I'm sorry for everything, for running, for ignoring you. I'm sorry I can't be the man you need, and I'm sorry that I need to live a lie to do the thing that I've been dreaming of since I was a teenager. I miss you like fuck and I don't know what to do. I don't have anyone to talk to and I'm driving myself insane. I don't want you to hate me, but I know you do and I don't blame you." The words tumble out without control but I need him to hear them so he can understand.

"I don't hate you. I just couldn't be around you anymore. I couldn't watch you with her, Zeke. It was breaking my heart every god damn day." He gives me hope as he speaks. Hope for what exactly, I'm not sure, but at least he's talking to me. He hasn't shut me out like I expected.

"I'm so fucking sorry. I miss you so much." My voice is quiet and I'm not sure if he can actually hear me over the line, but when I hear his answer I know he has.

"I miss you too, more than you'll ever know." The silence between us is deafening and I don't know what to say. I don't know how to tell him what he means to me and that I love him. I want to say the words but I know it's unfair to him to tell him when I can't be with him.

Before I have a chance to say anything I hear him over the line, asking a question that I never thought I would hear. "Can I come over? I need to see you."

I answer without hesitation I, barely letting him finish talking. "Yes."

I hear the phone disconnect as my heart starts galloping in my chest again. I don't know what's going to happen when he arrives or what he wants to see me for, but the thought of being so close to him again has my dick hardening in my underwear. I need to get my body under control before he arrives.

CHAPTER EIGHTEEN

Bryce

I know this is a mistake, nothing good can come from seeing Zeke again, but I couldn't stop myself. When I heard his voice on the phone my heart felt like it might explode in my chest and the feeling of being complete again was overwhelming. I hadn't planned to call him back but when I saw his name on my mobile, I couldn't stop my finger from pressing the call button. I wasn't surprised that he called. I'd been expecting it when he saw me at the fight today.

That's another thing I hadn't expected to do. I haven't been in an arena watching a fight since the day I lost Austin, and I always said you would never find me in another one. There are too many painful memories that I had planned to stay away from and I would have, if I hadn't had a very interesting call from Asha. When the unknown number appeared on my screen I almost didn't answer it but the worrier in me accepted the call. I'm the type of person who always thinks that something bad has happened, that someone I know has had an accident and if I don't answer I won't be able to get to them in time. I know people think I'm a little insane, but it's just the way I am. So I answered the call and was completely shocked to hear Asha on the other end. She'd asked me what was happening between Zeke and me because she was worried about him.

She told me she had never seen him hurting so much and she didn't know what to do. She knew that anything she did wouldn't be what he needed, but she had a suspicion that I might be able to help him. I'd sat and listened to her, shocked that my leaving had made any impact on Zeke's life. He seemed to leave so easily when Dwayne caught us, even going as far as getting engaged to a woman to hide his secret. She told me about his upcoming fight and that I should go and watch him, but I explained that I couldn't. I had even moved house, despite not being able to afford it, just so I wouldn't run into him. I don't think I would be able to handle seeing him with her, watching them be the happy couple when I know all his secrets. I wonder if he told her everything that he had confessed to me, about his past and his desires. I'm pretty sure he hasn't since she's still planning on marrying him, unless it's for the money, but she doesn't seem like that type of person. If she were only after his fame she wouldn't have called me, in an attempt to make Zeke happier.

I went against everything my brain was telling me when I walked into the fight arena. My heart almost stopped in my chest when I saw Zeke in the ring, bouncing on the soles of his feet. He looked stunning up there. The energy bubbling under his skin made him look like a snake waiting to strike. His skin was shining slightly under the lights and he looked like a God, like he could take on the world. I stood in awe watching him, well that was until his opponent threw the first punch. Even though it didn't look like it had affected Zeke in any way, watching someone try to hurt him had my stomach in my throat. That's when I knew I had to leave. I couldn't stand there and watch this. I had just reached the aisle, working my way towards the door when I felt all the hair on the back of my neck stand up on end and that's when I knew he had seen me. Even from this distance my body knew when it had his attention. I fought against turning around but I knew it was a losing battle. When my eyes connected with his, it was like all the air left my body. It was the first time I had seen him in weeks and the intensity in his stare was immense. It drew me in until the whole arena faded away into the background. I could feel the pull of his eyes, the need to touch him, to hold him and I fought desperately against it but I knew I would give in if I didn't leave. Thankfully his attention was pulled away from me, allowing me to run before he looked back at me. I almost ran out of those main doors, knowing that I needed to get away before I did something stupid.

Now I'm standing at his front door, doing that something stupid. I just stand there, not wanting to ring the bell but not wanting to walk away. *When did I become this person?* I used to be decisive and be able to know exactly what do, but now I don't know what the hell I'm doing. The door in front of me opens and I stop breathing. Zeke is standing there in just his underwear, a small lamp illuminating him from behind. He looks like a fucking angel, one that I want to dirty up and make sure he doesn't get back into heaven. We stand and look at each other, neither of us making the first move. My eyes drift over his body even though I know I shouldn't. I'm pretty sure I came here to talk so I need to keep my eyes on his face.

"Are you coming in or are we staying here all night? Just so I know if I should go get a jacket or not."

I feel the edges of my lips twitch. I've missed his attitude, the fact that he doesn't give a shit about what he says, well unless it's telling people who he really is, always made me laugh. With that sobering thought I move forward, hoping it will keep me on track for the chat we need to have. I'm doing well until I step inside and Zeke shuts the door behind me. He steps close to me and overloads all my senses. His scent invades my nose and I have to close my eyes as I start to feel light headed. I can feel his body heat behind me as he stands closer than he should be, his breath breezing over the back of my neck making my hair stand on end. It feels as though he's pressed against me but I know he isn't touching me at all, and suddenly I want him to. I want to run my hands over his naked flesh, and my tongue, I want to taste every inch of him, inside and out.

I turn to face him and the look of lust in his eyes almost sears me. I refuse to touch him. I can't give in to my want for him. That thought is still going through my head as I grab Zeke by the back of the neck and our mouths collide with a passion that threatens to set the world on fire. His taste explodes over my tongue, making my already erect dick excruciatingly hard. I've been semi-hard since I spoke to him on the phone, but seeing him and tasting him takes it beyond anything I've experienced. I think I'm harder now than when we were together before. I know how good he feels now, so I know what's to come. I push against his body until he's moving, my lips not leaving his for a second. When his back collides with his front door I keep moving until my chest is pressed tightly against his, his hard dick pushing against mine. I grind into him and when he groans into my mouth I nearly lose the control I have on my orgasm. The next few minutes are a battle for control. We're all hands and mouths as we reacquaint ourselves with each other's bodies. The only time our lips disconnect is when he strips my t-shirt over my head. Flesh to flesh we move down the hall to his bedroom. We bounce off walls and I head butt the doorframe, but not once do I stop kissing him.

When his hands work on the zip of my jeans, I take a minute to try and control my breathing. I'm light headed from the kiss, the lack of oxygen playing havoc with my body and I don't think it will do any good if I pass out on the floor. My jeans hit the floor, closely followed by my underwear, and I step out of them as Zeke watches me. His eyes feel like they're caressing me, making my skin burn under the attention. He takes a step forward so our chests almost touch, sparks flying between the inch he's left between us. I reach out and pull him, closing the final distance between us. I take his lips in a softer kiss this time, trying to show him what he really means to me. His hands work their way through my hair as he keeps my lips on his.

I can feel my heart swell as emotions run through me. I can feel what he's trying to tell me, that I'm important to him. I run my hands down his back, pressing deep into his tense muscles until I reach the waistband of his boxers. I run my fingers under the elastic before slipping my hand inside, using my wrists to take the material with me. I push them down over his body, moving my hips away from him for a moment so they can fall to the floor. I press my fingers into his arse cheeks, pulling him into me so our dicks are finally touching skin to skin. It's Zeke's turn to push against me and forces me to move backwards until my legs connect with the bed. My knees buckle and I fall onto the mattress.

Zeke stares down at me, the hunger in his eyes making it look like he wants to devour me whole. A few seconds later that's exactly what he does. With no hesitation he leans over and takes me deep into his mouth. I cry out as my back arches off the bed. The feel of his warm mouth and the pressure of his tongue are taking me to the point of exploding, and as much as I want to come down his throat I want to feel him inside me more. I reach down and grab him by the hair, pulling him up my body until his lips are on mine again. I roll us over, pushing us up on the bed until we're in the center of it. I kiss all over him, from his lips to his jaw, his neck and down over his chest until I reach his weeping dick. I flick my tongue over his tip, collecting the pre-cum there, letting it coat my tongue while my hand works over him from base to tip. I close my eyes, tasting him and listening to his heavy breathing. I wonder if it's possible to come without any physical stimulation or attention to my dick, because I'm pretty sure it's about to happen.

"Bryce, I need you." I open my eyes and look up in to Zeke's face to see him looking desperate. A shiver of pride rushes through my body with the knowledge that I can still make him feel like this. Even though he ran away from me, I know that I still affect him and that he still needs me as much as I need him. I lean over and open the drawer next to his bed, grabbing the condoms and lube. I would make him wait and make him suffer a little bit more but I need him inside me. I need that electric connection of our bodies coming together. I lean back on my knees and rip open the condom packet. I place the condom on Zeke's tip, ready to roll it down on him in preparation but his hand on mine stops me. I look up, worried that he's changed his mind and doesn't want me anymore.

"I need *you*. I want to feel you inside me." His voice is soft but I can feel the certainty behind the words. I've never been inside Zeke and nerves suddenly attack me. I want this so badly, my throbbing dick is evidence to that, but I don't want him to feel like

185

he has to do this. I'm more than happy to have him top me. I get as much pleasure from that as he does.

"You don't have to, Zeke."

He smiles at me, the smile that shows his dimple and melts my heart. "I know I don't have to, I want to. I need to feel you inside me, Bryce. Please."

I take a deep breath to try and calm myself down. The thought of being inside Zeke is almost too much, but I must be taking too long because he moves my hand and places the condom over my straining hard on. Zeke rolls the condom over me before grabbing lube and dripping it on me. He rubs it into my length and I let out a groan from deep in my chest. Taking my hand he pours some lube onto my finger before lying back and opening his legs for me, pulling his legs towards his chest. My eyes focus on the tight hole that has come into view. It's so fucking sexy seeing Zeke like this. My breath comes out on a stutter and I feel like I might have a heart attack any minute. The rate my heart is beating can't be healthy. I reach out, rubbing my lubed fingers over his puckered hole, making his body jump. I look up at him, needing to make sure that he's still on board with this. I don't want to do anything he isn't comfortable with.

"I'm fine, it was cold." He laughs but it sounds breathy. I need to distract him until he relaxes. It's the only way I'm going to be able to stretch him without hurting him. I lean down and take his dick into my mouth, working my tongue around his tip. With a groan I feel Zeke's body instantly relax and I go back to massaging his rim with my finger. I press against him and when I don't feel him fighting against the pressure I push the tip of my finger in. I take him deeper into my throat at the same time and he yells as the dual pleasure becomes too much for him. When his hands grab my hair I move back off him and look up into his eyes. He watches me lick his erection while my finger fucks his arse. I slip a second finger in and watch his face for any signs of pain, but all I see is fire burning in his eyes. He pulls my hair until his dick leaves my mouth and bounces against his stomach.

"I need you inside me. Now."

I remove my finger from his body, grab myself and press my head against his tight hole. "Are you sure?"

I feel his body pushing back against me, my dick popping through the ring of resistance until his body is hugging me. I stop and breathe quickly as I try to resist the urge to pound into his body. He's far too tight to do that, and truthfully I would only last one thrust. I move gently, easing myself in until I am fully inside him. I study his face the entire time for signs that he isn't enjoying this but all I see is pleasure. I still, letting his body adjust to me being there but he doesn't lose any of the tightness. *I am only going to last a couple more thrusts if his muscles don't relax.*

Movement catches my eye and I look down to see Zeke's hand caress his weeping dick. The sight makes me twitch inside him and he groans which causes him to tighten around me even more. I honestly didn't think that would be possible.

"Keep doing that, Zeke. I won't last long when I start moving so I need you to come."

I watch his eyes as they darken and it's such a fucking turn on. Everything about this man I'm inside turns me on. When I feel his body start to tense I move, hoping I might last long enough to come with him. I press my hands on the back of Zeke's knees and press them closer to his chest. Pulling out of him, I leave barely an inch inside before pushing back in gently. When I try to ease out of him, it's like his body is trying to suck me back in, like it doesn't want me to leave. I increase the power behind my thrusts, my balls crashing onto his arse as I pound into him. The sound adds to the thrill of what's happening, knowing that I'm not being gentle but he's taking everything I give him. I feel the tingling build at the base of my spine as my orgasm makes itself known. I push down on Zeke's legs again, changing my angle and hitting that special place inside him every time I thrust. He cries out and I watch as the first spurts of his orgasm start to coat his stomach. That's all it takes for the tingling sensation in my spine to spread through my balls, pulling them into my body as I come hard. I collapse onto his chest, burying my face into his neck as I enjoy the last few moments of one of the best orgasms I've ever had.

I feel his hand rubbing up and down my back which makes me want to lie here forever with him, but with his cum cooling between us and my dick shrinking in his arse, I know I have to move. I hold onto the end of the condom as I pull out of him, feeling lost the second I leave him. I'm hoping that Zeke's groan is for the same reason and not that I hurt him too much. I go to the bathroom to dispose of the condom and grab a wet sponge. I quickly return to the bedroom and clean him up. When I'm done I move to put my boxers on but Zeke grabs my hand and tugs on it until I look at him.

"Please stay. Just for a little while. I think we need to talk."

I sigh, knowing he's right. I climb back into the bed and settle down next to Zeke without touching him. I know that if I do, there will be no talking. He does something to my concentration.

"Why did you leave?"

I turn my head to look at him and see a sad expression on his face. "I couldn't do it anymore. I can't watch you with Asha knowing that I can't have you. You're getting married, Zeke. Do you not understand how much that crushes me?"

He looks down, his cheeks coloring as he listens to me. "You just left, you didn't tell me you were going. Coach had to be the one to tell me, that hurt, babe." The use of his pet name for me pulls at my heart and makes me want to tell him that he can have me, even if I'll be a secret all my life.

No, I refuse to be that guy, I deserve better than that.

"It wouldn't have made any difference if I'd told you myself. I was still leaving. I won't be your dirty little secret. You can't be married and have a life with her while I wait around for you to throw me a scrap of attention." Being honest with him is the only way to go now. I know that tonight won't change anything between us, but hopefully if we clear the air I will be able to move on and let my heart recover a little. I know I will never love anyone the way I love Zeke, but I need to move on and try to make the most of my life.

"Someone knew."

I look at him and I can feel how wide my eyes are. Someone knew. Oh my god, this can't be happening.

I hear the laughter in his voice as he speaks again. "Coach caught us one night, in the locker room. I'm pretty sure he went home and bleached his eyes. But I told him about us, so you aren't a secret."

Shit, I can't believe we were seen. I would worry more about it, but my need for his answer to my next question wins out. "Will you tell anyone else? Your friends? Will you leave Asha for me?"

He looks down and I don't need him to say the words. If he can't meet my eyes then I know that tonight means more to me than it does to him. "I'm sorry, Bryce. I just can't." His voice sounds softer and I see his eyes droop as sleep wins the fight with him. "I wish I could be the man you deserve, but I'm not him."

I watch as he drifts off, and just before he slips completely under he says four simple words. Words that make a sob catch in my throat and tears flood my eyes.

"I love you, Bryce."

CHAPTER NINETEEN

Zeke

I stretch my body out when I wake up the next morning, feeling better than I should the day after a fight. My body is usually tight and sore, but between a half-assed opponent and the amazing night with Bryce, I feel really fucking good. The sudden thought of Bryce has me opening my eyes and sitting up instantly. I look around for him but all I can see is a head shaped dent in the pillow next to me, the only evidence that he was here at all last night. My heart drops knowing that he's gone. *He's* run away this time and now I understand how fucking much it hurts to be left.

I collapse back onto the bed, suddenly not feeling as good as I did when I opened my eyes. I would think last night hadn't actually happened but I have a comfortable ache in my ass, proving that Bryce has been there. The thought of why my ass aches brings a smile to my face, knowing that I shared something so special with him, and even though I don't plan on doing it with anyone else I enjoyed it more than I thought possible. The feeling of him inside my body made me feel complete. I didn't think it was possible for sex to be any better than it was already with Bryce, but last night proved me wrong. I have never experienced a feeling like that before and I wish it was something I could feel for the rest of my life. I don't know what this means for who I am, what label I'm meant to give myself, and it's confusing. When I was younger I thought I was gay, but I'm pretty sure that gay men don't sleep with women. I used to get enjoyment out of them, the feeling of their soft bodies and wet pussies something I couldn't get enough of, but now? Now I can only think of Bryce. Does that make me gay, or bisexual, or just really fucking confused?

My alarm goes off next to me, making me groan. I need to get up and meet with Asha, maybe finally grow a pair of balls and call this whole thing off. If last night showed me one thing it's that I can't let this go on when I know that I will never love her. There is only one person in this world that has my heart and nothing will ever change that. I'd called her before Bryce arrived and asked her to come over because we needed to talk. I'm sure she knows what's happening, she must be able to see clearly that I'm not invested in this relationship. Something happened between us the night that Bryce left and while I still don't remember anything, I know that we haven't had sex since then and I've barely seen her. So today I will end this farce and beg for her forgiveness. I hope that she understands, and that maybe one day she can forgive me. God I hope she doesn't cry. I don't do crying women.

****

I take a deep breath before opening the door to Asha. She looks amazing today, her tight little body is dressed in a form fitting dress. Normally when she would wear something like this I would have dragged her straight to my bedroom and buried myself in her body. Not today though, today I can appreciate how she looks but it does nothing for me. It also sparks a little panic inside when I wonder what's happening to me. *Fuck.* If I'm not turned on by Asha and the only guy that wakes my cock up is Bryce, does that mean I'm never going to have sex again? A cough brings me back to the situation at hand, and I make a note to return to this thought. It's something I need to figure out later.

I stand back from the door and motion for her to come in. She walks slowly past me and I'm not sure how to act. Normally I would kiss her but I think that for the purpose of today's visit it would be inappropriate. I close the door behind her and walk towards the kitchen, hoping she'll follow me.

"Want a coffee?" I walk over and turn on the kettle without waiting for a response. I need something to distract me, and I take a few moments to make us both a cup, anything to stop me from having to look at her.

All too soon I have to turn and face her as I carry both cups over to the table where she's sitting.

"So how long are we going to avoid this conversation?" Asha picks up her cup and takes a little sip of the hot coffee.

I follow her lead, taking a mouthful to give me a few more seconds to work out what I'm going to say. "I just don't know how to start." I'm thinking that being truthful with her is the best way to go. I need to control my bullshit and just tell her how I'm feeling and what I've done.

"Why don't we start this with the fact that you're engaged to me but you are in love with Bryce?"

The cup stops half way to my mouth and I look at her over the top of it in shock. I expect to see anger or hurt. What I'm not expecting is to see her smiling. "But ... how?"

She reaches over and takes my hand in hers, squeezing it gently. I look at our joined hands and notice that she isn't wearing her engagement ring. Thinking about it, I honestly can't remember the last time I saw her with it on. The realization makes me feel even worse.

How long has she known and why hasn't she called me out on it before? Why isn't she screaming at me and throwing the coffee in my face?

"You talk a lot when you're drunk. I have to admit, I'm surprised I didn't see it before. Once you told me you missed him I could see it all so clearly, the way you used to look at him, the way your moods were always dependent on his, all those little looks between the two of you." She squeezes my hand again but I'm not sure what to say to her. I think I'm in shock that I confessed my feelings when I was drunk. Her smile fades a little and I'm scared what she's going to say next. "I know I've been distant lately but I needed to step away. I wanted you to think about what you want,

192

Zeke. I don't know why you asked me to marry you when you're in love with someone else."

I go to protest but she holds up her hand, stopping me before I lie to her some more. "If you do love me, it's only as a friend and it's okay. I understand."

I take a deep breath. Now is the time to tell her everything and completely clear the air between us. The fact that she isn't angry shocks me a little and I'm hoping that she will still feel that way when I finish.

"I'm not gay. God, even saying it sounds so fucking lame. It's not that I'm not gay, it's that I *can't* be gay. I'm gay … holy fuck … *I'm gay.*" The words sound foreign to me but they don't sound wrong. They don't make me panic or make my heart race like I thought they would.

"Then why are you pretending to love me? If you love Bryce then you should be with him." I expect her to look hurt but again, I'm surprised when all I see is confusion on her face.

"How can I be with him? I can't be gay and still fight. I had to make a choice and he knew that we couldn't be more than what we were."

Now I see some anger flashing in her eyes, but I'm not sure what's caused it. "Wow. That's pretty fucking cold, even for you, Zeke. That guy is in love with you and you with him, and you found it so easy to just dump him when he wasn't any use to you anymore. I always thought you were a decent guy, but now I'm beginning to think that you're an asshole."

I stand and start pacing across the kitchen floor. I know what she's saying is the truth, that I haven't handled this situation well at all, but I'm dealing with a lot. I thought I was doing the right thing. My career is important to me; this fight is the thing I've been concentrating on for the last few years. I can't give that up for love and no one would expect me to.

"It's not like that. You don't understand. I can't come out as gay in this sport. No one would fight me. I would be shunned. This is the only thing I've ever dreamt about, the only thing I've wanted to do with my life. Are you telling me you would give up your dream for love?" I grab my hair as frustration takes over.

"That's the thing, Zeke. Being with the person you love is not giving up something, it's gaining everything. To spend your life with someone knowing that they know you inside and out, knowing that they will be with you no matter what, that's what's important. That's the prize right there."

I stop pacing and turn to look at her. I don't understand why she's being like this. Why is she pushing me towards Bryce, and why isn't she being a bitch after what I did to her? "Why are you being so fucking nice?"

She laughs and it just weirds me out even more. I mean I faked being in love with her, asked her to marry me and basically used her to get over the man I love. She shouldn't be sitting here smiling. I know *I* wouldn't. I'd be throwing everything in my reach at me right now.

"Do you want me to scream and shout at you? Maybe I should come over there and beat your chest in anger. Will that help you feel better? I can't say I'm happy about what happened but I can't hate you for falling in love. Don't get me wrong, if you had spoken to me the day after you confessed your feelings I probably would have cut you, but I've had time to think about it all. We were friends before we were anything else, so we will still be friends now."

I'm not used to people being nice to me. I'm used to anger and blame, so this feels foreign to me. I think I have a deep down need for Asha to hate me. I think that's why I say what I do next.

"I slept with Bryce last night, I cheated on you."

Her eyes widen and I brace myself for her anger, maybe some crying that will make me feel like shit.

"You saw him? Oh my god, where is he now?"

Fuck, this isn't working. I need her to yell at me. Her being nice isn't getting rid of my guilt, it's adding to it.

"God, will you stop being so fucking nice about it. I was an asshole and cheated on you... with a *guy*. I asked you to marry me

194

when I've never loved you that way. Fucking hell, woman, can you just show some emotion?"

She gets up from her chair and walks over to me. When she stands in front of me, she pulls her hand back and before I know it she's slapped me across the face. My hand flies to my stinging cheek, mouth dropping open in shock.

"Feel better? Is that what you wanted?" She has a cute little smile on her face and I can't help but laugh at her. She does this stupid girly clapping thing before getting back to interrogating me again. "Okay, now that's done tell me what happened. Are you getting back together?"

I let my head collapse backwards until I'm looking at the ceiling. I wish it was that easy to explain about last night, but I'm not completely sure what happened between us myself. I know that everything we did felt right. Being with Bryce and letting him touch where no one has been before was like heaven on earth.

"You fucked it up again didn't you?"

I lift my head and look at her with a sad smile crossing my lips. "I don't know. Maybe. All I know is I woke up alone and I still don't know where he lives. I think this was his way of telling me goodbye. It's for the best really, my fighting has to take priority."

Asha looks at me with a sad expression on her face, before reaching out and caressing my cheek with her hand.

"I want you to take a good look inside, Zeke. Can you tell me that you're happy, truly happy and that this is the life you pictured? I think if you were being honest with yourself you would see that it's not. Since he left you don't smile anymore. Maybe fighting isn't everything to you now, maybe you have seen another way to live, one that makes you happy. If you can really say that you're happy then carry as you are, but if you have to think too long about it, then maybe it's time to change some things. Will your championship belts love you when you're old? Will they hold you on the cold nights?" She leans in and kisses me on the cheek before walking away. Just as she's about to leave the kitchen she looks over her shoulder. "And just so you know, I'm keeping the ring." She winks at me and I let a small laugh out. I'd buy her a house right this second if she wanted one just for being here for me and accepting me.

I walk to the hall and grab my gym bag from the cupboard, deciding that I would be better off working out than trying to answer the questions she just asked. If I do something energetic then my mind might switch off. Thinking is not an option for me today.

Bryce

I feel arms working their way around my neck before lips connect with my cheek.

"Hey, sexy." The whispered words in my ear make my cheeks color. I'm used to Trey calling me this but today it just makes me feel guilty. After last night I feel like the lowest kind of person. I always swore I would never be the kind of guy that would cheat on someone, and then one call from Zeke and I'm slipping my dick into him without a second thought. Trey takes a seat next to me while Nathan sits across from us. I met the guys when I moved into my new apartment. They helped me up the stairs with my sofa and we just hit it off. I didn't know anyone so it was nice to have some friends to talk to. It didn't take long to realize that Trey was gay, especially after he cornered me in my closet and kissed me. I was shocked to begin with and almost pushed him away, but then I realized that I needed to move on and there was no better way to do it than with a new guy.

I haven't officially dated someone since Austin. What I had with Zeke was intense but it wasn't dating. Dating doesn't happen behind closed doors or in secret, and nothing we did was in public. The only time we had been seen together was to do with work.

A hand on my thigh pulls me from my thoughts and I smile at Trey. His dark hair is down today, messy looking, and I think it makes him look hotter than normal, more rugged. Usually it's more styled, the sleek look working for him when he wears his suits to work. He's a gay rights lawyer working in the local area, and from what I've worked out, he's a force to be reckoned with. He looks sexy as hell in his work suits, especially when he rolls his shirtsleeves up his forearms and his tattoos peek out. I don't have tattoos myself but since all the guys I find attractive have them, it's obviously my thing.

"So how was your night? Did you get up to anything exciting without me?" He winks at me and I feel my stomach drop. I really want to be honest with him and tell him what happened last night, but here in front of Nathan isn't the right time or place.

"Are you feeling okay? You look kinda pale?" The look of concern on his face makes me feel even worse, and I quickly decide that I will tell him about Zeke, just not today.

I lean forward and kiss him, my lips lingering longer than they probably should in public. "I'm fine. I didn't sleep very well last night and I think it's just catching up with me now."

He runs his thumb across my jaw as he smiles at me. "You need to have better respect for bedtime. Maybe tonight I can tuck you in?"

I haven't slept with Trey yet. I can't bring myself to do it while I'm still so confused about Zeke. I always thought it would be like cheating on Trey, but I suppose that boat has sailed now. *Shit*. The thought makes me feel like crap, and I realize that not sleeping with him until I was ready only gave me time to be with Zeke.

Maybe if I give myself to him fully I'll realize that I don't need Zeke as much as I think I do. Maybe I'll be able to move on. "I think that would be a great idea."

He raises his eyebrows and a smile creeps onto his face as his eyes light up. He leans forward and kisses me again before whispering against my lips. "Thank you."

"Oh my god, will you two get a room? We came here to eat lunch and I swear you're putting me off my food."

I turn and laugh at Nathan. I forgot he was there. PDA is something I wouldn't normally do.

"Jealousy is a terrible thing, Nathan. I've told you before, we don't mind if you join in." When Trey teases him, I can see he's lucky to have such a good friendship with Nathan. Some straight guys wouldn't be able to handle being around gay guys, but he just takes it in his stride. He has never looked uncomfortable around us, and if Trey and me want to spend time together he just excuses himself. No hassle, no bother.

As Nathan gives Trey the finger over the table, I pick up my menu and have a look. I know what I'm going to order. We've been here several times over the last few weeks because it's Trey's favorite place. As I listen to the two guys argue, I let them drift away as I think about last night. I need to check on Zeke and make sure he was okay this morning and not too sore. I know I shouldn't. I know I need to just leave him be and let us both move on, but I can't. I still have this deep need to make sure he isn't hurting and alone.

The waitress approaches the table and we all order, chatting about a big case that Trey's working on. Some company has fired Simon, one of their upper level managers, citing that he'd broken some company rules. However, Simon believes he was replaced because the bosses found out that he was gay. Trey's sure that he will get a big settlement for his client, and he also has a position for Simon with another company when the case is over. I love watching Trey when he's talking about his work. He's so passionate about the job and you can see it shining through in his eyes. It's like it lights him up from inside, the determination and drive making him almost unstoppable.

Lunch is good, but it's over before I know it and Trey has to go back to work. He kisses me passionately before telling me that he will be back after he finishes work and that he will bring food with him. I tell him to forget the food, to just hurry and get to my place, and it makes him smile before kissing me again. The thought of having sex with him makes my stomach flutter with nerves. I've seen him topless but nothing more than that, even that sight had my mouth watering.

198

Trying to clear my head I grab my phone from my pocket. I open up the messages and my finger hovers over the buttons. I want to text Zeke, but I don't want to at the same time. It's probably healthier to just cut him out of my life completely but I know I'm not strong enough for that. I quickly type out a message and hit send before I can change my mind.

How are you feeling?

It only takes a few seconds for an answer to ping on my phone, like he was sitting on his phone just waiting for me to text him.

I'm okay. A little tender but good.

I smile as I read his answer, memories from the night before flooding my mind and making me hard. Knowing that I was the first guy to do that with him, that he trusted me enough to let me take him, just blows my mind. Being inside him was something that I will never be able to explain. I don't think anything will ever be that good, and I'm so fucking glad I got to experience it at least once. Now that it's done I'll have to be content with just the memory of the best sex of my life.

Are you sure you're okay? I didn't hurt you?

I had taken him hard in the end. I had pounded into his body like it wasn't his first time. I hadn't meant to, I had wanted to keep control but as usual, Zeke made me lose my mind. The phone pings again in my hand and I read the message he sent back, laughing as I read his response.

Again I'll tell you, I'm fine. It does feel like I have sat on a fucking gate post, but it's not an unpleasant feeling.

This is why I fell for Zeke so badly, he has a way of making me feel settled, less worried. No matter what we've been through, I feel bad that we couldn't remain friends, but I know that's not possible with the feelings we have. I see a second message come in, one that has my steps faltering.

Will you tell me where you live?

I lock my phone and put it in my pocket. There's no way I'm telling Zeke where I live. I need to make this break. I need to move on.

CHAPTER TWENTY

Bryce

I hear the front door open as I stir the tomato sauce that's cooking on the stove. The sound is closely followed by Trey shouting out to tell me he's here.

"I'm in the kitchen." My apartment isn't very big, so I don't have to shout very loud. I had to be careful when I moved. Money became an issue when I stopped working for Zeke, and my savings will only get me so far. I need to start looking for a new job soon but I hate the thought of training anyone else.

I smile over my shoulder as I hear Trey's footsteps hit my tiled floor. I turn around properly to see him enter and put a bottle of wine on the table. He walks over to me, taking my face between his hands and kissing my lips gently. He pulls me towards him as he continues to kiss me, my heart rate picking up with the passion in his lips. I drop the spoon onto the worktop before turning fully into his arms again, kissing him back just as passionately. I work my hands into his hair, pulling his mouth closer to mine as my tongue attacks his and the heat between us starts to rise. There has never been a lack of spark between us, when we come together it's like we can't get enough of each other, but I always stop us from going any further. I knew that there would be no emotions involved and it makes me feel like shit knowing that Trey feels a lot more for me than I do for him. I just need to get over Zeke, try and give Trey more. I need to try and find some happiness for myself. I never meant anything to Zeke and it's time to move on.

Trey rubs his erection against my own, making me groan into his mouth. I hear the sauce boiling behind me and I force myself to pull away from his lips. "I need to save the sauce if you want to eat tonight."

He doesn't let me move, keeping me close to his body as he kisses me again. His tongue flicks out and caresses my lips. I close my eyes and sigh, loving the feeling of what he's doing.

"There's only one thing I want to eat tonight and that's you, baby." When he calls me 'baby' I feel my stomach somersault and guilt builds inside me when it reminds me of Zeke. He would always call me his baby, but only in private, it was never a name that he would use in front of anyone. As far as everyone else knew I was just his trainer and, maybe at a push, his friend. That's why I need to put him to the back of my head and concentrate on Trey. Trey isn't embarrassed to be seen with me; he wants a relationship with me privately and publically. He isn't hiding me from the world. He wants everyone to know I'm his.

I turn and stir the sauce, leaning back into his chest when he wraps his arms around my waist. This is what I've missed the most in a relationship. The closeness with someone, being held and loved, knowing someone is always there for you. Zeke showed me that I had been hiding from the world so I couldn't get hurt again, but all I was doing was cutting myself off from the chance of feeling again.

I watch as Trey reaches around me to turn the flame off from under the pot before taking the spoon and laying it on the rim of the pot. His lips brush over my neck before settling next to my ear. "I don't want you to feel any pressure, I will wait as long as you need. But I just want to let you know how much I want you. You are the sexiest thing I've ever seen and I swear just thinking of you makes me hard." He presses his erection into my arse, making me lean my head back against his shoulder. "I can't stop thinking about what you'll feel like and what you'll look like naked. Fuck, I want to taste you."

If I had any doubts about my attraction to Trey, they all vanish when he whispers in my ear. My heart rate spikes when his hand travels down my abs and over my jeans. He cups my aching balls, causing a groan to leave my chest on its own accord.

I concentrate on the movement of his hand and the way he brushes over the front of my zip before he slowly lowers it. He's taking his time, letting me stop him if I need to. Moving his fingers up to the buttons of my jeans he stops, silently asking my permission to carry on. I answer his unasked question by grinding my arse back into him, loving the feel of his sudden labored breathing against my neck. The button pops and his hand immediately moves inside my boxers, his fingers brushing over my head, rubbing in the pre-cum that's leaking from me. He's turning me on more than I imaged he would be able to, and his fingers feel so good against my skin. I'm concentrating so much on the feel of his fingers that it takes me a few moments to realize that my jeans and underwear are down around my knees. With the first few strokes of his hand over my dick I forget about anything else other than what he's doing. The only thing I care about is thrusting into his fist.

"You feel so fucking amazing, Bryce. So much better than I imagined. I want to make you come, I want you to explode in my mouth." His dirty words make my skin tingle, and I want nothing more than to come in his mouth. The need for release is taking over and I can't focus on anything. I reach behind me and my fingers work on opening the buttons on his pants, quickly pushing them down his legs. I groan as I feel his dick hit my arse as it's released and I grasp his erection in my hand. He's hot and heavy in my hand, and I want to feel him inside me more than anything.

"Fuck, baby. Can I have you, please?" It's like he's reading my mind but I'm beyond speaking at this point to give him an answer. The sensations running through my body cumulate in my balls and I need to stop him before I come over his hand. I try to tell him that he needs to slow down but my words come out on a stuttered pant and I'm not sure if he hears me.

"Trey… oh god… Trey… I'm gonna… fuck… Trey." I know I don't make any sense but he must understand because he slows his movements. I remove both of my hands from his body and use them to support myself against the worktop in front of me. I take some deep breaths, trying to get control of myself. I think it's working because the tightness in my balls relaxes slightly, but Trey isn't in the mood to play fair. He moves in close behind me until his hard dick pushes in between my arse cheeks. He rubs his entire length over me, squeezing my cheeks together for more pressure.

"Tell me if I need to stop, Bryce. I will if you need me to, but if you don't answer me I'm gonna fuck you right here, right now. I'm going to bend you over and slip inside your body, fucking you hard against this work top." I always thought that Trey would be sweet and our first time together would be gentle and romantic. This side of him surprises me, and turns me on more than I thought it would. I always thought I'd be with a quiet guy who would let me lead the way, but I'm beginning to think that my type is the complete opposite. I'm starting to see a trend with the guys I've been attracted to recently. The stronger the man, the more he pushes my limits and takes control, the more I want him. I never thought of myself as a bottom, preferring to be in control, but I seem to be learning a lot of things about myself.

Trey must take my lack of response as acceptance because I feel his hand on the center of my back, pushing me down until my chest is flush against the worktop next to the cooker. I'm breathing so hard that I'm starting to feel a little light headed, and I try to calm myself down. I can't believe he has me so worked up, the anticipation of him slipping into my body making me lose all coherent thought. My body shudders as I hear a condom wrapper ripping, my arse clenching in anticipation. I feel something cold drip onto my arse and I jump slightly. I would make a joke about him being prepared but I can't get the words out my mouth as his finger brushes over my opening. He pushes it into me and I feel my hole clench around him.

"God, you're so tight." He leans over my back to whisper in my ear, sucking the lobe into mouth as he pushes a second finger inside me. He wraps his hand around my erection as he brushes over that special spot inside me, and I know I won't last much longer.

"Oh fuck, you're dripping baby." I feel him run his finger over my tip, spreading pre-cum down my length.

"You need to stop, I can't take any more."

Both hands leave my body immediately, and I'm about to complain until I feel his hard dick against me, pushing through my tight muscles and stealing my breath. I feel my body accepting him, my muscles relaxing as I become accustomed to his girth. He's thicker than I'm used to, and I feel my body stretching to an almost painful degree, but the pain is welcomed. I push back against him, needing him to fill me quicker. I'm worried that if he doesn't get inside me I'm going to come all over the floor. His loud groan makes me tighten around him and he tries to still my hips but I still push against him, my strength winning out until he's fully seated inside me. Once he's filled me completely, we both stop moving, the only sound to be heard is our harsh breathing. When Trey pulls out from my body, leaving just hit tip inside, I bite into my arm to try and focus on something other than the sensations in my body. I can already feel my balls draw up and start to tingle in preparation for my orgasm.

After a few gentle thrusts Trey unleashes the power behind those amazing thighs of his and he begins to pound into my hole like he's trying to make me feel him for weeks. He grabs the back of my hair, pulling on it until I have to stand. I support my weight on my hands, the throb in my head adding to the ache in my balls. I close my eyes, trying to concentrate on not coming, wanting this to never end. His hand works its way around my throat, pulling back until my head is on his shoulder, but he doesn't ease the pressure.

His voice is rough when he speaks into my ear, the lust clear. "Reach down and make yourself come. I want you to fill your hand for me." The combination of him filling my body, the pressure on my throat and his words have me filling my hand like he asked within a few strokes. The orgasm takes over all my senses, blurring the world around me.

I'm pulled back from my happy place when Trey lifts my hand to his mouth, his tongue coming out to clean the mess that's filled my palm. If I hadn't just come hard, I'm sure the erotic act of him licking my cum off my hand would send me over the edge. I feel him still suddenly behind me, the hand on my throat tightening as he twitches inside me, his own orgasm hitting as he fills the condom.

Just as I'm starting to panic about Trey's hand on my throat and not being able to breathe, he releases his hold and drops his head onto my shoulder.

"Fuck. That was… fuck. I knew you would be amazing, but that was… fuck."

I laugh at his incoherent ramble, knowing exactly how he feels.

****

I'm lying with my head on Trey's shoulder. We moved to my bed after our impromptu sex session in the kitchen, cleaning ourselves up on the way. We've been here for about an hour, just chatting about our lives.

"So you train MMA fighters? How did I not know this? The way I was pushing you around in the kitchen, I'm pretty sure you could have kicked my ass with one hand." He kisses my forehead, making me feel special and wanted.

"I train them, I don't fight myself." Our fingers twine together as we hold them in the air between us.

"Yeah but you must know some moves if you're training them."

"Oh, I know some moves." I look up at him, wiggling my eyebrows and making him smile as I speak. His smile turns to laughter and before I know it he has me flipped over onto my back with him pressed up against my body. He leans down, biting gently along my jaw and up to my lips. Even after an amazing orgasm not too long ago I feel my dick twitch to life, causing a cocky grin to appear on Trey's face.

"I bet you have lots of moves that I would enjoy. But what I meant was, I'm surprised you don't fight. Or did you? Did you start as a fighter?" My gut twists a little at his question and I know I should tell him the truth but I don't. I won't lie, I just won't give him the whole truth. No one knows about that part of my past apart from Zeke, and it makes me wonder why I won't just open up to Trey.

"I prefer to train, there's less blood and pain involved. Well usually." The memories of the times that Zeke winded me, or knocked me on my arse flash through my mind and I force myself to focus on Trey, trying to think of only him and me.

"So would I know any of these fighters that you've trained? Any big names?" This isn't a road that I want to go down. I don't feel comfortable talking about Zeke yet, the pain he caused is still too fresh.

"Do you follow MMA?" If he does and I mention Zeke's names it might lead to more questions, ones that I'm not willing to answer.

"Well, no. I might though if I will see your handy work. That's what boyfriends do, they support each other."

I grind my hips against him while he kisses me. It's not like the gentle kisses I'm used to from him, this one is full of passion and promise. He groans and pulls back, putting distance between us.

"Before we go any further, I think we need to talk about something."

I raise my eyebrows again but this time in confusion. "How much further can we go? You've already taken me, but if you don't remember that then we might have problems."

He groans above me as I feel him harden against my body. "Don't worry, I remember every second of it. What I meant was, before we do it again. I need to know, was there anything you didn't enjoy?" I'm hoping my confusion at his question is showing in my face because I think he might be losing his mind.

"Um… again… you might not remember how much I enjoyed it, but you licked the evidence off my hand."

He groans again and I decide I like this little game. Being able to turn him on so much and so easily is a boost to the ego. To have a guy who wants me and isn't embarrassed to show it is refreshing. I spent so much time hiding everything with Zeke that I forgot how much I wanted normal.

Trey leans down and rubs his nose against mine and I love the little sign of affection. "You're trouble, Mr. Tanner. I just need to make sure you're okay with everything I did to you. Sometimes I like things a little… rougher, and I need to know if you're comfortable with it. I will totally understand if you're not, not everyone is…" I kiss him, stopping the words and making him lose his train of thought. I feel his body relax on top of mine as he lets the kiss take over. I'm fine with everything he did, a little bit of roughness isn't something that would chase me away, but there is something I need to know.

I pull back so I can see his eyes as I question him. "What you did was amazing, nothing was too much. I need to know something though, and maybe it's something we should have discussed before now. Do you bottom?"

The look that flashes over Trey's face tells me my answer but I let him tell me with words. "It's not something I've done in the past, Bryce. Bottoming is usually a hard limit for me."

I wonder if that's going to be a problem between us. I told Zeke that it wouldn't be a deal breaker between us, but I don't know if that was because I knew he hadn't been with a guy before. Now thinking about spending my life with a guy and never being inside him is making me question this relationship. I don't always top. I've always been verse and enjoy receiving just as much as giving, but to know I'll never have the option again makes me feel uneasy.

I'm pulled from my musings by Trey's hands caressing my cheeks. My eyes move to his and I see the gentleness in them.

"I said it's *usually* a hard limit, but for you I'll try it. I'm not saying that I'll love it, but I will try."

I bite my lip as my throat tightens with emotion. The fact that this guy is willing to try something he isn't into just to keep me happy, makes him suddenly more important in my life. It proves that he's willing to compromise in this relationship and I won't be the only one working towards what could be a great thing. I need to make this work with him. Zeke doesn't want me but Trey does. Trey is such a great guy, he is kind and he honestly makes my heart beat faster, I just need to let myself give him a chance. I need to draw a line in the sand and move on from what's happened in the last few months. This is what's good for me. This is a healthy relationship.

"You keep saying things like that and a guy could really fall for you."

The smile I get in response makes my heart flutter. I think I could be happy with this man.

"I have the day off tomorrow, how about we do something together? I know of a gym about ten minutes away that has a shop next door that sells all the equipment that you probably know how to use." This catches my attention. I haven't managed to find a local gym that I've liked so my training has somewhat diminished. If this one is any good then it might be worth the drive every day to get a good workout.

"I think spending time with you in one of my favorite places sounds like fun. And you never know, you might like what you see and join with me."

He looks down at me with mischief in his eyes "I already like what I see." And for the next hour he proves just that.

CHAPTER TWENTY - ONE

Zeke

I hate this part of not having a coach. Having to buy my own supplies is boring and time consuming. I don't even know if I'm going to remember everything I need. I'm reading my list while I walk aimlessly around 'Fighting Fit' trying to find everything. It's the best fighting equipment supplier in the area, and even though it's a forty-minute drive it's worth it to get everything in one place. It took me an exhaustive Internet search to find a place that stocked my favorite wraps, so the long drive isn't a problem, or it usually isn't because I'm not the one who normally does the driving. This is why I need to start thinking about replacing Bryce, even though the thought causes me physical pain. My chest aches when I think about finally giving up on the idea of having him in my life. If I fill his position then it's admitting that he's never coming back, and I'm definitely not ready for that.

The experience of being with him the other night was something I would never change, and if I was to be completely honest it's something I want for the rest of my life. That's all I've been thinking about since I woke up alone yesterday morning. I don't know why it suddenly hit me, but I made a very important discovery about my life. I can live without a lot of things, but I know I can't live without Bryce. I only have a few days before my big fight against Dwayne and if I win, it will be a kick-start to a new, more lucrative fighting career, but all I can think is that I don't want to do it alone. I want Bryce by my side to celebrate every win or to hold me through every loss. I just need to decide how to beg him to come back to me. I'm not stupid. I know that I've pushed him away too many times and that when I confess that I want him he might laugh in my face. I know he might feel like I'm using him, that when he wanted something more from me I ran, but now that I've finally decided what I want, I expect him to come back to me. It sounds bad no matter how you look at it, but I can't change that now. I just need him and I hope he understands.

I shake my head, determined not to spend the entire day thinking of him again. I just need to get what's on my list and get back to the gym so I can work out some of my frustrations before heading into the steam room. This sounds like a fantastic plan and one I'm pretty sure will keep Bryce out of my mind. This plan would work perfectly if, when I raise my head, he wasn't standing on the other side of the store right now. He's looking at the supplements, picking up different bottles and reading them before putting them back on the shelf. He's wearing tight, black denim jeans that mold to his sexy as fuck ass, making me want to run my hands over it. His white shirt is tucked in and the sleeves are rolled up his forearms showing off his perfect arms. I get goose bumps when I remember how those arms felt around me, holding me against his chest as he slept. Those were the times that I want back. I've never experienced them with anyone else and I miss them. I miss him.

I just stand and watch as he looks around, moving from the supplements to another part of the store. I know I must look like a stalker but I don't care. It feels like it's been forever since I saw him and I want to get my fill of his sexiness. I don't think anyone else has ever looked as good as he does right now. He's simply the most stunning thing I've ever seen.

I take a deep breath and build up the courage to approach him, but before I move I see something that has my heart breaking in my chest. A really attractive guy walks up behind Bryce, working his arms around his waist and leaning his chin on his shoulder. I can see Bryce leaning into his body, relaxing into the embrace before kissing the guy on the cheek. They look comfortable together, like this isn't a big deal for them, that being in public together is natural. It's the kind of relationship I wish I had with him and watching them makes it hit home that I have completely missed my chance. He's got someone who won't keep him a secret, someone who won't only kiss and hold him behind closed doors. The realization hurts more than I want it to. I want to pretend that this means nothing to me and I'm happy to move on, but I can't lie to myself this time. It's time to be honest and admit that I am one hundred percent in love with Bryce Tanner, not that the truth will make any difference now.

I turn to leave before I lose it, the ache in my chest making me want to scream, but my foot catches the bottom of a display unit. I watch in horror as every single can of muscle spray shakes on the shelf before settling down again. I say a silent thank you that I didn't bring any attention to myself and I carefully move away from the unit. As I take my first step there's a tug on the backpack I'm wearing and my eyes widen in horror when I hear a crash behind me. I stand and watch as dozens of cans fall all over the floor, the crash echoing the whole store. I close my eyes, praying that maybe the incident didn't make as much noise as I thought it did. Maybe no one noticed? I know that it's a useless thought. There's no way that anyone inside the store didn't notice the idiot who knocked over a display of noisy cans. I open my eyes and my worst nightmare is realized when I see Bryce standing in front of me, and he's holding the hand of the guy he's with.

"Zeke?"

I can't take my eyes off their joined hands, the hand that gave me so much pleasure just the other night. I wonder if he's told the guy that he was with me, because this doesn't look like a new relationship, they look too comfortable with each other.

"Zeke?" This time his voice pulls my eyes up to his and I feel myself blushing. He's standing there looking as hot as sin, holding hands with an equally attractive guy, and I'm surrounded by a mess that I made, probably looking like shit.

"Hi, I… uh… knocked them over." I cringe at my inability to sound like a normal human being. Of course I knocked the fucking thing over, anyone with eyes can see that. There's an awkward silence between us and I can't tear my eyes away from Bryce.

Someone clearing their throat has me finally turning away to find the guy with Bryce holding his hand out to me.

"Hi, I'm Trey Colby." He doesn't sound like a jerk as he says it and I hate him for that. I don't want him to be nice, I want to be able to say to Bryce that he deserves someone better, someone like me, but I can't if the guy is nice and polite.

Fucker.

I take his hand, putting a little more power into the shake than necessary. "Zeke Raine."

He doesn't give any sort of reaction when I say my name so I think it's safe to say that he's not been told about me.

"Are you a friend of Bryce's?" He looks between us and I don't know what to say, so I raise my eyebrows at Bryce to let him know that the ball is in his court. I don't know if I can trust myself not to tell this guy exactly how I know his boyfriend, and that I *knew* him only a few days ago.

"I used to train Zeke. He's an MMA fighter." It actually hurts that he introduces me this way. I didn't expect him to confess his undying love for me, but I wanted a little more than just 'he trained me'. I think I meant a little fucking more to him than that.

"Oh come on, Bryce. We were more than that."

The look of horror that crosses his face makes me feel like shit, but I don't have any intention of spilling his secrets. If he wants to build a relationship on lies then who am I to stop him?

I look towards Trey before continuing. "We became pretty good friends too. I think it's hard to work so closely with someone without there being something more." I emphasize the 'more' and part of me hopes that this guy picks up on it. I can see Bryce's cheeks color out of the corner of my eye and I know I need to stop being a dick but it's coming so naturally. I've always been this way, when someone hurts me it comes out in my attitude. I need to get away before I say something that I can't take back, something that will hurt Bryce.

"I'm sorry, I need to get to training. It was great seeing you, Bryce, I hope I see you soon. It was nice meeting you, Trey." I don't even wait for them to reply before I rush out of the store, stepping over the cans that still litter the floor.

****

I pound my fists into the bag in front of me, trying to get rid of some of the pent up anger that's coursing inside me. I've been here for hours and nothing is working, nothing is making me feel better. I keep replaying the scene with Bryce, of how happy he looked with that guy Trey. *What a stupid fucking name. Trey Colby.* Sounds like a porn star or some shit. Yes, yes, I know I'm sounding like a jealous ass hating on the guy who has my man, the man I pushed away until he couldn't take anymore, but it's making me feel better about everything. I need something to hate and I know that it will never be Bryce.

I feel a twinge through the top of my hand and I swear loudly, knowing it's my old injury playing up. I don't know if it's the extra training or if my technique is suffering but something isn't right. I wish I had someone to tell me what to do, because I need to win this fight as if my life depends on it. If I can't have the man I love, then I need the career I love. I really wish Bryce was here to tell me what I'm doing wrong with my posture though. I think that's what's causing me to throw my arm wrong which is then causing tension on my wrist.

I start to punch again and just like my wish is granted...

"You're dropping your right shoulder. There's no way you will last the entire fight like that."

I don't stop hitting but lift my shoulder, instantly feeling the difference when my fist connects with the bag. Why does he have to be so fucking good at this? I don't turn to look at him but I can feel him moving to the other side of the gym. My curiosity finally gets the better of me and I turn to see what he's doing. Of course, just as I look at him, he strips off his shirt and throws it over the weight bench. I watch him and the way his muscles move as he tapes up his hands. He turns and walks towards me, flexing his fingers before stepping onto the sparring mat. He cracks his neck, waiting for me to walk over to him.

Like a moth to a flame I move to him, preparing to fight. "Where's the boyfriend?" I can't help but ask, hoping that maybe they had a huge fight over me and he's here to claim me.

"Trey had some errands to run. I thought it was a good time to maybe come and see you. Talk about what happened the other night."

I take the opportunity to swing at him, but just like old times, he moves out the way before I connect. It's like he can read my body and knows the moves I'm going to make before I do.

"Is there anything that needs to be said? We had a moment, and then you went home to your boyfriend. Was he not putting out, is that why I got the bootie call?"

Color works its way through Bryce's face but this time I know it's caused by anger, and I know that I might suffer for the comment but it's how he made me feel. It's his turn to take a swing, but the difference is that he connects with my left shoulder, knocking me back a step.

"You weren't a fucking booty call. I had no intention of sleeping with you when I called. I wanted to talk, to clear the air. I can't help it if my attraction to you got in the way." Even though I can hear the anger in his words, I still smile upon hearing that he's still attracted to me.

"Did you tell him?" I punctuate my question with a kick, hitting him high on the leg so his knee collapses slightly. He recovers quickly and circles me. I match his movements, keeping my guard up.

"Not yet, I don't... I don't know how to explain it." His voice lowers as he speaks and his eyes drop to the mat. I use it as an opportunity to make my final move. I grab him by the arm, pushing my hip into him and throwing him over it. He lands on his back and I collapse on top of him, no longer trying to win the fight, just wanting to talk to him.

"Explain what?"

He looks up at me, recovering quickly from my surprise attack. "Explain what happened. Explain us."

I watch his lips, wanting nothing more than to kiss his confusion away and let him see that it's me he should be with. "You could tell him the truth." I say it as though it's the simplest thing in the world but I know it's not. And it's not helped by the fact that I don't think either of us know fully what the truth is.

"That's the thing, I can't tell him that. How do I tell the guy I'm trying to make a life with that I slept with the guy who still has my heart? How do I tell him that I had sex with you because I felt like I would die if I didn't? The truth is that spending the night with you is something that I will never regret. I know I cheated on him, but I would do it again in a heartbeat if it meant being able to feel your body around me."

I don't get a chance to answer before he tilts his hips and throws me off of his body. I land on my back and watch as he rips the bandages from his wrists and grabs his shirt. He rushes towards the door, buttoning up as he goes.

"Bryce?"

He stops, but doesn't turn towards me as I sit up.

"Will you be at my fight on Saturday?"

His head drops and I can almost feel the pain flowing from him. "I can't, Zeke. I just can't."

I watch as he leaves the gym, and I don't know why, but I have a feeling that this might be the last time I ever see Bryce Tanner.

Bryce

I rush from the gym before I give in to the urge to go back and kiss Zeke. The whole time I was in there, it took all my control not to tackle him to the ground and take him again.

I shouldn't even be here. I told Trey that I forgot I had a job interview with a new 'up and coming' fighter, someone who was travelling and could only fit me in today. So apparently I don't just cheat on him, I now lie so I can go to see other guys. I couldn't tell him the truth though, not yet. After meeting Zeke in the supply store, Trey had started asking a lot of questions. With his lawyer mind, I know he saw something that made him slightly suspicious, and I didn't want to have to tell him about my past with Zeke. I don't know why I thought that coming here was a good idea, I thought that maybe we could put what happened between us to rest so we could move on and not be so awkward around each other. I should have known better. We can't be in the same room without pissing each other off or letting our attraction take over.

I never wanted to admit to him how I feel about him out of fear that he might use it against me. I can't give him all the power and I know I feel more for him than he does for me so I need to keep my emotions hidden from him. He's made it perfectly clear that he doesn't want anything more than fucking with me, and I have finally accepted that now. If he truly loved me the way he said he did in his sleep, he would fight for me, show me that he doesn't care what the world says about us. But I know his career is more important and that's easier to keep in the forefront of my mind when I'm not standing right in front of him. When I am, the only thing I can think about is the memory of how he feels and tastes, and that leads to nothing but problems. I have this pull to him, something deep in my soul that hears him calling out to me and it's nigh on impossible to ignore. I bang my head back against the headrest in my car, confusion making me frustrated. Maybe I should go back to being alone. At least then I knew what was happening in my life. How did I end up torn between two men?

Trey is amazing. He's smart, kind, sexy as hell and wants to be with me. He's happy to be seen with me, to admit how he feels to the whole world and would never hide me. The only problem is that I don't know if I will ever love him like he deserves. He should be with someone who can give him one hundred percent of themselves, and no matter how hard I try there will always be a part of me he can't have. Zeke holds that part of me that I will never get back, the part that only the guy I love can have. But, he's also the one who doesn't want me in public and refuses come out of the closet to be with me. I know it's nothing to do with me personally but it also hurts that he doesn't think I'm enough for him to pick me. Then on the other hand, he also turns me on more than anyone else I've ever met. A simple look, a small touch and my body is on full alert, ready to act on anything he's willing to do. Why can't I combine both of these guys and make the one perfect partner. I try not to think about how the only thing I would change about Zeke is the fact that he isn't openly gay. If he could change that part of himself then he would be everything I want.

I shake my head, laughing at myself and my pro and con list. It's official, I've turned into a teenage girl who's torn between the nerd and the football star. When I feel my phone vibrate in my pocket, I grab it and see a message from Trey, and even after everything I find myself smiling.

Sorry something's come up, I won't be able to come over tonight. You up for a visit tomorrow night?

I'm a little disappointed that I won't see him tonight, but a night on my own is probably a good thing. It gives me a chance to really think about everything, and maybe I can work out how I'm going to come clean to Trey about Zeke. I don't know how I even bring it up, and I don't think he'd be able to forgive me. I know that there is a good chance that this will rip us apart but I can't have this hanging over our head. I don't want the risk of Zeke saying something in the future. That is ammunition I can't let anyone have. I thought he was going to say something at the gym store today and my heart had been racing in my chest. I still can't believe that I cheated on Trey. I would never have thought I would capable of that. I've always thought cheating was the lowest thing that

218

someone could do, and I suppose I still do. I laugh at the irony of the situation before replying to Trey.

I'll miss you, but tomorrow is great.

I put my phone in the center console and, putting the car into gear, I drive away from the gym and towards a night of thinking. A night to finally decide what I want.

CHAPTER TWENTY - TWO

Bryce

Trey looks stressed as I watch him walk in the front door. It's an unusual state to see him in. I'm used to seeing him cool, calm, and under control. I don't even ask him if he wants a glass of wine, the look on his face telling me he might need the whole bottle. I have the glass poured by the time he walks into the kitchen and collapses into the chair next to the table.

He gives me a smile as I pass the glass to him. "Thanks, babe."

I lean down and kiss him gently before grabbing my bottle of beer. "You look stressed. Is everything okay?"

The groan that leaves him tells me that he's had a terrible day, and I'm hoping it's something that can be easily sorted. I know he deals with a lot of high pressure, high profile cases that attract a lot of attention so I'm wondering if one of them have gone wrong or garnered him some unwelcomed attention.

"It's been the day from hell. An important piece of paperwork went missing and we had to spend the entire day looking for it. No one admitted to moving it but I'm pretty sure it was Quincy, and yes I swear that's his name, that lost it. The guy causes more problems than he solves. The only reason he's still with the company is because his uncle is a friend of the senior partner. I don't see why I ended up with him and why I should have to carry the dead weight. I win more cases than anyone in that firm so I should have the best staff, not that I'm being big headed... but yeah, I am." I know he's telling me about his bad day but I can't help but laugh at his rant. Watching how serious he is when talking about work is funny as hell.

"I'm glad I'm amusing you." Even though he's trying to sound serious, I can see the humor in his eyes as he flips me off over the top of his wine glass, which causes me to laugh harder.

"Oh you are. You amuse me a lot. Usually when you're naked." I realize what I've said when he chokes on a glassful of wine. "Shit, no, I didn't mean it like that. I meant… well… it was… shit." I can't seem to get the words to come out of my mouth to explain what I meant. I was trying to say that last night in bed be made me laugh with all his questions, but now I realize how bad it sounded.

His hand dramatically flies to his head as he exhales a pained cry. "I can't believe you said that. My naked body isn't anything to laugh at, it is something to be adored!" He gets up from the chair, continuing the dramatics as he walks out of the kitchen, making it really hard not to laugh at him. "If you don't want me, I'll go find someone who finds me irresistible. I'm in demand you know. Demand, I tell you!"

I slowly follow him down the hall, watching as he sways from side to side like an old forties actress suffering from palpitations. I let him reach the front door before I rush after him, spinning him round and pinning him to it.

"Don't leave, I don't think I could take a moment without you and your stunning naked body." I steal his lips in a passionate kiss, and it isn't long before the atmosphere goes from light and humorous to heavy and thick with desire. Passion takes over and we struggle to get each other naked quickly. With our clothes around our feet, I show Trey that he's not the only one who can be in control, and from the way he screams out his orgasm, I think he likes it.

****

I close the door behind me and walk into the kitchen with the Chinese takeout that's just been delivered. I'd planned on cooking tonight, but after the impromptu sex against the door with Trey earlier I couldn't find the energy to finish preparing it.

I place the bag down and start taking out the containers while Trey grabs plates and cutlery. I can't help but notice how domesticated the scene is. I find myself imagining what it could be like having this every day, the comfortable feeling between us is something that I've always wanted in a relationship. And then there's the passion, when he touches me my body comes alive. He's sexy and alluring, and has a body that could turn a straight man gay. It's not the same as Zeke's body. It's not as sculpted but with his tattoos and the way his muscles are perfectly toned, it's a huge turn on. I feel guilt when I compare him to Zeke. It's not fair to Trey when I do that. He can't possibly win against the memories he doesn't know I have.

An arm around my waist brings me back to the present, making me smile as I kiss Trey's cheek. He really is a great guy, and if I give myself enough time, I really do think I could learn to love him. He rests his chin on my shoulder as I open all the food boxes and place them in the middle of the table so we can help ourselves. When I'm finished I just stand there and let him hold me. We're quiet as we take our time to move, both of us obviously caught up in our thoughts.

"I like this, just being here with you. I don't know when I've ever been this happy just staying in and spending time with someone. It's been forever since I let anyone in like this. Thank you for letting me trust again." His words have my heart stuttering in my chest. He hasn't told me much about his past relationships but Nathan had hinted that he'd been hurt in the past, and that it had taken him a long time to get over it.

I pull out of his hold, walking around the other side of the table and taking a seat. Sitting across from each other we fill our plates before I find the courage to ask the question that's been on my mind all day. "What happened with your ex?" I don't look at him and focus on pushing the food around my plate.

It takes a few minutes for him to speak, but I sit patiently as I wait for him to answer. "I was with Dustin for about seventeen months before I realized that he was cheating on me. I had been asking him for months to move in with me but he kept making excuses as to why he couldn't. I never thought to question him fully, I just thought he wasn't ready. Anyway, the reason he couldn't move in was because he was actually living with another guy and had been for about a year. That was the day I knew what it was like to have my heart broken. It took me a long time to trust anyone again, but I let you in. People who cheat are the lowest people out there, and it's a very hard limit for me."

I feel the color drain from my cheeks as he speaks. Without knowing it, I've gone and done the one thing he would never forgive. I had treated him just like his ex did and hadn't taken his feelings into consideration at all. But when I went to see Zeke that night, I had no intention of sleeping with him. One look at him standing there and all I could think about was giving into my cravings and having him. I hadn't thought of Trey once, well not until I was leaving Zeke's bed did the guilt hit me. I never imagined I would be the type of guy who would stray but one moment in Zeke's company had me forgetting who I was.

Trey's hand on mine makes me jump and I look up quickly, realizing that I've been lost in my head again. I seem to have spent too many months stuck in some internal battle between my heart and my head, and it's caused me so much stress. Now I have to add hurting Trey to that fight, and I know when he finds out what I did he'll leave me.

"Are you okay, baby?" He looks worried as he watches me carefully, making me feel awkward. Here he is spilling his guts to me and I manage to make him worry about me.

Fuck, when did I turn into this guy?

I fake a smile at him, hoping he believes the poor attempt. "I'm good, I think I have a headache coming on."

He squeezes my hand before returning to his meal. As I eat I can see his eyes watching me and it looks like he wants to ask me something but he just smiles before grabbing more fried rice. We eat in comfortable silence but I'm forcing the food into my stomach, the level of guilt eating me alive has increased tenfold since the start of the conversation.

When we're finished we clean up the table, moving around each other as though we have done this hundreds of times before. It's times like this that I wonder if I'm meant to be with Trey. It just feels like we are made for each other. I would jump into this with both feet if it weren't for one simple fact: I'm still in love with Zeke. When Trey is finished washing the dishes, he dries his hands and walks over to me. He traps me against the kitchen unit, his hands caging mine and leans in to kiss me gently. He lingers on my lips, licking and nibbling on them until I'm hard and pushing against the front of my jeans.

"How's the head?" He breathes against my lips and I can't help but groan in response. He really makes turning me on look so easy. He has such power over my body, it's just my heart he needs to conquer.

"It's better now. I think I was just hungry."

He rubs his nose over mine, kissing the tip before leaning his forehead against mine. "You didn't eat enough for the food to make you feel better. There's something bothering you tonight, and I wish you would tell me what it is. I'm here for you. Only you." I close my eyes as he speaks, pain ripping through me as I listen to him being wonderful. I can feel a tear work its way down my cheek, like my body is trying to release some of the guilt. I feel Trey's finger wipe it away which causes a silent sob to work through me. This has been building for so long. Everything that's been happening since I arrived here is making me want to get on a plane and go back to the UK.

"Baby, I wish you would tell me what's wrong. I hate seeing you in pain."

I let my head drop until it's leaning on his chest. I enjoy the feel of him against me, for what might be the last time. I need to tell him what happened with Zeke, no matter how much it hurts the both of us. It's better to get it out in the open now than later on. Maybe if I explain how and why it happened, he will let us move forward together, both of us with fresh starts. We are only just getting serious about each other now, so when I cheated it wasn't like we were in a full relationship. Another sob wracks my body as I recognize that I'm trying to convince myself that everything will be okay, but I know it won't. I know when the words come out my mouth I'm going to have to watch Trey walk out of my life, leaving me alone.

"I'm sorry." I'm hoping the words are loud enough, because I don't know if I'll manage to repeat them around the lump that's appeared in my throat.

His hands cup my cheeks and raises my head, forcing me to look at him. I see a look of confusion on his face that is soon going to turn to one of hate. "Why are you sorry?"

Another tear falls and his confusion continues. I can see the moment that he comprehends what I'm trying to say, the look of pain in his eyes destroying me. It makes me want to hold him, but I doubt he would let me touch him. He's backed away from me slightly, telling me that he knows and doesn't want to be near me any more.

"Who?" His voice is strained, like he's trying to hold himself together.

"Zeke." I can't say anything other than his name. It's too hard to speak. It must take him a few moments to realize who I'm talking about but then he closes his eyes and I know he's made the connection.

"When?" He takes another step back, creating space I don't want between us.

"About a week ago."

Trey grabs his hair and I barely recognize the noise that comes from him. It's a mixture of pain and anger, and I don't like it. I try to walk towards him but he holds his hand up, stopping me dead in my tracks.

"Don't come near me." He turns away from me, his hands dropping to his knees as he tries to catch his breath. I don't know what to do or what to say. I need to make this easier for him but I don't know how. He stands and faces me, a serious look on his face.

"So you slept with him before our first time?"

Fuck. I don't want to answer that, but I know there is no way to avoid it. He already knows the answer, he's just looking for confirmation. I can't even say the words so just nod my head at him. He closes his eyes and I move back slightly, convinced I'm about to get a black eye. I wouldn't blame him. After all I did cheat on him, keeping it secret while I moved forward in our relationship. I should've told him before we had sex and given him the chance to make the decision on whether it happened or not.

"I can't fucking believe this. How do I pick the wrong guy every single time?" I don't think he's actually talking to me as he walks past me towards the front door. I follow close behind him, not wanting him to leave but fully aware that he's going to.

"Trey, talk to me. I can make this right. It doesn't have to be this way. Let me explain."

He doesn't stop moving as he grabs his belongings. I just want him to slow down to give me a chance to explain why I slept with Zeke but he's not letting me. He grabs the handle on the front door and I try one more time to get him to stop. "Trey, please wait!"

He turns towards me, a look of pure hate on his face. "Answer me this, did you sleep with me out of guilt? Is that why you suddenly gave yourself to me?"

I feel color burning my cheeks as he talks. I know it wasn't the only reason I slept with him, but there is some truth in what he's asking. I wanted to move on, to prove to myself I didn't need Zeke.

Trey's face contorts into an angry snarl as he opens the door. "Fuck you, Bryce. I can't believe you did this to me. How could I be so stupid and not see you were hiding something? Thanks for breaking my fucking heart." The tone of his voice lowers and is full of emotion. "I was falling for you. I thought you were the one." He looks at me with eyes full of disgust as he leaves, slamming the front door behind him.

I stand and stare at it feeling completely numb. I don't feel the same heart wrenching loss I felt when Zeke walked away from me, but there is an ache deep in my stomach. I may have just lost the best chance I ever had at having a happy ever after.

****

I sit in the empty bath, putting the bottle of vodka to my lips and taking a large drink. I don't remember how I ended up in here, but I know that I've been here since Trey left. I drop my head back against the wall behind me, repeatedly hitting my head against it again and again. I don't know what the fuck I'm doing anymore. My life seemed so simple when I moved here for this job. It felt like I was finally getting over Austin, like I was actually moving on with my life and nothing could stop me. But something stopped me. A tall, sexy motherfucker who goes by the name of Zeke 'The Storm' Raine. I can't even wish that I hadn't met him, because the time I spent with him was honestly the best time of my life. I thought I loved Austin but it was nothing compared to how I feel for Zeke. I just wish he would get his head out his fucking arse and see I'm here waiting for him.

I take another long drink from the bottle, praying it takes away the pain or at least makes me pass out so I don't have to feel it for a while. I grab my mobile to look at the time and see that it's well after midnight. I don't know what time Trey left, so I can't even guess how long I've been drinking. I do know that my arse is numb and feeling left my legs a long time ago. Taking another drink, I unlock my phone and see that the last window I had opened was the contact details for Zeke. I don't even remember using my phone, so I don't know why it's on that screen. I stare at his details like I'm hoping that they hold the answer to sorting my life out, but like always it doesn't help me. I get so angry looking at his number and picture. *He has made me lose everything: my job, my apartment, and my boyfriend. I hate him.* And suddenly I need to tell him that. I press the call button and put the phone to my ear, waiting for him to answer. When I hear his voice he sounds sleepy, like I woke him up. *Ha, I'm glad I called now.*

"Bryce, what's wrong?"

I'm quiet. Now that he's on the other end of the line, I don't know what to say. I go with my gut and bluntly tell him exactly why I called. "I hate you." My voice doesn't come out as strongly as I hoped and I wince as I hear pain lacing my words.

I'm met with silence, his breathing the only thing I can hear. I close my eyes and listen to it, the sound giving me a strange sort of comfort.

"What happened?" I don't even have to tell him something's wrong because he just knows, like he's part of me.

"He's gone. He left me because I slept with you. You're stupid, with your stupid hair and stupid muscles so why can't I just move on? You don't want me, and I still can't get you out my head. I need to fucking move on because I hate you." I'm impressed that I managed to make sense considering all the alcohol that's running through my veins. I thought I would feel better after speaking what's in my heart, but instead I can feel it shattering all over again. *Just my luck.* My chest tightens and I feel the tears start to flow, but this time I just let them. I'm tired of hiding everything, of how much I miss him, of how much I hurt. I just want all the pain to stop.

"I never said I didn't want you. Not once have those words ever left my mouth. I want you so badly it physically fucking hurts, Bryce. Knowing you're with someone else has been eating me up. I can't fucking survive without you."

The first painful sob rips through me and I almost drop my phone from the power of it. I don't know if I can listen to him telling me that he can't be with me again. I'm a glutton for punishment but I can't take another rejection from him.

"Fuck, baby. Please don't cry. I don't want to hear you hurting."

I cry freely, unable to control it any longer. "Do you want me, Zeke?"

I hear him sigh, the sound coming clearly down the phone. "I want you more than anything in this life."

"Will you be with me?"

There's a moment's silence and it tells me what I need to know.

"Baby..."

I can't bring myself to listen to him answer, the ache already too much. With a final sob I hang up the phone, dropping into the bottom of the bath. It pings a few seconds later, my screen lighting with a message from Zeke.

Tell me where you fucking live. I need to know.

I grab the mobile again, pressing the off button until the whole thing goes dark. I can't deal with any more tonight. There are changes that are going to happen, a new road to take, but none of that can start tonight. I lie down against the cool enamel of the bath, pulling a towel from the towel rack and cover my arms with it. I just need to sleep for a little while. Tomorrow when I wake up I will be in a better place to decide what I need to do.

CHAPTER TWENTY - THREE

Bryce

    I look around my living room to make sure I haven't left anything behind. I've spent the last few days packing so I'm ready for my flight on Saturday evening. The morning after Trey left, I'd made the call I had been putting off for a few weeks. I had been offered a new coaching job in another state, but with starting a new relationship with Trey I hadn't known what to do. When everything crumbled around me I knew that it was time to go. This way I could have a fresh start with a new state and job and leave everything behind. After accepting the job they had asked how soon I could be there, and since I had nothing keeping me here I told them any day after Sunday. That would have worked out great if they had flights on Sunday, and after a lot of compromising I will be flying out late Saturday night, after my plans.

    I know I shouldn't, but I'm going to see Zeke fight in the final against Dwayne. I'm hoping that it'll give me the closure I need to close the door on this part of my life, and if I'm honest, I want to see him smash Dwayne's face in. I still hold the fucker responsible for everything that went wrong between me and Zeke. If he hadn't have made those smartarse comments, Zeke might not have run.

    I grab my mobile when it rings, seeing Eddie's name on the screen. I take a deep breath before answering, wondering what this is about. "Eddie, how's things?" I don't know why I try to make conversation, Eddie doesn't do small talk and his next words just prove that more.

    "You're leaving the state? Craig called and said you'd taken a job with him."

I was hoping that I would be on the plane when everyone heard, but I should have known that luck wouldn't be on my side. I swear I must have done something really fucking bad in a past last life because Karma is really kicking my arse in this one.

"Yeah. He approached me a few weeks back and now I think it's for the best."

I can hear him muttering but I can't hear what he's saying. I keep going to speak to him, but every time I open my mouth I hear him curse under his breath, so I close my mouth again. When he calms down he must remember he's still got me on the phone.

"I thought you would've come back to the gym. I haven't filled the position yet, I didn't want anyone else but you."

I feel a pain in my chest as he speaks. I loved my job there, I moved across the world for it, but there is no way I could ever go back now, too much has happened.

"I'm so sorry, Eddie. There's just no way that I could come back, not after... I just can't come back." I nearly tell him Zeke's the reason that's stopping me, but I can't let that get out. Even after all the hurt he's caused, I would never do anything to tarnish his reputation.

"You know, I left you two to sort this out, thinking that maybe you could both be adults, but apparently I was wrong. I don't see why you fucking each other means I need to lose one of the best coaches I've had at the gym. I should have known that he would fuck this up for me. And you, you should be the bigger man and stay."

I don't even have a chance to respond before he hangs up on me, leaving me standing with the disconnected tone in my ear, not able to move with the shock I'm in. Zeke had mentioned that Eddie had walked in on us once, but with everything that happened after that conversation I completely forgot about it. I feel my cheeks heat as I think about what he probably saw. I know what we got up to in that locker room and most of it would have probably gotten us a thousand notes on Tumblr.

I throw my phone onto the couch and grab a roll of tape. I need to get a move on. The moving company will be here any minute and I still have some boxes to finishing packing. I make a mental note to never move again, especially to a different State. I hate the feeling of packing up your life, knowing that you're leaving somewhere that was important to you. Also I hate packing all my shit into boxes. I don't know when I managed to gather all this stuff; I don't remember half of it. Another mental note that I make is to never sleep with a coworker, like ever. I let out a dry laugh, there is no way I'm going down this road again. In fact I don't think I will be dating in the future at all. If this situation has taught me anything it's that I should just be alone. I'm not good at being with someone, I've ruined every relationship I've been in so I think it's time to quit before I hurt someone else.

I move to another box and I'm taping it shut when I hear a knock on my front door. I open it to find a huge guy standing there, and he offers me his hand as he introduces himself as being with the removal company. I let him and a few more guys into my little place, unsure how they will be able to move properly with the size of them all. I show them what has to go before telling them that I'll be finishing up the last few boxes. I'm thankful I have something to occupy me, because watching them remove everything makes my heart hurt. I thought that I could have made a life here, but it just wasn't meant to be.

****

I take a bite out of my sandwich as I look around my now completely empty apartment. Everything is in lorries on their way to my new place; a place that I'm hoping to make my new home, leaving all the heartache behind. I know that's wishful thinking, a new location will never remove Zeke from my memories, but maybe the distance will make it hurt a little less. When I leave tomorrow evening I'm hoping it will be a new chapter in my story, and I'm hoping this one has less drama than the last.

I hear my phone alert me to a text, my mobile vibrating in my pocket as I put my food down. I pull it out of my pocket and lean against the wall behind me. I'm currently sitting on the floor, having not thought through what I was going to do for the next twenty-four hours since I have absolutely no furniture, which also means no bed. I open the text and smile when I see it's from my mum. I don't hear from her as much as I would like, but calling over here is more than she can afford. She's also a complete technophobe, meaning that trying to explain Facetime caused a twenty-minute crying session. And I was the one in tears.

Hi Son. I added your new address to my book. Please make it the last address you have, I'm running out of space. I hope the move goes well, let me know when you land safe. Love Mum xx

She always signs it, 'Love Mum', even though I know it's from her. I've tried to explain it to her so many times but I've just given up. I know I need to reply to her, easing her nerves for my flight tomorrow. She hates it when I fly, convinced that the plane will drop from the sky. When I was coming over here the first time I think my dad had to sedate her for the whole nine hour flight. He said he got sick of her nonstop pacing and talking. I type out a reply and press send.

I will let you know as soon as I land. It's a short flight, only a couple of hours. I'm looking forward to this job so not planning on leaving any time soon.

I close my phone, not expecting her to message back quickly but she does, and her text cuts through my heart. I haven't told her what happened with Zeke, so I know she is only making an observation, but it still hurts like hell.

233

That's what you said about this one. Maybe it's time to settle down?

I lock my phone and drop it on the floor next to me. I can't answer her. I have no response to that. How do I explain that that's what I was trying to do, that I found someone I wanted to spend the rest of my life with but he wouldn't choose me over his career? He picked his lifelong dream over me, and I don't blame him, but Mum wouldn't see it that way. I gave him my heart easily, but that isn't his fault. He never once lied to me. I chose not to listen to him. I can't blame him for my stupidity.

****

I listen to the thunderous sound of the crowd inside the arena. As normal, the final has brought out all the true fans of the sport, and I can hear them chanting both fighters' names. I walk down an aisle and grab a seat a few rows back from the reserved family seating. I don't want to be noticed or affect Zeke's concentration, but I want to hear what his coaching team's telling him. I want him to win this fight and I need to make sure they're making the right decisions for him. I was a little shocked the last time I was at the gym, the fact that no one had picked him up on his poor stance. If he drops his shoulder today there's a chance he will get seriously hurt, and no matter what's happened in the past, I can't let that happen.

I'm about to sit when I hear his opening song start. I feel my heart racing in my chest as the lights dim in the arena. The noise of the crowd is deafening and the floor is vibrating under my feet. He might have lost his last title fight, but Zeke is the crowd favorite. The spotlight hits the door on the other side of the arena and I stop breathing with the anticipation of seeing him. I've never seen him enter before. I've always been hiding in the changing rooms to escape the visions of my past. When a figure appears in the center of the light I let the breath I was holding leave my lungs in a stuttered fashion. Zeke stands there in nothing but his shorts looking like a fucking god. He hates wearing a robe like the other fighters, says he looks like a fucking idiot in one. I take him in, from his sexy shorter than normal hair to his body that looks more toned than usual, right down to his legs that are making my hands want to reach out touch them. He looks like everything you would picture a top fighter to be: strong, in control, and powerful.

I watch as he makes his way down the stairs, punching the air and bouncing from side to side. Women have taken all the chairs next to the aisle and they are currently fighting to get his attention but he's too focused. Nothing will get inside his head right now. He gets to the edge of the cage, stretching as he enters it and I can't help but focus on his muscles. They're defined and strong, and I want nothing more than to run my tongue over them. My cheeks flush as my body remembers what those muscles can do to me, the pleasure they can give when they're focused on me. My body temperature heats up, and I pull the collar of my shirt away from my neck trying to get some sort of relief from my sudden bout of sweating. It's difficult to get control when my eyes are stuck on Zeke bouncing around the cage. I have every part of his body memorized, so I'm a little surprised when he turns his back to me and I see a new tattoo on his back. I try to think back to when I saw him last. *Did he have it then?* I don't remember seeing it, but I wasn't exactly paying attention to his back that night. I scrunch my eyes and try to focus on the words that are written across both his shoulder blades. When I finally manage to read it, the meaning of them steals my breath. In beautiful black script, the large tattoo reads 'My only regret is losing you'. I can't help but wonder if it's meant about me, but I try not to dwell on it.

Movement in front of me catches my eye. If I had been able to steal my eyes away from Zeke, I would have seen her before since she is standing waving her arms at me. I can't help but smile as I watch Asha jump over seats in front of her to get to me, not caring about the people she is stepping on.

She throws her arms around me when she finally reaches me. "Oh my god, you came!"

I nod my head, not knowing what to say to her. Zeke is in the cage working the crowd, causing the volume to get even louder.

She hugs me again and when the crowd quiets down slightly she talks again. "He will be so glad you came. He honestly thought you wouldn't be here. He knows it's not easy for you. Come sit down here with me, there's plenty of room." She tries to pull me towards the seats at the edge of the cage but I don't budge. She turns back to look at me with confusion on her face.

"I'll stay in this seat. I don't want him to know I'm here. He needs to focus... and I will be leaving straight after the fight."

She tilts her head like she's trying to work out what I'm saying, and I wonder if maybe I suddenly started speaking another language.

"What do you mean leaving?"

I take a deep breath, not sure how much to tell her. I know she will tell Zeke everything I say, and I don't want him to know where I'm going. "I have a job in another state. I just came to see the fight before I catch my flight. I need to leave as soon as it finishes."

Her mouth drops open and I see a look of pain flash in her eyes. I don't know why she looks upset, it's not her I'm leaving behind. I know we have spoken a few times but I wouldn't consider her a friend, more of an acquaintance. "You're leaving him?" She grabs a hold of my hand, holding it between both of hers.

"I'm not leaving him, I have a new job. I can't leave him when he isn't with me. I can't wait around for him to decide that he needs me to satisfy him, and then watch him leave again." Anger replaces the pain and I want her to drop my hand but she has a tight grip on it.

"Is that what you honestly think? That he just wants you for sex? That he doesn't want you? You are *all* he wants, Bryce. I was there the night he found out you'd left. I was the one who had to

236

hold him as his heart broke. Do you know what it's like to see Zeke cry? It's the most painful thing I've ever witnessed."

I look up to the strong man in the cage and I can't imagine him breaking down in front of anyone. He is too closed off, too put together to let anything affect him that much.

"He might want me, Asha, but he's made it more than clear that he can't be with me. I can't spend the rest of my life watching him from a distance. I don't think my heart could take it."

She bites her lip as she watches me, looking for something on my face but I don't know what. "Fine, but one last question. Do you love him?"

I feel the tears I thought had dried up flood my eyes again. I try not to blink in case I send them rolling down my cheeks. I can't cry again, especially not here. "I love him. I don't think I've loved anyone as much as him, but that just makes this harder. It hurts so fucking much Asha. I can't stay here." A single tear escapes and I angrily wipe it away, refusing to be weak any longer.

"Oh, honey." It's the only warning I get before she pulls me into her arms, wrapping them around me and hugging me tight. I return her embrace, happy to finally have someone to hold. For a few moments I don't feel so alone, but it doesn't last long enough.

Zeke

I hear Dwayne's music come over the speakers and I bounce in place to keep from storming up the steps to meet him as he exits his tunnel. I want to get this fight started, I want to just stomp him in to the mat and walk away the winner. Coach is shouting at me to not use all my energy in the first round and to save something for the second. If I have my way there won't be a second round.

I see Dwayne appear at the door of the tunnel, and that cocky as fuck look on his face makes me want to just punch him even more. I can hear sections of the crowd booing him and I can't help but smile. Apparently I'm not the only person who thinks he's a fucking asshole. I'm going to beat his ass into a bloody mess, and not just because he's the only thing standing between me and the winner's belt. I also blame him for me losing Bryce. If he hadn't made his smartass jokes I might not have panicked and run. I know it's wrong to blame him when it was all my own fault, but I'm finding it easier to put it all on him. I know the reality is anyone could have made a comment and I would have panicked. I lost the only good thing I've ever had in my life, and there's no one to blame but me.

I look over to where Asha's sitting. She came today as my support. No one knows we've split up so it's not strange for her to be in my family seats. She's the only person I want here, well apart from one man, but there's no way he would come. When I see that her seat is empty I look around the arena and my whole body stills when I see her. She's not alone, and the person she's talking to is the one that has been haunting my dreams for months now. She's having a very intense looking conversation with Bryce, and he doesn't look happy about what's being said. My eyes are stuck on his face, just drinking in how fucking amazing he looks. I didn't think I would see him today, especially not in the arena. I know how uncomfortable being here will make him, so to think he came to watch my championship fight has a strange feeling working through my chest. I don't think anyone has ever put me first, not my parents, not any of my friends, but there he is doing just that.

He must feel my stare because he turns to look at me. When our eyes meet, I'm lost. I don't even notice when Dwayne enters the cage, I don't notice when Coach tries to get my attention, and I don't notice when the referee calls my name over and over. I'm stuck to the spot, scared that if I take my eyes off of Bryce then he'll disappear. I don't pay attention to anything until Bryce smiles and mouths the word 'focus' at me before pointing behind me. With a smile on my face, I turn to face the man I need to beat into the mat. *I will do this. I will win this fight.* As I say the words in my head, I wonder what fight I'm talking about.

CHAPTER TWENTY - FOUR

Zeke

I'm pretty sure this guy is on something. No one fights like this. Every single time I've hit him he hasn't faltered. I step back to my corner as the bell rings and grab my water bottle.

"What the fuck are you doing out there?" Coach's harsh tone has me biting the inside of my cheek. I know I haven't exactly got control over the fight yet, but I'm doing everything I can think of.

"Feel free to grab some wraps and show me how it's done."

He mutters under his breath as he walks away, leaving me holding onto the side of the cage. Just when I'm about to turn around to face Dwayne, knowing I need to start gaining some points, I see someone coming towards me. I focus on the figure to see Bryce trying to get past security who stop him because no spectators are allowed near the ring. I shout at them but my voice is lost in the noise of the crowd. Bryce hears me though and looks at me with a pleading look on his face. I get Coach's attention and point towards Bryce, hoping that he gets the message. Thankfully he does and gets the security to let Bryce through without any hassle. Bryce reaches me just as the bell goes. He jumps onto the ledge surrounding the cage, holding onto the ropes, his fingers mere inches from mine.

Bryce talks quickly, so I focus on what he's telling me. "He's favoring his right side, I think he has hurt his ribs on the left. Get some good shots there and it will send his balance off. Stop dropping your fucking shoulder or you're gonna end up injured, and it makes it easy for him to read your next move. Go in hard. He's on something so he has more energy than normal, but it's making him do dumb shit. Don't try and outpace him this time, use what I told you and go kill the fucker." He pulls back and he winks at me and it sends my heart racing. After everything I've done to him, every ounce of pain I've caused, he's here helping me win this. I step away from him and it takes all my will power to tear my eyes from his. He looks amazing standing there. It's the view I want to see at all my fights.

When I turn I see Dwayne standing there with a shit-eating grin on his face as he watches my interaction with Bryce. "How's the boyfriend? I hear that he left you for another guy... maybe you don't give good head."

I feel emotions boiling up inside me, but I'm shocked to find that shame or embarrassment isn't any of them. Oh no, I'm pissed off. *How dare he talk about Bryce like that?* My anger fuels my ever-present hatred of Dwayne and I don't waste any time attacking the fucker. I keep in mind what Bryce told me as I concentrate my punches and kicks to the left side of his body. After the fifth or sixth kick to his ribs I can see that he's losing the easiness in his movements and he's trying to turn his body away from me, which makes him sloppy. At one point I get cocky, moving too close to him and I end up with a split lip, but I don't let it deter me. I wipe off the blood and go back into attack mode.

It takes a full two minutes of kicks and punches to get him on the ground and I make sure to give him an elbow to the ribs as I collapse on top of him. I hear his intake of breath and I know I have him. He can't focus on what I'm doing because he's trying to keep his body protected. I go to do a choke hold on him, determined to finish this fight, but he has to go and open his big mouth again.

"Do you think Bryce will give me a blowjob tonight? He must be good with his mouth. It's the only thing I could imagine that would turn a guy like you."

I don't even register the first time my fist connects with his face. It's instinctive. The second and third punches I'm aware of and mean them with all the hate inside me. I keep going, unable to stop myself even when I can feel his blood dripping from my fist. The bell rings and I still don't stop, the need to make him stop breathing has taken ahold of me. My body is pulled off him by a pair of strong arms and then everything else is a blur.

My arm is held up above my head and I'm declared the winner. I blink a few times, trying to clear my head. *I won. Holy shit, I won!* I turn to see Coach with a huge grin on his face, which is about as excited as he gets. My arm is dropped and the crowd goes crazy as I'm announced as the new belt holder. *I can't believe it. I'm number one.* A body comes flying at me across the ring and I grab it as it jumps into my arms. Asha attacks my face with kisses, causing me to laugh. I look behind her for Bryce. I need to see him. He helped me get here. This is his win as much as it is mine. When I don't see him I look at Asha and see that she has a sad look on her face.

"He's gone."

My ears block all other noise and zero in on just what's she's saying.

"What do you mean he's gone?"

She grabs my hand and gives me a very serious look. "He's leaving the state. Trey left him after Bryce told him he had been with you." She slaps me across the head as she mentions us being together, and I know it's because I've been so fucking stupid. "So he took a job at some guy's gym. He's on his way to the airport right now. You need to decide now Zeke. Is he the one? Is he worth the fight?"

I look at her, realizing for the first time that he is. He's worth risking everything for. I don't have anything if he leaves. He's my friend, my heart, he's my *everything*.

"Yes he is."

She claps her hands as I give her my answer, but quickly starts pushing me towards the open side of the cage. "Then go, he only just left. You can catch him."

I pause, only quick enough to kiss her on the cheek, before taking off. I run over to the door and jump, not taking the time to walk down the steps. As soon as I land on the main floor I take off, running for the exit. I can hear the people around me shouting their

241

congratulations but I can't pay attention to them, the only thing I'm thinking of is Bryce. As if by magic I think his name in my head and he appears in the aisle in front of me.

"Bryce!"

Thankfully he hears me and turns with a gentle smile on his lips. *Fuck, he's so beautiful.* I slow to a stop in front of him, suddenly doubting myself. *Why would he want me after everything I've done to him? How could he forgive me?*

"Congratulations, Zeke. Now you have everything you ever dreamed of." I can see flashes from cameras going off around us and I suddenly wish we were alone. He deserves better than me laying all this out to him in front of a big crowd.

"No I don't. There is something very important missing." If he leaves after I speak my heart then so be it, but I can't live with him not knowing how much I love him.

"Zeke, please don't. I can't do this with you. I have a plane to catch." He turns to leave but I grab him, making him turn back to face me.

I step into his personal space until we are chest to chest, our lips so close that I can feel his warm breath across my face. I wrap my arms around his waist, fully expecting him to pull away from me but he doesn't. There is a look of shock on his face but I ignore it as I speak.

"I'm so fucking sorry. I know I have no right to touch you, no right to think you would want anything to do with me but please hear me out." When he doesn't move from my embrace I brave continuing, not sure where the hell I'm going with this. All I know is that I need to get him to understand and try to forgive me. "I spent my whole life being told my feelings were wrong, that I needed to find a nice woman to settle down with and I tried. Well not the settling down part, but I tried women, lots of them, but there was something missing and I didn't know what it was. I didn't realize I was hiding who I really was. I fucking love you Bryce, and now I know the thing that was missing was your dick."

His fingers cover my mouth as a laugh escapes him. "You

were doing so well there. I suppose no one could ever accuse you of being a romantic." He drops his head, and I can feel a heavy sigh leave him. I just want to make everything right. I want to show everyone that he's mine.

"I can't be a secret, Zeke. I can't be someone you hide away to protect yourself. I love you... fuck, I love you so damn much... but I love myself more." When he looks up at me, I can see the pain in his eyes, the doubt, and I hate that I'm the reason it's there. I lean down and kiss his lips gently, trying not to show my passion. This time I need to show my love. It takes a few heartbeats, and just as I'm about to give up and move back, his lips move against mine. In that single moment I think I'm happier than I've ever fucking been. He's letting me in. He's thinking about giving me another chance.

"Look around, baby. I think this whole arena has a camera pointed in our direction right now. I give it roughly five minutes until the videos are on YouTube with the title, 'Zeke 'The Strom' Raine kisses his onetime coach'. There's no way in hell you could ever be a secret now. The funny thing is couldn't give a damn. I don't know if I'm gay, or bi, or what the fuck ever, all I know is I fucking love you. The type of love that means I can't breathe when you're not next to me, the kind of love that makes me think about us when we're old and grey. Well that will be you, I'll never be old." I kiss his nose as I feel his chest move against mine as he laughs. "I love you, Bryce. I fucking love Bryce Tanner!" I shout the last part loudly and get a thrill as I feel Bryce burrowing his face into my neck. It feels real, so fucking right.

"You know you're crazy, right?"

I capture his lips in a passionate kiss this time, breaking apart only to whisper against them. "Crazy about you, baby."

A groan comes from Bryce before he pulls back from me laughing.

"Seriously, you're going there? You are using a lame arse, cheesy movie line on me?"

243

I can't help but laugh along with him. "I never claimed to be good at this shit, and it usually works on the ladies."

Bryce gets an annoyed look on his face, before he smacks me on the back of my head. "Let's not go there shall we? The last thing I need to hear about is all the women you've seduced, Mr. Raine."

I grab his face and pull him to me, attacking his lips until we are both gasping for breath and I'm as hard as fucking stone. I hear my name over the speaker again and Bryce pushes me towards the cage.

"Go get your belt, you won it."

I grab his hand, pulling him behind me. There is no way I'm letting him out of my sight, and there is no chance he is getting on that fucking flight. As we walk down the aisle I see that everyone is watching us and a slight hush has come over the audience. I don't know if it's the shock of me kissing someone, or the fact it's a man. *Fuck them.* The only thing that's important to me today is Bryce. There is nothing else I need in my life.

I pull him into the cage with me, if this is the last championship I ever win I'm going to make the most of it, let Bryce live it with me. I accept the belt from the chairperson, lifting it up to the crowd. It doesn't take long until there are cheers and cries, people applauding my win. With a smile on my face I turn to claim Bryce's lips. I've spent too much time without him and I can't stop kissing him. I need to get out of here so it can be just the two of us and not hundreds of people.

****

I'm lying in bed, my limbs tangled with Bryce's and I couldn't be fucking happier. We'd barely made it in the front door when I tackled him to the ground, showing with my body how much I'd really missed him. Somewhere in between our second and third orgasms we found our way in here, but not before I got rug burns on my ass and knees. *Totally fucking worth it.*

"You know we still have a lot of things to work out. And I have a job that I need to catch a flight for... about three hours ago." He laughs as he speaks, but I can tell he's worried about where we go from here. I don't know what we will do, or how the fighting world will take my coming out, but as long as I have Bryce I am more than prepared for what they throw at me.

"You need to quit that job. There's no fucking way you are leaving, even if I have to tie you to the bed." I kiss his head and feel him lick my nipple. I didn't think it would be possible for my dick to get hard after everything we've done tonight, but just like always after some attention from Bryce, it's as solid as a diamond.

"I need a job, Zeke. I need to be able to pay my way. I also have my Visa to worry about. If I'm not working I need to leave."

Holy shit, I can't believe he thinks he's getting to leave. Maybe I should let him in on my secret. "What the fuck are you on about, babe? You have a job. You own a gym."

I watch as his head slowly lifts from my chest until he's looking into my eyes. "What are you talking about?" He looks so adorable when he's confused. I had a long time to work out what I was going to do after I won this fight. There were a lot of roads I could have taken, lots of management and endorsement offers, but somewhere along the way my dreams have changed. Now I just want to be happy, and the only way that can happen is if this guy stays in my arms forever.

"Well, you see, it's like this. Coach has wanted to retire for a while now, personally I don't think he's old enough for that shit, but his wife has been incredibly ill, and he wants to spend what time she has left together. I didn't want my gym to fall into the wrong hands, so I bought it. And if it belongs to me, then it belongs to you. I want you to help me run it. If the fighting world is ready for their number one to be gay, then I will need a coach. Know anyone who would be interested?"

His eyes open widely and he looks a little like a goldfish as he tries to find something to say. "But... I can't."

245

I lean up and gently kiss his lips before pulling him until he's lying on top of me. "Yeah, you can. I thought I bought it on a whim, but I think maybe, deep down, I did it because I knew I was coming after you. I knew I couldn't let you get away. I want you with me, Bryce. Every minute of every single day will not be enough time with you. It took me a while but I can see it all so clearly now. You are my everything."

Tears fill his eyes and I start to worry that I've made a mistake again, said something wrong. "I love you, Zeke. God, I will never get bored saying that, and you never stop surprising me."

I wipe the tear from his cheek and smile like a lunatic, but I don't care. Seeing the man I love in my arms and happy, has made me feel complete for the first time in my life. Growing up and being constantly told that my feelings were wrong and that I needed to find the right woman had messed with my head. I had spent my life feeling like I was locked inside a skin that wasn't my own and that I was lying to myself. I didn't know what I felt until I met Bryce. He was the one who unlocked my heart and showed me that what I felt was the most amazing and natural thing in the world.

This man currently lying in my arms is everything to me and I will live my whole life knowing that when it came to the biggest fight of my life, I won. I have his heart, and he was more than worth the fight.

The End

EPILOGUE

Trey

I down another glass of Scotch and motion for the waiter to come over so I can order another. I've been sitting here for what feels like five days now but I'm pretty sure it's only been a few hours. I don't even know why I came here; it's not my usual hangout but I needed something different. Sitting with a glass of wine while listening to fellow lawyers talking about cases just wasn't going to settle my mind tonight. I needed to get drunk and that's how I ended up here. I've heard of the bar before, but since it's known for its half-naked dancing men, it's not really a place I would bring clients or prospective dates.

With the thought of dating I throw back another Scotch, thankful that I ordered a few the last time the waiter came over. I sit back in the seat, letting the flashing lights distract me from what's going on in my mind. I can't believe that I didn't know Bryce had cheated on me. I thought I was an expert in spotting that shit by now. *Fuck. Why can't I find someone who doesn't lie to me?* I don't know what it is about me that screams 'Tell me whatever you want, I'll believe it all'. I'm a fucking lawyer for fuck's sake. I'm meant to be able to spot liars a mile off. I pride myself on it. I have a reputation that is known around all the big firms; people know that they'll lose if they come up against me. But apparently when I stick my cock in someone I lose all rationality and I'm unable to see what's right in front of my face.

I really thought I had something with Bryce. He was everything I look for in a guy. That first day I saw him I thought I was going to trip over my tongue. He was perfection like I'd never seen before. Tight perfect muscles, eyes that held so much

247

passion, and lips that I wanted to spend a lifetime getting to know. I should have known there was someone out there that already had his heart. A guy like that can't be single. Especially when you add his rocking body to the equation and the fact that he was a really nice guy. He thought of others and was genuine. Well he was if you don't count the fact that he cheated on me. I knew there was something between him and that guy in Fighting Fit. The way looked at each other was just too intense to be innocent. If I'm being honest, I don't blame Bryce for wanting the other guy. He was a beast, one that I would have loved to try and tame myself, but apparently he had his sights set on my man. *Fuck.*

I'm happy when I see the waiter approach and I don't even wait for him to put the drinks on the table, grabbing one straight from the tray before drinking it in one gulp and putting it back. I sit back and let my mind empty as I look around the room, finally taking in the place. I had tried to get a table towards the back of the room but it was already so busy when I arrived that I had to sit close to the stage. Most of the dancers are dressed in costumes such as sexy sailors, policemen or soldiers. They look good and I can see that their skin is all oiled up, but I don't think I'm in the mood for anything like this tonight. Maybe it would have been better if I had gone to a quieter place. But I didn't want to be recognized by anyone. Talking wasn't high on my to do list tonight.

The room goes dark around me and I notice the dancers leave the stage and podiums. Obviously something is about to happen as the seats in front of the stage are quickly filled. I turn my seat a little, interested in what's about to happen. A light appears towards the back of the stage as *Candy Shop* by 50 Cent starts to play. The crowd starts going crazy and it takes me about four seconds to realize why everyone flocked to their seats when the most beautiful man I've ever seen appears on the stage in just a pair of shorts. He's tall, but it's hard to tell how tall from my seat, and his body is lean with the definition of someone who spends a lot of time swimming. It isn't a gym body like Bryce's. This guy is less bulky and a whole lot sexier.

When he starts moving to the music it takes everything I have to keep breathing. The fluidity of his movements are making me hard as I think about how good he would be in bed. He grinds against the floor and I want to jump up there and see what he feels like. He works his way along the front of the stage letting the men in the audience slip money under the waistband of his shorts. He is the first dancer of the night who hasn't stripped completely, and he seems to be more popular than the rest. Maybe it's the pull of the unknown that keeps men slipping dollars into his shorts. Perhaps they're hoping to touch something other than his tight, toned stomach. He works his way towards me and I can't look away, my heart racing as he gets closer to me. I'm finding it harder and harder to breathe as I watch him dance and before I know it, he's standing in front of me. His eyes widen when they land on me and he has a look of surprise on his face, which I don't understand.

I get up from my seat, grabbing my wallet from my back pocket as I stand. I take my time, anticipating the touch of his skin. He drops to his knees as I walk to the edge of the stage, bringing his body close to mine. My eyes don't leave his as I tuck a hundred into the waistband of his shorts, a deep groan emanating from me as I rub my hand over his stomach. He's all hardness and warmth, and I want nothing more than to bite him. His breath falters as he moves away from me, his eyes leaving mine only when the song ends, and he walks backstage. As soon as he disappears through the curtains, I let out the breath that's stuck in my throat. I have no fucking idea what just happened, but I'm hoping he keeps the business card I tucked inside the money, because I want to see that guy again.

Coming soon...

MAKE ME *TRUST*

T.A. MCKAY

Acknowledgements

For anyone who has read my other books, you will know that this book has stepped away from anything else I've written. Deciding to listen to the male voices in my head, leading me to this genre was a scary step but I'm glad I did it. I hope that you, as readers, feel I've done the genre justice and that my men led you on a story that you enjoyed! I love reading m/m stories, they have been a passion of mine for so long. The voices in my head led me down this path, telling me their story that sometimes had me laughing and sometimes making my heart break.
There were a few people who stood out when it came to helping with this book, and here's the soppy bit to say thanks.

My husband Stuart: As always you were the most important person when it came to making this book possible. You took over at home and dealt with the constant tapping of keys in your ear. You couldn't really help with the investigating with this book, but you totally accepted when I was 'researching'. I just want you to know...I love you!

Ellie: Again...you took my garbled words and made a story out of them. I know this one must have been a labour of love...and yes I know...clauses!!!!

Claire: No matter what time I messaged you, you were there to read words and be my sounding board. You told me when it sounded crap, and also when you thought that the words were sizzling. Thank you for being there all the time!!

My betas: Vickie, Laura, Rae and Elisia...thank you for reading this before it even hit my editor, for looking past the typos and missing words to let me know what you thought of the story. You don't know how much it meant when I doubted everything.

Nicola Haken: What can I say? You kinda made this happen. You made a flippant comment one day we were talking, I can't even remember what it was but it planted a seed. That seed grew into two loud voices in my head that couldn't be ignored anymore. Thank you for making me grab the bull by the horns and write the story that was there. I promise the next book is coming, and your boy will be fine.

Mike Elcock: Thank you for keeping me right in the whole world of MMA. Your input helped more than you will know, making this story feel real to me.

To everyone who has read this book, who has pimped me or just simply shared a photo. Thank you for everything you do.

Other information

The Into The series:

Into the Deep ~ Rocco and Makenzie's story is available now

Into the Dark ~ Mason and Niamh's story is available now

Into The Fire ~ Noah and Madison's story out now

Leaving Marks series:

Leaving His Mark ~ Out now

Leaving Her Mark ~ Out now

Clay ~ Coming soon

Hard To Love series:

Worth The Fight ~ Out now

Make Me Trust ~ Out now

This Isn't Me ~ Out now

Standalone Novels:

Undercover ~ Out now

Someone To Hear Me

Keep up to date with all my news:

Website: www.authortamckay.com

Facebook: https://www.facebook.com/pages/Ta-Mckay-Author/1462902633937350

Twitter: https://twitter.com/tamckayauthor

Amazon author page: http://www.amazon.com/T.a.-McKay/e/B00JFF1R80/ref=sr_ntt_srch_lnk_1?qid=1411487268&sr=8-1

Goodreads: https://www.goodreads.com/author/show/7750967.T_A_McKay

Made in the USA
San Bernardino, CA
09 May 2017